Miriam Graves lay supine in the middle of her carpet, bulky and still as a beached whale, her round face white in the electric light. Tessa was bent over her, stethoscope applied to the broad bosom where the jacket and shirt were buttoned.

"Is she dead?"

The doctor straightened up. "No. But she is concussed. Lift her onto the bed for me."

"What happened? Did she fall?"

Tariq directed his attention to an object on the floor. "Sure. She was just contemplating a little late-night baking when she tripped and fell headfirst on her rolling pin."

Richard stared. "You mean—someone *hit* her?"

"It didn't go off while she was cleaning it."

"Bannister superbly develops this tale's understated menace..."

—*Publishers Weekly*

JO BANNISTER
THE LAZARUS HOTEL

WORLDWIDE.

TORONTO • NEW YORK • LONDON
AMSTERDAM • PARIS • SYDNEY • HAMBURG
STOCKHOLM • ATHENS • TOKYO • MILAN
MADRID • WARSAW • BUDAPEST • AUCKLAND

THE LAZARUS HOTEL

A Worldwide Mystery/April 1999

First published by St. Martin's Press, Incorporated.

ISBN 0-373-26307-4

Printed in U.S.A.

THE
LAZARUS
HOTEL

ONE

HE DIDN'T KNOW what to expect and he lay awake all night restless with apprehension. It was a timely reminder, if he needed reminding, of why he was doing this. Eighteen months ago the unknown was a joy to him: no situation was too alien, too alarming then. He'd left for the bloodiest of foreign wars with a spring in his step, his elf-green eyes bright with curiosity.

Now he lay on sweat-damp sheets, aching with the effort to be still while his wife slept curled peacefully beside him, fretting over an encounter with a psychologist in a London hotel. It was pathetic. He was ashamed of his timidity, didn't know where it had come from, why he couldn't shake it off. At first he'd refused even to acknowledge it: everyone at the TV station knew he was in trouble except Richard Speke. But he had to seek help when he couldn't get out his passport without his hands shaking.

This was the solution the station medico came up with: a Personal Discovery weekend with a psychologist and a bunch of other misfits. Eighteen months ago it would have amused the hell out of him; now he lay sweating in the dark, anxious about what waited for him at Lazaire's Hotel

At six o'clock he gave up the pretence of rest and dressed in the half-light. When he finished Fran was propped up on the pillow, watching. 'Did you sleep at all?'

He shook his head, avoiding her gaze as if it were a confession.

She wasn't surprised: he hadn't slept properly for months. 'I'll make some breakfast.' She padded through to the kitchen. She wore a choirboy mop of short brown hair that fell into place with a shake and one of Richard's T-shirts that came to her knees. She was everything he was not: small, neat, self-contained. Oh yes: and sane.

Richard picked at the meal as he picked at sleep, without enthusiasm. Now he was up he felt exhausted. 'Oh God, Fran, this had better work.'

'I hope it does,' she said evenly. 'I'm just not convinced. You know my view.'

Endless rehearsals meant they knew each other's views intimately. Fran's was that it was not Richard but what he did that was the problem; that the solution was to do something else. His eyes rolled. 'It's my job, Fran. It's what I do, who I am. I'm not going to give it up without a fight.'

'Fine,' she said shortly. She didn't want to argue with him, not again. She knew from bitter experience that it would do no good: not shouting at him, pleading with him nor rational discussion. It wasn't that he wouldn't talk about it, more that the debate never resolved anything. His determination to crucify himself was unshakeable. 'Just remember that fights cause casualties.'

Richard raked long fingers through his sandy hair. 'I'll take my chances.'

Fran rounded on him for that, angry colour in her cheeks. 'And you think you're the only one in the firing line, do you? That your choices don't affect anyone else?'

A famously articulate man, he could be reduced to gibberish by her scorn, most of all when it was justified. He knew he'd let her down. He was trying to make things right again, how they'd always been. He didn't understand why that wasn't what she wanted too. He was confused, his voice a plaint. 'Fran, I don't know what else to do. There are only two things in the world I care about, and one of them's falling apart around me. And if I can't get it back without losing the other I think maybe I *will* go mad.'

Compassion and fury warred in her breast. 'Don't you *dare* put this on me!'

Richard winced; he'd got it wrong again. Words were the one thing he'd always been able to do: now they betrayed him like everything else. Couldn't she see that? Couldn't she *see* how it hurt, losing something that important to him, feeling it crumble to dust in the palm of his hand? 'Please—'

One word, cracked and stumbling, reached her where any amount of skilful oratory would not have. She blinked and looked at him, and saw the pain crowding the corners of his eyes. She sighed and reached for him, her arms going round his waist. He dropped his cheek on to the top of her head, resting there.

After a time she said carefully, 'I know how much this matters to you. And for the record, you'll never have to choose between your job and me. I love you, Richard Speke. That's why I hate what you're doing. You're hurting someone I care deeply about, and I don't believe it's necessary. You don't have to change what you do, only where you do it. You don't have to go to wild and dangerous places. There's plenty of work closer to home.'

She felt him shake his head. 'Oh sure. Political junkets, royal scandals, bishops and actresses. I cut my teeth on that stuff, I'd lose my mind doing it again.' He sniffed sourly. 'What's left of my mind.'

He'd become inclined to self-pity. When they met Richard Speke was a rising star of television journalism, ambitious, energetic, the least neurotic man she'd ever met. He did his job and lived his life at speed, snatching experiences and fast food, the good and the bad, with a sure instinct for what to keep and what to leave behind.

But perhaps the instinct was less sure than it had seemed, because that phase of his life ended in breakdown. Fran knew that people weren't allowed to have nervous breakdowns any more, had to have Post-Traumatic Stress Disorder instead. But she'd seen it happen, and there was no better description of how his personality cracked and fragmented. His last trip to Bosnia, that the station had to bring him home from, was only the climax: for months she'd been watching him grow thin and brittle and known it was only a matter of time before something hit him hard enough for the pieces to fly apart.

'There's nothing trivial about politics,' she insisted. 'You don't have to risk your neck to be a good reporter. Credibility doesn't depend on bullets whistling past your ear on prime-time news.'

He stood back, raking his hair again, automatically, unconsciously. Fran thought he needed another trip to the barber. These days his hair was the only energetic part of him. 'Mine does. It's all I know, Fran. I can't do the clever stuff. There are guys reporting Westminster who know more about politics than both front benches put together and always ask the right questions because they know what the answers are. Well, I can't do that. I don't know enough.

'What I can do—could do—is operate in places most people can't. I know which side of a street to walk to avoid snipers. I know my way around, even places I've never been before. I can get into areas that are supposed to be closed, reach people who're supposed to be inaccessible and get out with a story that makes sense to people whose experience of anarchy is limited to the buffet car on a football special. There aren't many things I do really well, Fran, but there's that.'

They'd been married five years. For four of them he really was among the best. She'd seen a room full of hoary old journos, print and broadcast, burst into spontaneous applause watching one of his dispatches. So she knew how good he'd been.

And she knew it hurt like an amputation, like flesh ripped

from his body, to have that taken away. The pain of it, and the grief, glittered in his voice. 'Only I can't do it any more. I remember how I did it, I know what has to be done, but I can't do it.' He turned away, his long body rigid with tension, his angular face flayed. 'You want me to cover Chelsea Flower Show and Trooping the Colour instead? I'd rather dig up the roads.'

It wasn't mere bitter rhetoric; he meant it. In fact he wasn't bitter. He was too honest to pretend anyone had done this to him, blamed only himself. He wasn't strong enough and he couldn't hack it any more: not because the job was too hard but because he wasn't hard enough. At thirty-four he was still young enough to think that a failing.

'So maybe this group encounter crap is a waste of time,' he went on, a tremor in his voice. 'Maybe nothing will come of it. But it's my last shot at getting back to where I was. I know the station won't sack me if it doesn't work— they won't have to. I'll leave. I know how this job should be done. If I can't do it I won't stand by while people who can make kind remarks and try to find something I'm not too scared to tackle.'

Fran laid her hand on his. He was so taut the tendons along the top stood up like guitar strings. She murmured, 'I still don't see how three days with a bunch of crazies is going to help.'

Richard let out a gust of laughter. It was part of the problem, that he could do nothing in moderation. His nerves were so close to the surface that he reacted instantly and often inappropriately. 'The only crazy there'll be me. It's a personal discovery course, not the Broadmoor annual outing.'

Fran went back to the bedroom, began brushing her hair. A couple of strokes would have served; all this extra effort was to keep herself occupied. She'd given up trying to talk him out of it, looked for something neutral to say. 'So what do people do on a personal discovery course?'

Long in the doorway, he shrugged. 'I don't know. The brochure talks about Expanding Personal Horizons—what does that mean?'

'Staring into one another's navels?' hazarded Fran, watching for his reaction in the mirror.

For a moment, when he grinned, he looked like the man she married. 'How to make Freud influence people?'

'Keeping Jung at heart?'

'Who cares what the others are looking for? I'm going because I need some help, and just maybe three days of personal discovery with Dr Miriam Graves will start shovelling out some of this garbage that's got into my head. Maybe there's a simple answer—it came from nowhere, there's no reason for it, maybe someone who knows the right mantras can exorcize it. Anyway, I've nothing to lose. And I don't want it on record that our medico came up with something that might help and I turned it down.'

'Come back talking psychobabble and I'll kill you,' promised Fran. He smiled but her eyes were serious. 'Richard, don't stake everything on this. I hope it works, I really do. But if it doesn't I don't want you thinking it's you that failed. All right?'

He kissed the top of her head. It was the only part of her he could reach without stooping. 'All right.'

But she knew even as he said it that, in the nature of his illness, it was a promise he couldn't keep.

TWO

THE BUILDING was so tall that from street level perspective distorted the shape, compressing the upper storeys so that as the eye climbed the walls seemed to curve in. It was like looking through a fish-eye lens: lines which common sense insisted must be straight bulged and narrowed according to rules that had nothing to do with load-bearing.

At first Richard thought an optical illusion also explained why one storey of the building seemed to be missing. He blinked and looked again. The first five hundred feet were complete, the blush-coloured stone rising from its plinth in a confection of steps and chunky Tuscan columns like a particularly durable birthday cake. And the penthouse on top was finished, capped with a pyramidal roof that emphasized how distance could compress solid masonry towards a vanishing-point. Apart from the plaza, which still had piles of building material under plastic sheeting where the plans showed lovers drinking wine under umbrellas, it looked ready to occupy.

Except for one thing. Immediately below the penthouse was a thin slice of nothing, the top floor with its high-pitched roof seeming to float above the building like a cubist helicopter inching in to land. Narrowing his eyes Richard could pick out a filamentary framework of brown girders like denuded ribs, as if the structure were a great animal that some other animal had been disturbed in the process of eating. He knew nothing about civil engineering but he thought it an odd way to build: like writing the headlines and the weather forecast, and trusting to luck for the news to fill the gap.

The letter confirming his reservation gave the venue as Lazaire's Hotel and a functioning hotel was what he'd expected. But the foyer at the top of the pink steps was screened by plywood and there seemed no prospect of finding a receptionist inside.

Richard Speke had regularly found his way to spots so remote they were missing from their own country's maps. Now, assailed by doubt, he studied the letter—irritatingly personalized with a picture of himself in one corner—wondering if he'd come to the wrong place.

Someone else had the same idea. 'Today's Friday and I think this is the right address. Was it a hoax?' The young man behind him was puzzling over a letter identical, except for the photograph, to Richard's.

'Personal Discovery?' He said it as if it were a joke. Now he was here he couldn't imagine why he'd ever taken it seriously. 'Dear God, where did they get these photos? Yours is worse than mine.'

At least Richard's had been taken by a professional, though he couldn't recall the occasion. He'd been wearing his suit so it must have been something formal. He supposed it came from the station's PR department, wished they'd sent something a bit less po-faced.

The photograph on the other man's letter was never more than a poor snapshot, grainy, out of focus and badly cropped. 'It's the sort of snap my mother used to have in her album,' he said in a quiet, rather colourless voice that went with the light brown hair that wasn't quite fair and the grey eyes. 'She'd start off with a family group, then cut off the people she wasn't talking to. I'm Will Furney, by the way.'

'Richard Speke.'

'I recognized you.'

'You've got a good memory,' grunted Richard.

A fractional lift of one pale eyebrow was Will Furney's

only comment. He was younger than Richard, smaller and neater, and he looked as much at home among the piles of pipes and cladding as a string quartet in a working men's club. Everything about him said desk job: his weekend clothes, casual only by comparison with a suit, his pale skin and economic movements, as if he worked where a careless gesture could send things flying. Accountant, Richard decided. Wife works in a building society, two point four children, family hatchback, cocker spaniel.

'I won this in a competition,' offered Will. 'When it said three days in the penthouse suite of a new luxury hotel, this wasn't how I pictured it.'

Richard pointed. 'There is a penthouse. The problem's going to be getting there.'

Construction workers wearing hard hats, nonchalant grins and those special drop-waist jeans designed for the building trade rode the front of the tower in cages. Will pursed his lips. 'If that's the way up they'll have to drug me first.'

'Excuse me, gentlemen?'

Even without the accent, which was that of a Scottish gentlewoman of a certain age, it may have been the oddest salutation ever heard on a London building site. The men looked round but she wasn't behind them in the boardwalk leading to the road; she wasn't on the steps, or where the entrance would be when they took down the plywood; she wasn't even—Richard checked—riding the facade in a cage.

'The Lazaire's Hotel banshee,' he decided. 'It's heard whenever someone's about to make a fool of himself.'

'Better get used to it then, hadn't we?' Will was regretting his good fortune already.

'Over here, gentlemen—the side door. Stay on the duckboards and you'll avoid the mud.'

There are few reliable photographs but neither man had

heard of a banshee that wore a navy-blue suit and sensible shoes, and brushed its hair into permed corrugations like ripples in concrete. So perhaps she was only a woman of about sixty after all.

She glanced at a list as they picked their way towards her. 'It's Mr Speke, isn't it? And Mr Furney?'

Will nodded. 'Dr Graves?'

The woman laughed as if he'd said something witty. 'I'm Mrs Venables. I'll be looking after you while you're here. Don't mind this.' She gestured at the chaos around them. 'We'll be comfortable upstairs. Lovely views. Dr Graves is there now. Let me show you to the lift.'

When he saw it the blood drained from Will's face. 'I'm not going in that!'

But Richard was enchanted. 'It's beautiful!'

The heart of the building was an atrium arising through twenty storeys. Though the soaring space was as yet unfurnished, the structure was advanced enough to imagine how it would look when the ground-floor mall was open for business, the galleries were filled with bars and restaurants, the spidery escalators arching over the void were carrying people to and from the offices in the mid-section, and the great crystal fountain rising like a stalagmite through the vault was playing, adding the music of falling water to the bustle of people and the cheery babble of money being made.

And the little gilt and glass elevators were rising and falling in their perspex tubes. That was what worried Will. He could cope, just, with a lift whose doors shut on one level and opened on another. But the idea of sailing through this great space in something as insubstantial as a Victorian birdcage turned him cold.

A glance told Richard the man was genuinely afraid. To Mrs Venables, who already had the door open, he said quietly, 'Is there another way up?'

She frowned, perplexed. 'I don't think so. At least, there must be a staircase but, man dear, it's forty storeys! Why, what—?' Then she saw Will's ashy pallor and her tone softened. 'There's nothing to worry about, I've been up and down a dozen times.'

Richard had too many hags of his own to ridicule anyone else's. 'I'm sure she's right—lifts have to be pretty fool-proof to get approved. On the other hand, this isn't something you have to do. You could go home.'

'I have a ground-floor flat,' said Will. The strain was audible as a creak in his voice.

Richard nodded. 'I'm sure that's wise.'

'My office is in a basement. I don't even travel upstairs on buses.' He shut his eyes. 'I knew it was going to be high up. But it's a big solid building. I thought I could keep my back to the window and ignore all that sky outside. I never guessed they'd want to get us up there in a bucket!'

Richard was inspecting the little glass gondola. 'No problem. Just face me and don't look away. I blot out quite a bit of scenery.'

There was something engaging about Richard Speke. He looked like an overgrown schoolboy: tall, gangly and freckled with wiry ginger hair. Apart from the one suit which he dug out when absolutely necessary, he wore jeans on all occasions. Early in his career editors tried to do something about his appearance. They gave up in despair when they found that, however good the clothes they forced him into, by the time Richard had worn them half an hour they looked as lived-in as his own. After that it was decided that battered jeans were his trademark; like Kate Adie's earrings.

The other thing that made people warm to him was the fact that he was plainly a decent, trustworthy man. Will trusted him now. He might have joined someone else in what all his instincts told him was a death-trap, but he'd have agonized over it a lot longer first.

But nothing could make him enjoy the ride. His first thought was to fix his eyes on the floor and keep them there until the lift either arrived or crashed in a litter of broken glass and broken bones. But to his horror the floor too was transparent. Looking down was worse than looking out.

So he fixed his gaze on Richard's chest, on a broken button on his shirt. He was conscious of the movement as the gondola started up, of the passage of the galleries through his peripheral vision, but he kept his mind on Richard's button. He wondered where he'd broken it. He wondered how. He wondered if he'd no one to sew him a new one on or if he couldn't find one that matched. He wondered whether, if he broke another button, Richard would then consider the shirt done; and if not, how many broken buttons he would tolerate.

Then the gondola left the open space of the atrium and plunged into the mid-section, a bright bullet fired into darkness. That troubled Will less than space around him: Richard heard him breathe out for the first time.

There was one more bad moment when the black tube through the thorax of the building yielded momentarily to a clear tube through the gap below the penthouse. 'It must be a viewing deck. It'll be glazed in when they've finished, probably for a restaurant. On a clear day you'll be able to see halfway to Birmingham.' Then Richard remembered this wasn't the sort of information Will wanted.

Even as the building closed once more around it, the gondola was slowing to a halt, solid external doors sliding into slots to let the clear curved doors of the gondola swing open. From across the corridor came the hum of voices.

'We're here,' said Richard. 'Are you OK?'

Will said thinly, 'A lot of laundries will replace shirt buttons, you know.'

THREE

'I'M MIRIAM GRAVES. I'm glad you could come.'

The psychologist was a substantial woman, both tall and broad, big boned and well covered. Aged about fifty, her large frame was upholstered in tweed suiting and her pepper-and-salt hair styled by reference to a pudding basin. She might have been making the point that she was strong enough to do without props—the diet, the couture, the cosmetics, the expensive hair-do—but Richard suspected that she hadn't realized she needed them. He found that rather endearing.

'Wouldn't have missed it for worlds, Doctor,' murmured Will Furney.

She shook the pudding-basin crisply. 'Miriam. The Doctor isn't an affectation—I was a GP before I got interested in this—but it's of more use on the stationery than in this context. I'm not here to diagnose or to treat. My role is that of a moderator: I'll guide, I'll prompt, I'll give you the odd nudge in directions you'd probably sooner not go, but this isn't a patient-doctor thing. Also, first names cut through a lot of mental gymnastics. So call me Miriam, at least for now. Later you'll call me other things.' The unfettered grin transformed her plain round face. 'Come and meet the others. Sheelagh, let me introduce Richard and Will.'

Sheelagh Cody made little effort to hide her feelings. It wasn't anxiety barbing her voice so much as exasperation. 'Welcome to the madhouse.'

Miriam's apple-cheeks dimpled. 'Sheelagh is not one of our more enthusiastic participants.'

'Sheelagh has better things she could be doing this week-end,' the younger woman retorted acidly.

Richard had heard of power dressing but didn't often see it close up. Women reporters prefer a kind of practical chic, as in parka and pearls. The last time he'd seen something this sharp it was in the hands of an Afghan tribesman and he'd run for his life.

Inside the designer suit—lime-green shoulder-padded jacket, short narrow black skirt—Sheelagh was small but strongly made, well proportioned. Jogger, Richard decided. No, rower: sculls up the Thames from Limehouse every morning to avoid the traffic. Not yet thirty but runs the sort of women's magazine that would sue if you called it a women's magazine. Long black gypsy hair with a powerful curl fell down her back and her eyes were a hard dark blue.

'Then why are you here?' It was the sort of obvious question only a reporter would have been brazen enough to ask. Richard's freckled face was amiable but he waited for a reply.

Sheelagh had arrived in a bad mood and nothing that had happened since had improved it. She resented his curiosity. Whether she refused to answer, answered honestly or offered some polite dissimulation instead, he'd win on points. As a businesswoman she hated being outmanoeuvred.

'Well now,' she said, pursing carmine lips. She wore a lot of make-up for a young woman, used it combatively like warpaint. 'In the advertising world there are clients, Clients and CLIENTS.' She made the distinction with vocal and facial modulations that had Miriam making ticks on a mental check-list. 'When a *CLIENT* tells you about the wonderful weekend he's had learning how all his problems stem from being pushed off his rocking-horse by his sister at the age of three, you don't say what you're thinking, which is that anyone who'd believe that should get the word PRAT tattooed on his forehead. You smile and nod,

and steer the conversation back to how you're going to shift
a million pounds' worth of his useless bloody product.

'And when a week later he gives you an idiot grin and
an envelope, and explains that since you were so interested
he's treating you to a Personal Discovery weekend of your
very own, you don't say that the only thing you need less
is herpes and can you have the money instead? You thank
him, and say it'll be most revealing, and add the cost of
your time to his bill. And you come. But you don't feel
obliged to pretend it's anything more than an excuse for a
bunch of losers to blame someone else for their own inadequacies. That's why I'm here, Richard. You want to tell
us why you are?'

'Sure,' he said, without missing a beat. 'I'm a loser looking for someone to blame for my inadequacies.'

Others had gathered round. A powerfully built Asian si-
dled up to Sheelagh with a consciously handsome smile.
'You're in advertising? We should compare notes. I'm in
promotions. Tariq.' He stuck out a large hand.

Sheelagh eyed the big man, his pony-tail and his out-
thrust hand with blanket disfavour. 'Aren't Indians usually
rather small?'

Seeing it wasn't about to be taken, Tariq Straker took
his hand back. It wasn't the first time he'd had to. 'My
mother's from Pakistan. My dad's from a long line of Can-
ning Town dockers.' His accent was ambivalent; he'd
erased all the clues to his origins that weren't indelibly
branded on his skin.

Richard ambled to the window. 'You could give them a
wave from up here.'

All London and half the Home Counties stretched below.
The Thames was a grey ribbon dropped in loops across a
pointillist cityscape. There were other high buildings but
none was close: Richard was looking down mostly on
roofs. Though he knew the city well it took him time to

get his bearings, to recognize the threads that were main thoroughfares and the matchboxes that were important buildings. The boats on the river looked like cracker novelties. A movement caught his eye: a helicopter following the line of the river. He was looking down on the helicopter too.

Tariq grinned, the slight—if that's what it was—already forgotten. Insults had the same lasting effect on him as allegations of misconduct on a politician or water on a duck. He ran his life as he ran his business: adding up the profits, writing off the losses. 'Hardly. I bought them a retirement cottage in the Peaks.'

'Excellent choice,' said the last man heartily, sticking out a hand. He'd been waiting patiently to be introduced, finally decided to do the job himself. He was older than the rest of them, a big bluff man with a Midlands accent. 'Joe Lockhead. I'm from Derbyshire. Lovely county. Nothing to beat it in all England, I always say.'

'I bet you do,' said Sheelagh waspishly.

'For pity's sake,' groaned Richard. 'You're not going to start on him now, are you? What happened—miss your breakfast?'

Short of calling her sweetheart he could hardly have put himself at greater risk of physical assault. Sheelagh Cody had carved a place for herself in a competitive field by hacking through the tangle of custom and practice with a determination as sharp-edged as a machete. She was used to fighting—for acceptance, for respect, for success. She always reacted to a slight; quite often she reacted first to pre-empt any slight which might have been coming. She didn't mind her reputation for aggressiveness. She did sometimes worry, in the privacy of her own head, that aggression had become a way of life, that she was addicted to the stench of battle, that fighting was no longer a means to an end but an end in itself. She would not have admitted this even to close friends and colleagues, but it remained a gall on her psyche that quite casual comments could irritate.

If she'd sketched a brief apology, explained that the situation had got her a bit twitchy, it would have been readily accepted by people who were themselves on edge and glad she'd made a spectacle of herself before they could. Half of her wanted to do just that. But the other half had the casting vote and she squared up to the long-limbed man like a bantam threatening a heron. 'So what are you—his minder?'

'If you two will stop squabbling for a moment I've a little announcement to make.' Completing the group was a tall rangy woman in her early forties with fox-red shoulder-length hair and a dusting of freckles across her nose. Light hazel eyes travelled between the protagonists with good-humoured self-confidence, amused at their antics. She was dressed simply but expensively in fawn slacks, a linen jacket and lace-up shoes that could have been handmade.

When she had their attention she went on. 'Miriam knows already but I'd better warn the rest of you: I'll be writing about this. Don't panic: no real names and it's not for general release. I'm a doctor—Tessa McNaught. A medical journal I do some work for wants an assessment of this kind of course. It won't make you famous but don't be concerned if you see some reference to what went on here. You may recognize yourselves but no one else will.'

Sheelagh turned her back on Richard with a sniff. Her saving grace was that her mercurial temper passed as quickly as it blossomed: she could shed a quarrel as quickly as get into it. Unless Richard chose to prolong it this one would be forgotten within minutes. 'As long as you don't use these bloody photographs. Have you seen mine?' She showed it round. 'I must be about fifteen. I look like something out of the Wizard of Oz—a cross between the Wicked Witch and a Munchkin.'

'If you're using aliases,' said Tariq with a sly smile, 'can we pick our own? If Sheelagh's going to be the Wicked Witch I'll be the Tin Man—a poor lost soul searching for a heart.'

Possibly he was searching for something; conceivably it was the organ mentioned; but on mature reflection Richard decided that he'd never met anyone less like a poor lost soul. Whatever neuroses the others entertained, whatever anxieties lurked behind their eyes, Tariq's outlook was cheerfully uncomplicated. He'd come here as last weekend he might have attended a conference and the weekend before a party at some country house: for whatever he could get out of it in terms of contacts, gossip and entertainment. He would talk a lot, listen attentively, show off shamelessly and flirt with any woman under sixty; and on Sunday evening he would bore whoever he went home to with an enthusiastic appraisal of the encounter even though he had brought to it no problems and left with no insight. Ruefully, even a little jealously, Richard thought the big man needed three days with a psychologist like Abraham Lincoln needed a season ticket to the theatre. He murmured, 'In that case, I'll be the Cowardly Lion.'

'What's left?' asked the man from Derbyshire. 'The Wizard, I suppose. I can't sing soprano so that rules out Dorothy.'

It was a good reason but not the only one. If Judy Garland had sprained her ankle during her first dance routine, Joe Lockhead was the last person in the world the director would have called. He'd have tried Mother Teresa of Calcutta first; he'd have made discreet enquiries as to what Winston Churchill and Noel Coward were doing, but Joe's career as a printer would have been safe.

He was in his mid-fifties but he hadn't changed that much since entering Cartwright's of Derby as a fifteen-year-old apprentice. The curly hair was dark then instead of silvered, the jowls less heavy, the movements less ponderous. But that solid framework was the result of genetics more than time. He'd been a solid child and a substantial young man, and the idea of him tap-dancing his way up the Yellow Brick Road would have been hardly less ludicrous forty years ago.

'Printers served a six-year apprenticeship then,' he said. 'By the time a lad was twenty-one he was a journeyman. We hadn't the education they have today—the degrees, the diplomas. At least, I don't think we had them in Derby. I never heard of anyone taking a year off to ride a bicycle to Nepal. We were too busy making families and the means to support them. I met my wife when we were fourteen. We were engaged at sixteen, married at eighteen and still best friends when she died last year. How many of today's youngsters will be able to say the same when they're my age?' He raised a bushy, interrogatory eyebrow.

No one answered; but no one mocked either.

Miriam was doing mental arithmetic. 'Is that everyone now?' Her eyes travelled round the room, coming to rest on Joe.

Another thing they apparently didn't have in Derby was rhetoric. He looked concerned. 'I don't know.'

She smiled. 'Of course you don't. I'll check the list again, but I thought—'

She was interrupted by the sound of the gondola in its tube. It delivered Mrs Venables and a man in a navy-and-white tracksuit.

'You must be Larry.'

Everything about him said athlete: the muscular body stripped of fat, the lithe purposeful movements, the determined jaw, the piercing light blue eyes. Fair hair flecked with grey was clipped ruthlessly short, as if he'd no use for anything that didn't lend him speed. He might have been forty. He was not a handsome man but he was impressive. 'Yes.'

Richard didn't have to invent a background for him. He remembered when Larry Ford was the home crowd's best hope of a Wimbledon men's singles title. He never fulfilled that promise: there were bad draws, bad luck, injuries. Three years running he was among that small handful of Brits to survive the opening round. A week later he was the only survivor and the debate switched to how much further he could get: if this could be the year the host nation had a semi-finalist—a finalist—a champion? Then he bowed out at the quarter-final stage and told the Press the best man had won but did anyone know a good treatment for hamstring?

Larry Ford's tragedy was that he was never quite good enough to be a national hero nor bad enough to be an institution. For one week each year people were rooting for him, but when he suffered the inevitable defeat attention shifted elsewhere. There was never the affection that sustained other players, including poorer ones. For a few years after he dropped out of the singles line-up he was in the doubles; then that too came to an end. Richard hadn't heard his name in ten years.

'I think that's everyone,' said Miriam. 'Time's getting on and we've a lot of ground to cover. I suggest we make a start.'

FOUR

THERE WERE EIGHT CHAIRS in a circle at one end of the room. Miriam Graves watched who sat where as if their choices were significant.

All Will cared about was that he didn't find himself eye-balling the pilot of an inbound flight to Heathrow. He set his back to the window. Tessa took a chair beside him, marking her territory with an old-fashioned snap-jawed medical bag she pushed underneath it.

Richard liked the view and took a chair facing Will's. But it was low and, ill at ease, he couldn't think what to do with his legs. When he crossed them he couldn't see past his knees; stuck out in front they became a hazard to navigation.

Sheelagh tapped him on the shoulder. 'Swap?' Her chair was higher and when she sat back only her toes touched the floor. Changing places solved both problems.

Larry took the seat next to her simply because it was nearest. Tariq sat beside Tessa, the orientation of his large, supple body suggesting that the ten-year difference in their ages need be no obstacle if the chance arose for some other sort of personal exploration. Joe Lockhead held one of the remaining chairs for the psychologist before settling heavily on the other, palms flat on his knees, feet square on the floor, as if modelling for a toby jug.

Now they were assembled in all their idiosyncratic glory Richard began to think his wife had been right. Seeking equilibrium in this company was like a glue-sniffer going cold turkey at a model-plane convention. Of course they weren't actually crazy, but they were people who'd elevated individuality to an art form. A phobic, a paranoid, a gigolo, an android and a man who'd retired too soon. The only one who struck him as normal was Tessa and she was being paid to be here. Even the psychologist would have attracted uneasy glances anywhere else.

He knew he was being unfair. They had as much right to be here as he had; his motivation only seemed less frivolous to him. Perhaps they too had worries for which they wanted professional advice. Will's fear of heights, for instance, and Sheelagh's temper. Though she claimed to have been shanghaied it could have been an excuse; perhaps she too was seeking enlightenment. Presumably they each had an agenda, were probably as unimpressed with Richard as he was with them.

That coaxed a little inward grin from him—at least, he hoped it was purely internal; he didn't want to have to explain it. There was one positive aspect to all this. At work, at home, he felt to be riding an emotional rollercoaster. Among these people he felt like a paragon of self-control.

'Everyone comfortable?' Miriam smiled. 'Make the most of it. It'll be the last time for a while.

'We've got three days to give you people something worth the money you've shelled out'—her eye caught Sheelagh's and the smile turned impish—'or had shelled out for you. Right now you're thinking you made a mistake, but by close of play on Sunday I hope you'll feel it was the most useful weekend you ever spent. But it takes work, not all of it mine, and commitment and even some grief to get there.

'Don't be anxious about that: nobody's going to be hurt or humiliated. You may have heard of people being torn apart and put back together differently in encounter sessions but that's not personal development, it's brainwashing. Nor am I interested in sibling rivalry over nursery toys.

'Instead we'll be exploring the reasons you aren't making the most of yourselves: personally, professionally, in relationships, inside your own skins. We'll discuss areas where you'd like to be more successful and work out where these elusive increments might come from.'

Larry stretched in his seat, met her gaze in a deliberate challenge. 'What makes you think we're underachieving?'

'You're here. Why would someone who believed himself fulfilled come on a Personal Development course?'

'Because he was sent?' Larry spoke in a kind of clipped drawl, his tone sardonic. But it was an artifice: underneath he was tense.

'By whom?'

'You want to hear my life story?' He was fencing with her but there was a slightly troubled twist to his lips and in the narrowed corners of his eyes as if the tennis-player was afraid of being wrong-footed.

'I'm sure we'd all find it instructive,' said Miriam. 'But since we only have three days, give us the potted version. Who you are, what you do, why you're here.'

He was here because of an eleven-year-old girl called Selina, a pretty, energetic child with a modest talent for tennis. Larry was the professional at the club where she played and one of his duties was teaching the juniors on Saturday mornings. He called her Dumpling.

He gave all the kids nicknames but Selina didn't like hers. Eleven is a tender age: hovering between childhood and adolescence, she was too old to accept anything a grown-up chose to throw at her, too young to deal with it on an adult level—by letting his tyres down, for instance, or spreading gossip about his sex life. So she sulked. When her mother discovered why, she went round to the club with murder in her heart.

If he'd been in his office Larry could have contained the damage. But the working day was over and he was in the bar. He never drank alcohol—he cared too much about his reactions—but he could have done without the audience.

She did not, spat Selina's mother, pay her membership to have a washed-up tennis bum upset her daughter. If he had a problem with girls who were girl-shaped he ought to offer his services to the Anorexia Foundation because a family club was always going to challenge his delicate sensibilities.

Larry was genuinely taken aback. He had no great liking for children, except on rare occasions when he found one with the talent and hunger to be a competitor, but he considered himself a good coach with all grades of player and was amazed that so trivial a matter could give rise to such acrimony. He tried to be reasonable. 'Selina's a nice kid but she is plump. It's bad for her and you're doing her no favours by pretending it doesn't matter. A little encouragement now and maybe she won't be fat all her life.'

Selina's mother went ape. Whatever qualified him to advise her on bringing up a daughter? All he knew about children was that a few with enough natural ability and no one looking out for their welfare could be turned into tennis prodigies: great at twelve, stupendous at fifteen, burnt out at twenty.

He plucked his stars out of a healthy adolescence, enjoying their sport as part of a range of activities, and turned them into automata, not an ounce of spare flesh on their bodies or a surplus thought in their heads. Just eat tennis, sleep tennis, play tennis, and try not to look blank when someone asks if you're happy. Was it conceivable that he was *proud* of that?

It was possible, Selina's mother conceded icily, that Selina would grow from a plump child into a fat woman. That would affect her prospects of happiness hardly at all. Were Selina to acquire, thanks to genes, hormones or a taste for good living, a backside like a buffalo's, she would still be an intelligent capable caring person loved by her family and valued by a wide circle of friends. A future infinitely brighter than that awaiting those who sacrificed all the extras that did nothing for their game—like schoolfriends and riding lessons and pop music—to pursue another second-per-second acceleration on their service and another mile per hour across the court.

And almost none of them would see rewards worth half what they gave up. For a while they would play better and better, winning enough to keep them hooked. Their education, home life and social development would suffer but there'd be enough silverware on the mantelpiece that for a while no one would notice. By their late teens, however, the cracks would be showing. The constant stressing of immature bodies would cause injuries that were slow to heal; some of them would be in constant pain. Then it would dawn on them that they didn't have the ultimate degree of skill that would let them make a career of this.

Soon after that the game would be over. By their early twenties they'd be physically and mentally exhausted, with no idea how to spend the rest of their lives. They'd have no friends outside tennis, no skills outside tennis, no qualifications, no job prospects, no hopes, no dreams. And this faced not just an unlucky few, trapped with a bit too much talent and not quite enough, but almost all of them.

So he was worried about Selina's weight, was he? If need be, said Selina's mother, she'd force-feed the child cream eclairs to keep her out of the hands of men like Larry Ford.

A cheer went up from the assembled membership as if she'd beaten him in aces. After weeks of bad feeling and rumour, so that he wondered each morning if he'd still have a job by teatime, the committee made him an ultimatum and an offer. He had to change his attitude. To help him they would sponsor him on a Personal Discovery course.

Miriam nodded slowly. 'How did you feel about that?'

Larry sprawled in his chair in the casual attitude of a man telling a funny story. But the nonchalance of his pose was betrayed by his fingers, laced so tightly across his chest they'd gone white.

'I felt I'd wasted fifteen months. I'd sweated blood for those people. I'd got them fit, taught them to play a game they loved. I'd taken their snotty children and given them a glimpse of the magic world of the athlete. And this was my thanks. I felt like walking out. In six months they'd be back where I found them, patting the ball to each other like a bunch of old ladies, clapping whenever someone got a service in.'

'Why didn't you?'

He smiled tightly. 'Even an athlete has to eat. There aren't that many jobs for a tennis pro. You think twice before chucking one.'

'So you want some way of reconciling your professionalism with the gentler ambitions of your members.'

'I want to keep my job, Miriam.' He lifted the powerful head that was nothing more than bone overlaid with muscle to blast her with his ice-blue eyes. 'That's all. I came because I had to. But I don't want to be here and I don't expect to gain anything from it.'

He was a difficult, uncompromising man, possibly the last man in the world who should have been teaching tennis in suburbia; but his honesty won him a ripple of respect. Richard found within himself an embryonic admiration for someone who could face the ridicule of strangers in cold blood, unbuttressed by any sense of self-mockery. For a man who took himself as seriously as Larry, telling a story that made him look foolish must have been agony.

That he'd done it without hiding, without flinching, paradoxically made the Olympian rhetoric seem less absurd. The same strength of purpose, hardly distinguishable from courage, that made him hungry for victory lent him dignity in defeat. It occurred to Richard that he might have been wrong to dismiss these people as stereotypes. If Larry Ford was a little less than he himself believed, he was still rather more than Richard had given him credit for.

Others may have shared the same feeling, but Will wasn't one of them. Edgily wondering how the group would react to a cowardly reporter, scanning the watching faces to see how they responded to a martinet coach, Richard was startled to see an animosity bordering on hatred in the set jaw and blazing eyes of a young man he'd thought so mild as to have practically no personality at all.

He opened his mouth with the question already framed. Then he thought better of it, looked quickly at Larry to see if he'd noticed—he hadn't—and back at Will. But by then the murder was gone from his face, and his gaze had dropped to his knees where he was quietly picking a little lint off a trouser-leg.

FIVE

WHEN THEY BROKE for coffee Richard got Will alone, wanting to ask about what he'd seen. But Will got in first. No trace of the mute fury remained. His clear grey eyes were puzzled and he kept his voice low. 'Is there something weird going on here?'

Richard didn't know how to answer. 'You tell me.'

'Nobody's here of their own free will. Or am I wrong—are you?'

He was about to say that he was, but realized it wasn't strictly true. 'My station's medico booked me in. I'd no objections but it wasn't my idea.'

'And Sheelagh was sent by a client, and Larry by his committee, and I won mine in a competition.'

'What's weird about that?'

'I didn't enter any competition.'

A sensation like ants crawled up Richard's back. 'Did you tell them?'

'Of course. I called the number on the letterhead. They said the entry was in my name so the prize was mine. They suggested a girlfriend must have entered me.'

'Possible?'

Will's gaze went distant for a moment. 'No. I decided, though she denied it, it was my secretary. She tends to mother me. Maybe she thought I needed my head examining and was too polite to say so. I'd been a bit low—' He heard himself rambling, shook his head irritably. 'A relationship ended and I didn't get over it as quickly as I should have done. I thought maybe that was why she put me forward. But hellfire, Richard, it's bloody odd that *everyone*'s here at someone else's behest. As if we were—conscripted.'

Richard chuckled, feeling his spirits lighten at the rare sensation of being surrounded by people more neurotic than him. Whether or not this weekend helped him get back to work, it was going to be entertaining. 'You don't think that's a little paranoid?'

Will looked at him quickly, then sniffed. 'Just because you're paranoid doesn't mean they're not out to get you.'

'OK, let's find out.' Richard raised his voice. 'Excuse me, folks, but we're curious to know if everyone's here under duress or if some of you came from choice.'

Joe Lockhead stuck up his hand like a small boy anxious to get into teacher's good books. 'I did.' A moment later Tariq added, 'Me too. Well, more or less.'

'How much more,' asked Will suspiciously, 'and how much less?'

Tariq gave an elegant shrug. For a big man he was surprisingly graceful. He dressed confidently—a pale grey suit with a faint expensive sheen over a burgundy shirt with a diamond stud instead of a tie—which, combined with the theatrical hairstyle, argued scant desire to blend into the background. 'A friend did one of these courses and found it fascinating. She said she learnt stuff about herself and other people that improved her professional effectiveness. She thought I should give it a try.'

'Personal recommendation is the best advertisement,' nodded Miriam. If she was offended by the line the conversation had taken it didn't show.

Tariq grinned, a white slash in the olive skin. 'Oh no it isn't. A really good campaign devised by an outstanding promotions agent is the best advertisement.'

The psychologist chuckled. 'Are you sure you need help promoting yourself effectively, Tariq?'

He had no difficulty taking that as a compliment. If in

doubt he took everything as a compliment. Optimism was a creed that served him well: he saw business less as a rat race than a river of opportunities. And he liked women— any age, any colour, any shape. He basked in their attention. 'Perfection is the prerogative of God,' he said modestly. 'For the rest of us there's usually room for improvement.'

Sheelagh ran on high-octane fuel, impatience never more than a breath away. She said testily, 'What is this, a mutual admiration society? Can we get on?'

Miriam raised an eyebrow. 'That's interesting. You say you don't want to be here, Sheelagh, but you resent being left out. Is there something you want to contribute?'

Sheelagh glowered, a tetchy David squaring up to an intellectual Goliath. 'Since you ask, I'd quite like to put on record that I think you're all mad—sitting on top of an hotel that isn't even open yet, swapping CVs. It's like being on Miss World! "Tariq is a promotions agent, his main interest is himself and his ambition is to find someone who finds this subject as engrossing as he does."'

Miriam laughed out loud, a generous laugh without rancour. 'All right, so what do we tell the judges about you? "Sheelagh is in advertising—"'

'"Sheelagh is the proprietor of an advertising agency,"' she amended, torn between reluctance to play this game and the desire to win it.

'"Sheelagh is the proprietor of an advertising agency,"' agreed the psychologist. '"She has worked hard for this and is proud of her achievement. Her hobby is the same as her work. So is her ambition." Yes?'

The younger woman was fighting the urge to smile. 'Boring, huh?'

'Oh yes, being happy's a real bummer.'

Sheelagh looked surprised. 'Happy? Am I?'

Miriam gave a hefty shrug. 'Can't help you with that.

You are if you think you are. But as a rule, people who're not happy with their lot want something different, not more of the same.'

'So it's all right to be a workaholic.'

'I didn't say that. I said it made you happy. Whether it's good for you is something else.'

'Perhaps I should broaden my horizons.'

'Perhaps.'

'Get out and meet people?'

'Yes.'

Sheelagh nodded thoughtfully. 'See if any of them want to buy advertising.' It was hard to know if she was joking.

Before resuming, Miriam sent the group off to find their rooms. 'Mrs Venables has put your bags in them so if you recognize your own gear, that's where you're sleeping.'

'Don't we get a jolly dorm and pillow-fights after lights out?' murmured Tariq.

'You get,' said Miriam, 'seven of the best rooms in what will be, when it's furnished, one of the best hotels in London. The facilities aren't luxury standard yet. You have a bed each, a chair and a chest, but we haven't got a television between us. On the other hand, the view will never be better.'

'Oh, whoopee,' muttered Will.

Mrs Venables had a sense of propriety. Tessa and Sheelagh found their rooms on one side of the conference room, the men on the other. Two more rooms were in use on the women's side, presumably for the psychologist and the housekeeper. Beyond were some unfurnished rooms. Then the corridor turned a corner and ended in a blank wall.

'We must be the first people to stay here,' said Sheelagh. Her door squeaked on its new hinges.

Tessa had practical concerns: whether there was hot water in her bathroom, whether her cistern worked. She gave her bed an experimental bounce. 'Seems OK.'

Sheelagh was in her own room. 'Do you have a phone?'

'No. Nor a fridge, nor a radio, nor a trouser-press. I meant, what we have seems to be OK.'

'I thought there'd be phones.' Sheelagh sounded troubled.

'Miriam may have one.'

Sheelagh appeared in the doorway, shaking her head. 'I looked.'

'Does it matter?'

The younger woman gave a sudden smile that chased the thunderclouds out of her face. 'If you must know, I arranged to be rescued. Someone was going to phone after lunch and say I was needed in the office. There was a number on the letterhead. I assumed it was this place.'

Tessa laughed. 'You really weren't keen on this, were you?'

'It's a bit beside the point now.' She gave a snort of self-deprecating laughter, half-annoyed, half-amused. 'If I'm stuck here for the duration perhaps I'd better stop biting people's heads off and try and get something out of it.'

'Nobody'll raise any objection to that.'

Sheelagh eyed her sideways. After a moment she said, 'I do *know*, you know. I am aware that I have a foul temper. That even Jesus wouldn't want *me* for a sunbeam.'

'Well,' Tessa said thoughtfully, 'knowing's a start.'

It was the mildest reproof possible, but enough to push up Sheelagh's adrenalin level. A steely edge sounded on her voice. 'Tessa, you don't know me well enough to criticize.'

The doctor was unruffled. 'Sheelagh, none of us knows one another at all, and you've done nothing *but* criticize since we arrived. Now, it's no odds to me whether you join in or sulk, but don't expect people to be grateful because you think you might stop behaving like a spoilt child.'

One of the prices to be paid for success is that people

don't tell you the unvarnished truth often enough. Sheelagh recoiled as if slapped and the cobalt eyes flared; but a split second before the Geiger counter raced off-scale the best part of her, her sense of justice, recognized the other woman's words as fair comment and she diverted the burgeoning anger into a cackle of fishwife laughter.

'You have a point,' she admitted as it subsided into a rueful grin. 'I'd try going out and coming in again if we weren't so bloody far from the front door. Would you settle for an apology instead?'

Tessa was happy to meet her halfway. 'No apology called for. Like I say, I'm only an observer here. But if you're staying you might find the time passes quicker if you go with the flow a bit. If you can't take it seriously, think of it as a rather protracted party game.'

'What, like charades?'

'Just like charades,' agreed Tessa.

They obviously went to different parties. Sheelagh nodded. 'Only you keep your clothes on.'

Not meaning to stay, she'd packed only enough to support the pretence. Fortunately, in the cause of authenticity she'd included a washbag and nightdress. She put the latter under her pillow, the former in her bathroom. Then she ran the taps for a wash.

Blinded by soap, she heard the squeak of the door hinges and the mattress sigh. 'Better or worse than yours?' she asked through the open bathroom door.

'Sorry?' Tessa's voice came from further away than she expected, and when Sheelagh dried her face and went back into the bedroom it was empty.

She stepped into the corridor. In the next room Tessa was still putting things in her chest. 'What did you say?'

'Oh—nothing.' As Sheelagh looked round Mrs Venables emerged from one of the men's rooms with a stack of towels. 'Nothing at all.' She returned to her room, her momentary unease forgotten, put her nightdress under her pillow and went back to the conference room.

It was someone else's turn. Miriam picked on the man from Derbyshire. 'Joe, tell us why you're here.'

Joe was not merely a volunteer but a zealot, a man pursuing a quest. Personal Discovery may not have been the obvious answer to his problem but he'd already tried the things that were. 'I've had a right bugger of a couple of years, the sort of time nobody'd blame you for sticking your head in a gas oven.' He gave a fractional jowly smile. 'It's harder with an Aga. I'm not looking for sympathy, but to explain why I'm here I'll have to tell you some of it.

'Two years ago I had a wife, a daughter and a good job, and I was about as content as a man's any right to be. Then Martha got cancer. It wasn't a total surprise. She'd had treatment six years earlier. We thought she was in the clear, but it came back and this time the treatment didn't work so well. After six months we knew there was no long-term solution.

'She was home most of the time. I quit my job to be with her. It was funny—we weren't scared, either of us. I knew I was going to lose her. Somehow that seemed less important than making the most of the time we had left. We visited places we used to like, caught up on old friends. We had a lot of fun. I don't know if you get marks out of ten for these things, but I reckon we earned an eight and a half for sheer style.

'Then one day the police were at the door. Our girl had been in an accident and she was dead.' He looked up with tears in the seams of his cheeks, gravel in his voice. 'More than Martha's illness, that broke us. You expect to die, don't you? You hope it won't be soon and you hope it won't be hard but you know your time'll come. But you don't expect your children to go first. It's the consolation for your own mortality, that your children will be there after you're gone, and theirs after them.

'Losing a child makes a mockery of the seasons of life. I think after that Martha saw no point in hanging on. She couldn't bear the pain of grieving when she knew she wouldn't live long enough to come out the other side. Four months after our girl went, Martha went too. So now I'm a widower, childless and unemployed, and I can't seem to deal with it. I was a family man for forty years and I don't have the instinct, the behavioural vocabulary, for being single.'

He heard himself saying that and gave a self-deprecating grin. 'Oh yes, I've seen all the experts. My GP sent me to a psychiatrist who sent me to a grief counsellor who said I was grieving just fine and it would take time for things to fall back into place. That was all right for a few weeks, even a few months. But it's a year since Martha died and I'm still living one day at a time. I can't seem to move on. I could live another thirty years—I need to make some plans but I can't seem to get started.' He raised one bushy eyebrow. 'Does that make any sense?'

Miriam nodded. 'You were very happy. The happier we are, the more we have to lose. You don't want to let go of the time in which your family still exists.'

Joe nodded ponderously as he considered that. 'What do I do?'

'You're already doing it. You look for a way out. Looking creates the door. You want to move on so you will. All you need is the confidence to stop hugging your memories. They're like a dog on a lead—at some point you have to let them run free and trust them to come back. And they will. They'll always be there. You don't have to live in the past to hold on to your family. Joe, you couldn't forget them if you tried. They're part of you. Go on, enjoy your thirty years. Your wife and daughter will come with you.'

Joe stretched stocky legs into the circle, vented a deep sigh. There was the sense of a burden lifting, of his thick body unknotting and letting go.

Richard watched in fascination, half-embarrassed to be a witness at something so personal but more impressed than he could have said. This was what he'd come for: this process of exploration, understanding, catharsis. Maybe Fran was wrong, maybe he'd been right to hope. Maybe with a few perceptive sentences Miriam Graves could spear the worm that was eating the heart out of Richard Speke. Yearning sharpened his eyes as he searched Joe's face for confirmation. And though there was nothing to see he thought the grieving man had found what he'd sought.

In fact he hadn't. What he'd got might have been better than what he came for, but Joe's quest remained to be accomplished. Though he hadn't lied he had told only a fraction of the truth. He was not merely a man in mourning: he was a bitter, angry man seeking both answers and retribution. His mind spun with images—laughing faces and sombre faces and the stolid faces of people posing for photographs—that mocked him and gave him no peace, and he craved their erasure as an insomniac craves sleep.

SIX

AT THE OTHER END of the conference room was a dining table. 'I hope nobody's expecting cordon bleu,' said Mrs Venables coyly. 'I haven't much of a kitchen here.' Then she produced a lunch any of them would have been proud to give their mothers.

Personal discovery was not suspended while they ate but Miriam took steps to lighten the mood. 'Love and hate,' she announced briskly. 'Everyone, quickly, no thinking— one thing you love and one thing you hate. Starting with…Tessa.'

'I love my job, helping people, getting them well. I hate bureaucracy.'

Larry said, 'Courage and laziness.'

Will said, 'Generosity and injustice.'

Joe said, 'Compassion and treachery.'

Sheelagh said, 'Strength and cowardice.'

Tariq said, 'Frivolity and dogma.'

Richard wanted to say, 'I love my job too. I hate being too scared to do it any more.' Instead he said, 'Diversity and intolerance.'

Miriam made notes on a paper napkin. 'All right, comments. Tessa loves her job. Does that surprise anyone? What does it tell us about her?'

Will said tentatively, 'Isn't it a bit obvious? Nobody's going to go "Ah-hah!" on the strength of that.'

Miriam smiled at Tessa's expression, an amalgam of amusement and indignation. 'What conclusions can we draw from that?'

'That she didn't want to answer the question?'

'She's here in a professional capacity,' suggested Richard. 'She doesn't see herself as part of the group—she's responding as an observer rather than a participant.'

'Excellent.' The psychologist's enthusiasm was infectious. Whatever doubts her clients might have, Miriam believed in what she was doing and something of that confidence was beginning to rub off. The tensions between them diminished as they opened themselves to the process. 'I think I'll go home now and let you develop one another.'

'Just a minute,' interjected Tessa amiably. 'Do I get a right of reply?'

'Of course. Do you dispute Richard's assessment?'

She thought for a moment, then laughed. She had a strong, musical laugh and humour skipped in the hazel eyes. If he hadn't already known, Richard would have guessed she was a doctor. That degree of poise, of composure, of almost masculine confidence came from certain knowledge of her own worth, measured in qualifications and independent of anyone's opinion. But though she came across as cool, self-possessed, slightly detached, she had the kind of presence that generates magnetism much as a wire coil and a pulse of electricity do. Not a woman to have men buzzing round her at social gatherings, perhaps, but one for whom a few men would gladly give up everything else.

'Actually, no,' she said. 'He's right. But Richard should understand better than anyone. I'm here to report, not to get involved in the story.'

'You're not interested in a voyage of self-discovery then?' Miriam pitched the question just the safe side of impertinence, watching for Tessa's reaction.

The doctor responded professionally: smiled composedly, went straight for the jugular. 'Miriam, that's what I'm being paid to assess—if you do help people discover themselves, or just separate them from their money.'

Miriam roared with laughter, vastly amused. She was frustratingly difficult to insult. 'I'm glad you're not letting yourself be overawed by the responsibility. I'll be most interested to read your conclusions. All right, Will, how about yours? Generosity and injustice—isn't that a bit obvious too?'

Will looked surprised. 'Is it?'

'For a man in your line of work. I expected you to say you hated heights.'

'Oh yes,' he admitted readily. 'I'm useless on anything higher than a barstool, but there's no point hating a fact of life. I regret being'—he gave a Puckish smile—'elevationally challenged, but I hate injustice precisely because it's not an Act of God: it's the strong profiting at the expense of the weak. Actually, that's a major handicap to a lawyer. You need to be able to absorb the frustration, accept that some you win and some you lose.'

Not an accountant then, thought Richard. Solicitor?—near enough.

'And generosity?'

Will frowned. 'What's wrong with that? Oh come on, everyone admires that. Nobody sits grinding his teeth going, "If there's one thing I can't stand it's a generous bastard!"'

'Sheelagh might.'

She startled at the sound of her name. 'I opted for cowardice.'

'You also said you loved strength. Are they compatible, strength and generosity?'

'Actually I think they are.' In a man, even in a taller woman, that jutting jaw and the clarion note in her voice would have been called pugnacious. Sheelagh got away with being provocative because people who were bigger than her hesitated to seem like bullies. In fact she was as easy to bully as a bobcat. 'Generosity implies strength—the weak can't afford it.'

'Fair comment.' Miriam confounded her own argument by being both a strong and generous adversary. 'So is Will right? Does everyone admire generosity?'

'I don't,' said Larry bleakly. 'And I can't see that it's the opposite of injustice. Generosity is a form of injustice. It isn't fair putting people in your debt. If they can't pay you back it's patronizing. If they can it's just another investment.'

Tariq gave a soft whistle. 'Man, you are a sad individual.'

The athlete's pale eyes turned on him like searchlights. 'I believe in a market economy: pay the price and you get the goods. Generosity is the free lunch there's no such thing as. I haven't a generous bone in my body, but I've never short-changed anyone.'

Joe gave a disbelieving snort. Miriam glanced at him and quickly back. 'That's quite a boast, Larry. You never let anyone down? A colleague, a friend, a lover? Never delivered less than they were entitled to expect?'

'I don't believe so.'

Miriam sat back from her lamb chop with eyebrows still elevated. 'I'm impressed. What about the rest of you? Any more paragons who've never let their halo slip?'

No one claimed a share of the accolade. But nor did they explain why.

Miriam returned to her meal, talking over her cutlery. 'Two possibilities. Either Larry's a wholly reliable person and the rest of you are not. Or his concept of obligation differs from yours.'

He was too much a competitor to miss that volley. 'If you mean I don't accept responsibility for those who're old enough to be responsible for themselves, that's right. If I say I'll do something I do it. But I don't consider myself bound by other people's expectations.'

'Isn't that rather sterile?' Tessa seemed to have no reservations about discussing other people's motivations. 'It's a tidy arrangement but hardly a humane one.'

'That's a matter of opinion,' growled the tennis-player. 'Mine is that you're doing people no favours by protecting them. Life's full of knocks. You have to learn to take your own. You learn to see trouble coming, avoid it if you can, deal with it if you can't. That's what growing up is.'

Miriam nodded somberly. 'It's a point of view. Richard, you've gone very quiet. Where do you stand on this? Are people essentially responsible for themselves or should we accept duties towards one another? Do you feel badly when you let someone down?'

The professional communicator was a long time answering. Joe saw, because he was looking, that his eyes flinched as if he'd been struck. He forced out the word, 'Yes.'

At a time when there was some embarrassment about consulting a psychiatrist, which was not very long before it became fashionable, people like Miriam Graves were referred to as trick-cyclists. Though meant as an insult, actually it described what she did quite well: the balancing, the pedalling like mad to stay in the same place, the sudden pirouettes when what seemed like progress suddenly turned volte-face.

And like a trick-cyclist, it was vitally important for her to know when to sit still and when to push. They could all see that this was difficult ground for Richard. Miriam said quietly, 'Give us an example.'

He didn't know why his mind turned to the accident. He might have failed the girl but the situation was not of his making. Mornings when he woke sweating he'd been out of his depth in Bosnia, not the Thames.

Taking his statement afterwards the police wondered

why he was strolling beside the river at two in the morning.
They searched his sodden clothes for drugs. He explained
through chattering teeth that he was a journalist: constant
switching between time zones played hell with his body
clock and when he couldn't sleep he walked.

Remembering where he'd gone into the water they ex-
pressed incredulity. 'On muggers' mall?'

He shrugged. 'Last week I was in Sarajevo. When you
go for a walk there you put on a flak jacket.'

It wasn't bravado; it was true. Before his present difficulties he'd done things like that. It wasn't that he was
unaware of the danger: they all knew they were in danger
all the time, dealt with it on a professional level. They were
there to do a job; doing it exposed them to risks; they took
precautions and then got on with it.

So when he was home and couldn't sleep he had no
qualms about driving to the river and walking till the quiet
entered his soul. No one bothered him. Perhaps by that time
even the muggers had gone home. Or perhaps, seeing how
he was dressed, they gave him a wide berth in case he tried
to mug them.

He heard the car before he saw it—the sudden roar of
power, the change in the engine note as the weight came
off the wheels, the great deep splash. By then he was running and he reached the spot before the crown of white
water subsided. The pinkish gleam of moonlight through
city fumes glinted on the tail-end of a car rearing out of
the river. The lights were still on, red bobbing high above
the surface, white pointing an eerie trail into the depths.
Then they went out.

If he'd thought about it he wouldn't have gone in. It was
late autumn and the river was like ice; it was racing after
an ebbing tide; it was dark and there was no help at hand.
He was more likely to lose his own life than save someone

else's. He was a decent swimmer but he knew that decent swimmers are the ones who drown.

But there was no time to think. He hit the bank running and leapt for the car.

Icy waves closing over his head drove the breath from him. But by then his flailing hands had found metal and he surfaced, shaking water out of his eyes.

The weight of the engine had dragged down the front end but the windows were closed, slowing the river's entry. The driver was a dark shape behind the wheel. Richard couldn't open the door. He hammered the glass in vain.

So he gripped the door handle and braced his feet against the pillar, pitching all his strength against the pressure of the river. Finally the door opened. By then the water was over the driver's face.

She was a black woman. He dragged her out by a handful of crisp wet curls. She made no effort to help. He had to reach over her to release her seat-belt but then she came out easily. The car sank under them.

He hadn't realized how far out they'd been carried. Towing her behind him he swam for the bank but could make no headway against the tide.

But for the timely intervention of a buoy they would both have died. He didn't see it coming; he hit it at the speed of the river and it knocked the breath out of him. It was hard and smooth and wet and he couldn't hold on to it, bounced back into the tideway.

For a desperate moment he thought that was it: he'd been given a last chance and he'd blown it. The fingers of his free hand clawed at the thing as he was dragged past but failed to find a purchase. It hardly slowed his journey towards the sea.

By merest luck there was a lighter moored to the buoy, its chain dipping to the water between waves. His fingers closed and he clung to it with the strength of knowing his life depended on it.

Somehow he got one arm over the chain and hung there, water to his chest, holding the woman with the other. It may have been shock or concussion but her senses seemed to come and go. At times she only sobbed and whimpered, a dead weight on his arm. Then she'd rally and cling to him, her fingers clawing at his clothes, whining like a terrified child: 'Don't let me die. Please, don't let me go.' And of course he said he wouldn't.

But the chill of the river invaded him, and when the waves breaking in his face started to feel warm he knew his core temperature was dropping. Exhaustion enfolded him. He could feel it as a slow fire in his muscles, consuming them fibre by fibre. Every wave that hit him on its voyage to the Medway tried to take him with it, and the woman too. The constant drag sapped him. His muscles raged and cracked; later the agony dulled, his strength with it.

Like something breaking, his numb right arm straightened and the river pulled him off the chain. Only for a moment; then panic fuelled a desperate surge of energy and he found it again. All the strength he had left went into fastening his hand around it. He was too weak to do any more and knew he hadn't much time left.

The woman had gone quiet. Perhaps she was dead. She was lower in the water than he was. Perhaps as she grew colder she hadn't been able to keep her face out of the waves. Perhaps he was holding only a corpse. For a corpse he was going to die because he needed two hands to grip this chain and he had only one.

He held on for a minute longer. But when he felt the grasp of his right hand loosen again he let the woman go. Immediately the force dragging at him halved; with his left hand to help he hauled himself back on to the chain.

A few minutes after that, like a dying man's hallucination he saw an immensely powerful light quartering the river. A police launch drew alongside and strong hands pulled him on board. They had to break his grip on the chain first.

Half-coherently he told them about the woman. They searched for twenty minutes before other boats took over. But it was three days before her body was found.

He didn't dress his account of the episode in much detail, said only that a woman had drowned, that he tried to save her but couldn't hold on to her.

When Miriam asked for comments no one offered any. Around the table the faces were preoccupied. She identified compassion and shock and anger depending on where she looked. If all she'd known of the episode was what Richard had chosen to tell, some of those reactions would have surprised her. They didn't, because she knew about Richard, and the rest of them, much more than she had chosen to tell.

SEVEN

SOMEWHERE A PHONE RANG. Tessa caught Sheelagh's eye. 'We're not quite cut off from civilization, then.' Sheelagh grinned.

Large even teeth, white in the coffee-cream skin, gave Tariq a dashing smile, spoiled only a little by his knowing it. 'A secret joke?'

Everything about him—his size, his confidence, the way he fawned on women, his blithe assumption of their gratitude—grated on Sheelagh. Understanding why she resented him—because in their male-orientated business he'd strolled across a battlefield she'd had to conquer inch by bloody inch—didn't alter how she felt. Her transition to sweetness and light temporarily on hold, she said snidely, 'You not knowing something doesn't make it a secret. It just means no one's bothered to tell you. If you must know, I had an escape plan but it needed a phone and I couldn't find one. I'd have brought my own but the Rules for Inmates asked us not to.' She tapped the latter with the despised photograph in the corner.

Miriam wasn't offended. That was beginning to annoy Sheelagh too. 'The problem with mobile phones is they tend to go off just when somebody's struggling to open up. It undermines the whole purpose of coming up here away from the madding crowd. But you don't need rescuing, you know. You can leave any time you want.' She gave a sly smile. 'I won't tell on you.'

Mrs Venables brought in the desserts. 'Actually, she can't. Not for the next hour or so. That was the builders—they've cut power to the lift. I said we shouldn't need it for a while, and they said if we did to phone down and they'd reconnect.'

'While we're on the subject,' said Richard, 'why *are* we sitting on top of a half-built hotel? Are they that far behind schedule?'

'I don't think so.' Miriam ate with the same relish she brought to her job. It would be easy to poke fun at her appetites but that would be to ignore the fact that she was good at what she did, that the enthusiasm stemmed from a real interest in the human mind and how it could be helped to run smoothly. 'I think they've just about finished building. There's the viewing gallery to glaze in, but after that it's just a matter of fitting out. Come back in three months and you won't recognize the place.

'We're here now because I have a friend on the Lazaire's board. It suits us both. All I need is somewhere we can talk, eat and sleep without being disturbed. In return for minimal outlay—most of our gear's cast-offs from their other hotels—Lazaire's earn a bit of rent.'

Tariq nodded his approval. 'Good thinking. You should go into business.'

She chuckled delightedly. 'Tariq, I *am* in business. I'm a service industry. I service people's minds—decoke them, change the oil, polish them up and when they're purring nicely send them back to their satisfied owners. Speaking of which…'

She paired them off on some principle she didn't explain: Sheelagh and Tariq, Tessa and Richard, Larry and Joe. Will she took as her own partner. 'The name of the game is Empathy. Tell your partner the thing you like least about yourself, then act as defence counsel for one another.

'So if Will confesses, for instance, a tendency to shout abuse when magistrates trash his cases, I look for a positive side and tell him—yes, I know—that an arrogant magistrate is a threat to justice so it's a public service to remind them of their fallibility. So now we've both learned something. I've learned a little of how Will feels, and Will's learned that what he always considered a fault doesn't necessarily appear that way to other people. All right? Give it a try.'

'What I really dislike about myself,' Will said when pressed, 'is that I don't shout abuse often enough.'

Miriam frowned. 'Like, at football matches?'

Will chuckled. 'Do I look like a football hooligan? I'm the original seven-stone weakling. I kick sand in my own face to save bigger guys the trouble. No, I mean when it's time to stand up for something that matters and I back down. I don't *call* it that. I call it seeing the other point of view, or deferring to the will of the majority. But the bottom line is, I bottle out. I'm a pacifist not from conviction but because it's easiest. I worry how much I'd give up rather than fight for it.'

'Any fight in particular?'

Will lifted a narrow shoulder in half a shrug. 'Perhaps one more than others. Over a girl.' Memory softened his eyes. Miriam had to prompt him to continue. 'She was— Well, I'm a solicitor, yes? I do divorces and conveyancing, defend the lower grade of criminal on legal aid. And here was this beautiful, talented girl. And she found me *interesting!*'

'So what was the problem?'

'Most people thought it was me. This was a special girl, a girl with a real future—a profitable future. I still believe that's what the problem was. There were too many people with a vested interest in her success.'

'Did you tell her that?'

'I told her. She laughed. She said they were the experts and they had her best interests at heart. She said it was sweet of me to worry but there was no need, she knew what she was doing.'

'Only it turned out she didn't?'

'Only it turned out she hadn't realized the sharks she was swimming with. They used her, used her up and threw her away. By the time they'd finished with her there was nothing left.' He was a gentle man but there was a momentary edge of violence on his voice.

'Couldn't you help?'

'Me? I was history. They persuaded her I was holding her back and she persuaded me. That's what I mean. I knew she was wrong, that she was putting her trust in men who'd betray it and sooner or later she was going to need me. I should have fought for her. But she said she'd made a mistake, it wouldn't work out for us, we were too different. She said it was better to make a clean break before we got emotionally involved.'

At that Will gave a little despairing snort and let his head rock back. '*Before* we got involved? I thought she was going to marry me! But what do you do? Somebody tells you to get out of their life so you go. However you feel about it, you have to accept that people have the right to choose their own lovers. She thought she could do better— how could I argue with that? I was hurt: my pride, yes, but deeper than that. I loved her.

'Then I thought, What if it's true and I am holding her back? I'd no right to do that. I thought, Maybe I'm wrong about the sharks. Maybe they'll look after her. I never met them, I was only going off things she'd said. Maybe I'd got it all wrong. And she wasn't alone. She had family to turn to. And she was an intelligent woman, well capable of knowing what she wanted. So I walked away.'

'Had you in fact any choice?'

Will waved a dismissive hand. 'There's always a choice. Anyone with any guts would have fought tooth and nail before leaving her to a bunch of professional advisers who had only her best interests at heart.'

'What happened to her in the end?'
'She—went away.'

'GO ON,' glowered Sheelagh, 'give me a challenge. Tell me your grimy little secrets and I'll grit my teeth and say how you're a great up-front guy anyway.'

If he wasn't careful, thought Tariq, he could make a fool of himself over this little viper with her eyes like sapphires and her tongue like broken glass. Deadpan he said, 'I'm worried that I'm drawn to women who despise me.'

But Sheelagh had his measure. 'You lying rat, that doesn't worry you at all! If it's true, and it may be, it amuses the hell out of you. Come on, have the guts to tell me something that really bothers you.'

Impressed and needled in equal proportions he gave her an honest answer. 'All right. It's my reluctance to make commitments. Oh, I like people, I get on with them. I'm good at my job because mostly that's what it consists of—making yourself agreeable to people who wouldn't recognize you in the street. That suits me fine, it's the sort of relationship I'm good at. There's no harm in it, I don't hurt anyone, I don't pretend I'm looking for a life partner. I don't break hearts, and I don't mind being a thinking-woman's crumpet.

'Until I think maybe that's all I'll ever be, that I've made a career of being a bit on the side. It's one thing when you're twenty, another when you get to my age. I should be putting down roots, only that means commitment and I shy away from it. I don't know why. I've loads of friends, I go to all the best parties, but I'm thirty years old and still the only family I have are my mum and dad in Matlock Bath.

'And I can't see that changing. I see people with nothing to offer falling into relationships at the drop of a hat. Some of them work better than others but at least they tried. I never have. I boast about never hurting anyone, but I've never been hurt either. I've never wanted someone enough to be. That isn't right.'

Against her inclinations Sheelagh was becoming interested: to some extent in the exercise but more so in the man. The paradox intrigued her, the idea of superficiality as a disguise for something deeper. Most men she knew used a veneer of complexity to disguise how shallow they were underneath. 'There are a lot of unhappy, destructive relationships about. Maybe you're smarter than most, take care not to start something you won't want to finish. I don't wish to shock you but that could be a pretty responsible attitude.'

Tariq laughed out loud, a deep boom that drew curious glances. 'That's nice. I bare my soul, and all you can do is insult me!'

Sheelagh grinned but she was still thinking about what he'd said. 'Or maybe you expend all your commitment on professional relationships and don't have enough left for personal ones.'

That seemed to strike a chord. His large expressive face went still, as if she'd tapped into something he didn't want to talk about. His eyes were distant, shadowed. Sheelagh did nothing to prompt him, watched and waited.

Finally he said, 'That's not the reason. It's the same at work. I don't mean I short-change clients—I don't, I earn my cut. But it's always a business to me, and maybe an agent and a client should be more like a marriage: for richer, for poorer, in sickness and in health. Not just while the money lasts.'

Sheelagh shrugged. 'If you're on commission you have to know the difference between clients who'll pay their way and those who'll never be worth your time and effort.'

Tariq's gaze strayed to the window. His eyes were a velvety un-English brown. 'Sure. Ten per cent of nothing is nothing. Even twenty per cent of nothing is nothing. You have to discriminate. It's tough telling someone they aren't good enough, but I can't afford to be coy and they can't afford anything less than the truth. They have lives to get on with. They shouldn't waste them waiting for the big break that's never going to come.

'But how do you deal with someone who used to have talent, someone you once had a profitable relationship with, who becomes a liability? Do you tell them it was good while it lasted but it no longer pays you to represent them? Or do you carry them, spend time and money you should be using to promote new talent on shoring up a career that's reached its natural end? I don't know. But turning your back on someone who's been a friend and partner feels like—like having a brood mare who's given you winner after winner, and when she comes up barren you send her to the glue factory.'

But it wasn't a joke and Sheelagh knew better than to laugh. She said softly, 'This isn't hypothetical, is it?'

He didn't answer. He was toying with the letter bearing his photograph—a rather younger, even flashier Tariq Straker beaming at the camera, one arm draped round the shoulders of a female companion. The way the shot had been cropped it could have been anyone. Sheelagh wasn't surprised he kept looking at his picture like that; only that he took no pleasure in it.

Still looking at the thing he murmured, 'Common sense says one thing, common decency another. Do you listen to your heart or your head? And if you listen to your heart who feeds your family, and your employees' families, when you go down the tubes?'

Sheelagh shook her head decisively. 'You don't go down the tubes—that's the first priority. Who are these people you represent—performers, personalities, sportsmen?' He nodded. 'People for whom a career is a few good years if you're lucky. They know that from the start. Your job is to maximize their earnings in those years, not to prop them up when they no longer have anything to sell.'

'Makes sense.' His voice was even but Sheelagh sensed an old ache that wouldn't be salved by platitudes.

She said quietly, 'I hope it is one person in particular. You can't afford to bleed over every professional relationship that comes to an end.'

He forced a little laugh, folded the letter and put it back in his pocket. 'Take no notice. For an international whizkid of a businessman I'm a sentimental sod at heart. What about you? What's your heart made of?'

The unexpected sensitivity he had touched in her vanished like smoke. 'Stainless steel,' she said briskly.

Tariq didn't believe her. 'But under that?'

'Titanium?'

He smiled slowly. 'And under that?'

'What is this?' she demanded indignantly 'GCSE physics?'

'I know what bothers you,' he suggested, holding her gaze. 'The possibility that, under the steel and the titanium and the triple-cantilever multiple cycling locks, there's a human being who's not only very bright and very determined but also rather warm and funny and perceptive and kind. Is that why you're so spiky with people? Because if you got to like them, if you let them like you, you'd have to open the vault and take a look at what was in there?'

So intent were they on one another that the sudden mighty clangour backstage, that made everyone look up, sent the large dark-skinned man and the small dark-haired woman rocketing from their chairs. But they barely had time to trade a wry grin before a shrill scream had everyone piling into the corridor.

EIGHT

THEY FOUND MRS VENABLES in the makeshift kitchen surrounded by debris.

'Whoops.' Miriam knelt to shovel cutlery and broken china back on to the big tin tray. But the housekeeper kept staring wildly at the door. Miriam sat back on her heels, her brow furrowed. 'Esme? Are you all right?'

'I didn't drop it.' The older woman's voice was as tight as the top string on a violin; tight enough for a perceptible involuntary vibrato. Her face was powder-pale.

Joe stepped out of the press in the doorway, took her arm and guided her to a chair. 'Sit down, Mrs Venables. Get your breath back. There's no harm done. Nothing that can't be replaced at the nearest Woolworths.'

Her capable hands were fisted tight. 'You don't understand. I didn't drop it, it was knocked over. By—'

The man's heavy brows knitted. 'Who?'

She made an effort to get a grip on herself, sitting straight on the straight-backed chair. 'I'm not sure. I thought, an animal.'

Miriam gave up trying to salvage the tea, looked round as if it might still be there. 'An animal? What—a cat?' She tried to imagine how the heavy tray had been balanced that a cat could send it flying.

'Of course not a cat!' From the sharpness of her tone Mrs Venables considered that absurd too. 'A big animal reared up against the table when I came out of the pantry.' She indicated the open door behind her. Planned as a store-room, its shelves made a good repository for foodstuffs that didn't require the fridge.

Joe was more confused than ever. 'A dog?' They were six hundred feet above the street and the only way up was the lift. He'd have put the chances of a stray dog finding its way up here right around zero.

But Mrs Venables nodded slowly. 'It could have been a big dog. I barely saw it, you understand. I put the tray on the table, went into the pantry for the scones, and when I came back it was—right there. It must have heard me, though, because it was already heading for the door. It knocked the tray down as it went.'

Richard had found a broom and took over where Miriam had left off. 'Why don't you take Mrs Venables next door while I put on a fresh pot of tea?'

A tweedy arm around her shoulders steered the housekeeper to a quiet corner of the conference room. As they sat down Miriam murmured, 'I don't understand why you screamed.'

Mrs Venables flustered like a disturbed hen. 'I was surprised, I didn't know what it was. Then it knocked my tray flying.'

'And then you screamed. After it was gone.'

'I suppose I froze. You don't expect to see something like that.'

'Like what?' She waited but there was no reply. 'Was it a dog, Esme? You screamed because a dog upset your tray? It doesn't seem like you. You might have yelled and thrown something at it but I wouldn't have thought you'd have screamed.'

The housekeeper's eyes flared, alarm lingering in their depths. 'I don't know what it was. I barely saw it, just the size of it and the movement. It was dark and big, and it moved—'

'Like a dog?'

'I don't know. It was fast like a dog. But—'

'Yes?'

She shook her head firmly, refused to think any more about it. 'It must have been a dog. It couldn't have been anything else.'

Richard brought in the tea and scones and an assortment of crockery designed for other meals. Helping herself to jam, Miriam chuckled. 'Perhaps it belongs to one of the builders. Perhaps his wife won't have it in the house.'

Mrs Venables shuddered. 'I don't blame her.'

The incident had broken everyone's train of thought. They took the opportunity to stretch their legs, wander round, admire the view.

Richard took his cup to the window to watch the city closing down for the weekend. Midway through Friday afternoon, already everyone who could was heading out. The roads were twisting multicoloured ribbons of high-powered transport engineered for travel at a hundred miles an hour but here restricting one another to about three.

The tweed suit that had as much personality as some people he'd known arrived at his shoulder. He waited for Miriam to speak but for a while she just stood beside him watching the city wind down.

At length she said, 'Why are you here really?'

The directness of that edged him on to the defensive. 'I need—some help with my job.'

'You have a good career—even I've heard of you. I can't tell you anything about television reporting.'

'I *had* a good career. I lost my nerve.'

'What you call losing your nerve others might call learning some sense.'

Richard smiled. 'You've been talking to my wife.'

'Ah. An intelligent woman.'

'She wants me to cover Westminster and come home nights. She reckons dodging bullets is a young man's game.'

Miriam winced. 'She really knows how to put the boot in, doesn't she?'

Richard's grin broadened, then faded. 'Maybe she's right. Maybe seven years is enough. Maybe it's not something you should try making a life's work of.'

'But?'

He wasn't convincing himself either. 'But actually that's crap. There are some great foreign correspondents in their fifties. Till this last year I always meant to be one.'

'What happened this year?'

His eyes widened. 'What didn't? Mostly that charnel-house that for the sake of political correctness we call Former Yugoslavia. Look, I'm no virgin. I know what it is to look, and look carefully, at images no station could show. I know what it's like talking to people who've suffered acts of appalling barbarism, and then travelling five miles up the road to talk to the guy responsible who thinks it's all right to use people as kindling as long as their churches have a different symbol on the roof. Even so, some of the stuff they've done to each other—' He shook his head in helpless disbelief.

'But Bosnia isn't the only place where the inconceivably awful gets worse every time you look. People are killing one another, with guns and knives and bombs and famine, over half of Africa. Then there's the mad bastards in sheets.'

Miriam considered. 'Who?'

Richard grinned tightly. 'Sorry, journo shorthand. Muslim fanatics. You know, the ones who torture opponents and stone women and bomb tourists in order to show that Allah is merciful. There's so much mayhem round the world I don't know where to go for a holiday.'

'And it sickened you.'

He chewed his lip. 'Maybe. I mean, yes, it's always sickening. There's something wrong with you if you don't feel sick and angry when there are people literally dying at your feet. You stand there with your well-fed face and your ty-phoid jabs and your flak jacket, and you know all you can contribute is a four-minute soundbite for the evening news. You want to shout at someone. You want to bang heads together. You want to take one of them—just one—put her under your coat and take her home, get her out of the madness and make her safe. And you can't even do that.

'So yes, I was sickened. But it wasn't the first time. It's worse at the start till you learn to do your job in spite of it. You tell yourself—maybe it's not true but you tell yourself—that you don't care any less, you're not growing hard, but you're a professional and the best you can do is a good job that might wake the world up while there's someone left to benefit.'

He paused, long enough for Miriam to wonder if he'd finished. But she thought not, and finally he forced himself to the point he'd been circling. 'It wasn't feeling sick that stopped me. It was feeling scared. For seven years I accepted the risk. It was the price I paid for doing something that mattered to me. Because even when it makes you crazy, when you'd like to grab a gun and do some shooting of your own, reporting it well gives you a sense of achievement.

'Then one day I couldn't do it any more. Nothing had changed. I'd had close calls before, got drunk and moved on. But now every shot I heard, I felt the bullet. Every shell that burst I felt the shrapnel. If a bombardment started while I was on air, even if it was miles away, it was all I could do not to dive for the nearest doorway and bury my head in my arms. Sometimes I was shaking so much the cameraman couldn't hold me in focus.'

'Sounds a pretty healthy reaction to me,' said Miriam.

'After seven years? In seven years you've seen all there

is to see. Chickening out then is like a heart surgeon starting to faint at the sight of blood.'

Miriam didn't change the subject although for a moment she seemed to. 'Why did you tell us about the girl in the river?'

Surprised, Richard struggled to answer. 'You asked about letting people down. You can't let someone down worse than letting her die.'

'You tried to save her. You risked your own life. What are you ashamed of?' His eyes avoided hers. 'Was there more to it than that?'

Almost inaudibly Richard whispered, 'Yes.'

'Tell me.'

So he did. 'I could have saved her. I had hold of her and help was on its way. But I started to slip. I let go of her. I promised I wouldn't, but I did.'

She let her eyes shut for a moment, feeling his pain. 'Richard, you did the best you could. Your own life was in danger. You held on for as long as you could.'

He would have given anything to believe it. He shook his head. 'I could have saved us both.'

'You didn't know that. You don't know it now. It's easy to be brave after the event. It's also easy to be wrong. You're not a coward. You did everything for that girl except die with her.'

'But I let her go!' The passage of time had done nothing to soften the guilt. The whine in his voice turned heads. 'I told them—the police, even Fran—I told them the tide pulled her out of my hand. But it's not true. I let her go. I could have held her, and I let her go.'

'And you've let it haunt you ever since. You damn fool. What's been happening to you, it's nothing to do with Bosnia. It's that—having to choose between your life and that of someone who was depending on you. In that river you were forced to confront your limitations, and you still haven't come to terms with it.'

'But that's more than a year ago!'

'And your problems started soon afterwards, yes?—the next time you found yourself under stress, which in your line of work was always going to be somewhere like Bosnia. You came face to face with your own mortality in that river. In order to do your job you'd persuaded yourself that death didn't apply to you, and now you knew it did.

'Till then you'd got by on a cocktail of skill, luck and youthful self-confidence. Robbed of that you went into withdrawal. Suddenly there was no magic screen between you and death, and that scared you rigid. Trying to work it through instead of seeking help made it worse.'

'I thought, if the other guys could cope—and I used to be able to—'

'But they hadn't been where you had—drowning by inches while you tried to save someone who couldn't be saved. Then you tried to purge the fear by getting straight back to work. You thought that if you could do your work you couldn't be a coward, whatever happened in the river. Only it backfired. Your subconscious decided that if you were a coward you couldn't do your work. All the time you were fighting the wrong dragon—no wonder you kept getting the back of your neck fried!'

Richard stared at her, ashamed but almost daring to hope. Was she saying what he thought she was saying—that there was an answer? 'So?'

'Forget the job for the moment. Tackle the root cause. If you won't take my word there was nothing more you could have done, find someone you will believe—the River Police maybe or the Coastguard. Talk about it, understand it, accept it. You don't need forgiveness, Richard. Not being Superman isn't a crime. You couldn't hold on to her, that's all; and now you can't let her go. But you have to.

She's been dead for fifteen months: let her go. When you do you can start rebuilding your life. Not the way it was—you'll never feel invulnerable again, that's the prerogative of youth and you've grown up. But you'll be able to work. You'll be as good as anyone else. You can learn to live with not being better.'

She smiled at his expression, put her cup back on the table. 'Now if you'll excuse me, I want a word with Joe.' She took a purposeful stride across the room.

Then the door of the conference room banged open, the handle chipping the new plaster, and Sheelagh stalked in, her face red with fury. Her cobalt eyes blazed round the room, ignoring the women present, striking sparks off the startled faces of the men. 'Which one of you *perverts*,' she demanded in a voice quaking with anger, 'has been playing with my underwear?'

NINE

IF SHE HADN'T been so clearly upset the response might have been ribald. Miriam looked quickly at Tariq, in her judgement the man most likely to light the blue touch-paper; but Tariq was watching with an absorbed expression and whatever he was thinking of it wasn't a witticism.

Tessa was nearest. 'What's happened?'

'My things!' Sheelagh sounded close to tears: tears of rage, the sort that come with knuckledusters. 'Someone's been messing with my things. One of these *bastards!*' Her eyes flayed the five men by turns.

'Is anything missing?'

The thick black hair danced as Sheelagh shook her head. 'No. But I know how I left them and they've been moved. And it's not the first time.' She told of the nightdress she put under her pillow not once but twice. 'Jesus, I knew there were going to be some weirdos here, but I didn't expect them to be *sick!*'

Tariq circled the company with his gaze, his face passive. 'I wasn't going to mention this, but my belongings have been disturbed too. I doubt anyone was interested in my underwear but my briefcase was opened. God knows why, there's nothing of interest in it except to me and a few clients. Nothing valuable, nothing sensitive—must have been quite a disappointment. If somebody wants to say what they were looking for I'll be happy to help.'

The silence could have been cut with something much blunter than a knife. Richard felt a change in the air like a pressure wave crossing the room as people who had come here tense and had then begun to relax, to enjoy one another's company and start getting something out of the experience, were suddenly reminded how far from home, mentally and emotionally, they had strayed. They snapped back into themselves like overstretched elastic, suddenly wary of opening their hearts and souls to strangers whose motives they could not know and whose reliability they had no way of judging. Whoever rifled Sheelagh's clothes and Tariq's papers left them all feeling tampered with.

'All right,' said Miriam with ominous calm, 'who's playing silly buggers? Poking through each other's personal property is an intrusion.' The silence persisting, she looked at Tariq again. 'When did you notice your briefcase had been opened?'

'Five minutes ago. I went for a pen.' He smiled. 'I didn't say anything because I thought it was you.'

'Me?' The psychologist's eyebrows disappeared into her pudding-basin fringe.

'That's how fortune-tellers do it: they have someone palm your wallet, then impress the hell out of you by knowing your bank account's overdrawn and your mum's on holiday in Bognor.'

Miriam didn't know whether to laugh or cry. 'Is that what you think? That what I do is some kind of conjuring trick?'

'Excuse me,' Sheelagh interrupted acidly, 'but can we stick to the point? Somebody's way out of line, and I want to know who and I want it stopped.'

'Yes, of course,' agreed Miriam contritely. 'For the record, it wasn't me. There's nothing I can learn from your underwear or his papers that's half as useful as talking to you. That means, I'm afraid, that it was one of you.'

It was interesting, she thought then, to see where each of them instinctively looked: Richard at Will, Will at Larry, Joe at her, Tariq and Sheelagh at one another. Tessa was carefully looking nowhere, back in her safe neutrality.

Richard voiced what most of them were thinking. '*Why?* We're strangers—what motive could we have to spy on each other?'

Miriam cleared her throat. 'Let's be charitable and suppose it was a joke. But it wasn't funny, and if it happens again there'll be trouble. Everyone here is out on an emotional limb. It takes courage to do this: to parade your problems in front of strangers. It's difficult, it's embarrassing, but it's worth it for the support you can give one another. If somebody's going to undermine that they'd better hope I never find out who.'

She had another exercise for them. 'Who was your best friend at school?'

'A fat boy called Charles,' remembered Will. 'He was no good at games either.'

'My best friend was called Cathy,' said Sheelagh. 'We were both terrific at games.'

'Tracy Louise Walters,' drawled Tariq, his eyes misty with nostalgia. 'We played games as well.'

'My best friend at school was called Smelly.' With a grin Richard explained. 'The caretaker's Jack Russell—we used to go ratting in the air-raid shelters during break. And quite often during maths.'

'Tessa?'

'I was a dreadful swot at school,' she confessed with a peridot twinkle in her eye. 'I decided early on what I wanted to be. After that I was always working towards it. My best friend was another embryo doctor, Lynn—something. We studied Latin together, God forgive us.'

'Larry?'

The tennis pro looked at Miriam as if she'd called him out when he couldn't see the linesman for chalk-dust. 'I'm forty-one years old,' he said distinctly. 'I don't remember the name of anyone I was at school with.'

'I'm fifty-six,' said Joe, 'and I can remember the name of everybody in my class. *And* where they sat.'

'Well, bully for you.'

'*And* whose mum did them a proper lunch, and who just got bread and dripping.' Joe smirked. 'My best friend was Duncan Wilder. His mum baked Eccles cakes.'

'All right,' said Larry in mounting impatience. 'My best friend was the captain of the girls' hockey team. Charity Matchett. She scored the winning goal for England in the 1973 world championships. She went on to become a concert violinist and Labour MP for Bootle.'

There was a longish pause while people wondered if it was safe to laugh. Then Miriam said levelly. 'That isn't actually true, though, is it?'

'Not actually, no.'

'You don't see the point of this, do you?'

'Not even slightly.'

'Does anyone?' Looking round them expectantly she met only averted gazes and the odd embarrassed cough. She sighed. 'People are partly born and partly made. Some of our strengths and weaknesses are inherent, there from the moment of conception. Others are acquired in the course of our development. It's useful to know which of our problems are programmed into our genes and which we've created for ourselves. By looking back to childhood we can see ourselves in something close to our native state, without the emotional baggage we've picked up since.'

There was a bemused pause. Then Will murmured, 'She means, Were we born weird, did we achieve weirdness, or was weirdness thrust upon us?'

Miriam chuckled deep in her throat. 'I like that. I may use it in my advertising. All right, we know about Smelly. Sheelagh, tell us about Cathy.'

Momentarily Sheelagh hesitated; then she began. 'We were eleven. We met on the junior athletics squad. She beat me over a hundred metres, I beat her over five hundred. She was stronger, I had more stamina. For three years we carved up sports day between us.

'What she was really good at, though, was tennis. By the time she was thirteen it was obvious she was wasted on school matches. There was a place in Richmond that gave tennis tuition as part of the syllabus. When her family were sure it was what she wanted they sent her there.

'We kept in touch but we had less and less to talk about. Selina's mum was right: the price Cathy paid for her first professional points was everything else. All she knew about, all she was interested in, was tennis. But it paid off—she got to Wimbledon. Twice she was the last Brit in the women's singles.'

'Do you still see her?'

'I didn't see her for years. Then about eighteen months ago she turned up out of the blue, dropped into my office for a gossip. It was lousy timing. I'd have loved to catch up on her news but I was expecting a client. We swapped phone numbers, promised to get together, but somehow it didn't happen. I was busy. I expect she was too.' She took a deep breath. 'Then it was too late. I picked up the paper one day and she was dead, killed in an accident. She only twenty-six.'

Something odd was happening. The silence was no longer a polite absence of chatter while she spoke. It had become an entity in itself, huge and oppressive, squatting in their midst like a great toad, using up the air. Waiting for it to end was like waiting for a volcano to erupt.

Miriam scanned their expressions, reading shock and pain in equal proportions. Sheelagh merely looked puzzled at the electric silence she had provoked. Larry, his jaw clenched like a clam, showed no emotion at all.

Will's voice was as bloodless as his cheek. 'A road accident. She died in a road accident.'

Richard shook his head. 'A car accident. She drove into the Thames.'

Startled as if the ground had moved under her, Sheelagh looked from one to the other. 'You knew her? Cathy?' Her eyes hardened, sank claws into Richard's face. 'The woman who drowned was Cathy Beacham?'

Richard nodded a numb assent.

Her eyes scored him, moved on to Will. 'You knew her too?'

'I loved her.' Cracks appeared in his voice. 'She drove into the river?—I never knew that. I was—out of the country when it happened.' The fractional pause where none was called for hit Richard like a blow. With a certainty born of years listening for such clues he thought, He's lying! Why on earth is he lying? What the *hell* is going on here?

'When I got back—' For some moments Will couldn't continue but no one jumped into the hiatus. They waited for him to regain control. 'My secretary told me. She said Cathy died in her car. I assumed it was a crash. But it was suicide? His voice climbed.'

Richard nodded soberly. 'That was the finding at the inquest.'

Sheelagh was on her feet in the circle, her short fuse burning dangerously close to detonation. Her eyes found Miriam. 'You don't expect us to believe this is a coincidence? Two total strangers sharing an acquaintance I could just about swallow, but three?'

'Four,' Tariq said emptily. 'I knew Cathy too. I represented her for a time.' He reached inside his jacket, drew out the letter with his picture photocopied on to it. 'That's her, that I had my arm around. We were celebrating her first sponsorship.'

They looked. It could have been anyone, just the shoulder and sleeve of a white dress. It wasn't possible to tell the age of the occupant, or even that she was black.

As if they were playing poker, Will matched Tariq's picture with his own. 'She was in that one too. It was taken in Paris, the weekend we got engaged. She gave the camera to some children and they took it. She was on this side'— he tapped with his fingertip at the uneven border—'with the Eiffel Tower behind her.'

Richard's letter made it three. 'I don't wear a suit that often so I'm pretty sure where it was taken. At the inquest.'

'And mine was taken at Beckenham when I went to cheer her on one summer,' said Sheelagh. 'Cathy took it. So who else? Larry? Joe? Tessa?' None of them offered a contribution. Sheelagh's voice became viperous. 'Well, Larry, the one thing we know about you is that you're a tennis bum. It would be pretty odd if you *didn't* know her.'

He wouldn't answer. Will answered for him. 'He knew her.' The hatred that had startled Richard returned to thicken his voice. 'He coached her. But only while it paid him. He used her, and he broke her, and when she was past mending he threw away the pieces. Not as if she was a person: as if she was a thing. A tool, something he used till it was done and he needed a new one.' The words were running up out of control but he hardly seemed aware of it.

Larry's eyes were glacial and his voice growled like bergs in an icefield. 'Sonny, you don't know what you're talking about.'

But Will was too angry to back down this time. 'I wondered if it was you. I wasn't sure, we never met. But when you talked about the trouble at your club I was certain. It takes a special kind of bastard to turn talent into a bludgeon to beat someone with, but if that's how you behave it's how you're going to go on behaving. The tragedy is that Cathy's mum didn't take you apart when you took an interest in her. What did you call Cathy? I know what she called you—the Iron Maiden.' In his passion he poured such scorn into the words that what might have been mere satire came over as a deadly insult. The tennis-player reacted with speed and ferocity: he slapped the younger man's face.

That right hand was still capable of hundred-mile-an-hour serves and Will reeled under the impact. But this was a confrontation he'd had many times in his mind, that he'd dreamed of, and probably nothing Larry could have done that left him standing would have stopped him. He straightened, his cheek flaming, an unimpressive figure cloaked in shining rage. His eyes raked the room for Tariq. 'And if he was one of Cathy's sharks, that makes you the other.'

Tariq's lips moved as if to reply—not to deny it, perhaps to attempt an explanation. Then his gaze slid sideways to the psychologist, observing with quiet intensity and making no effort to intervene. 'All right, Miriam,' he said softly. 'We can see what you've done. Do you *want* to tell us why?'

Miriam responded obliquely. 'What makes you think this is my doing? I didn't invite you on this course—you applied.'

'Or someone sent us,' said Richard. 'I thought Will was being paranoid but he was right. Almost nobody's here by choice. Joe says he is, and maybe Tariq is though the idea was sold to him. The rest of us are here because someone else fixed it. Did anyone get a choice of dates?' A few heads shook uncertainly. 'And these photographs—where did they come from?'

Miriam bore their hostility unflinchingly. 'What can I tell you? There were seven applications. I accepted them all. I asked for a photo of each of you and they came with your cheques. It may be you were referred by third parties— many of my clients are. That's where the pictures came

from—Richard's station, Sheelagh's client, the organizers
of Will's competition and so on. If you want to know where
they got them you'll have to ask them.'

The silence returned, stretching and crawling. There was
no doubt they'd stumbled on to something meaningful but
the meaning eluded them. The silence was made up of a
million tiny biochemical noises as synapses fired and mis-
fired and the cogs of mind and memory turned and meshed
and slipped and turned again.

Larry shook his sculpted head once, deliberately. Everything he did was deliberate, either to conserve energy or to
exploit it. He wore an aura of dynamic stillness as if the
potential for explosive action was implicit in every breath
he took. 'No, we don't. I don't have to do anything. All I
have to do is leave. I'll bid you all goodbye now. It's been
interesting, but I don't imagine we'll meet again.' He carried every eye with him as he left the room, and some
admired his courage in walking out and some despised his
cowardice for the same reason. But no one made a move
to follow him.

None of them had many belongings here. It took only
moments for Larry to throw his into his grip. Then he went
to the lift and punched the button. There was no distant
whirring of gears so he punched again.

Mrs Venables appeared at his elbow. 'I'll get the builders
to reconnect it.' Breathing heavily, Larry dumped his grip
on the floor to wait. After a moment he leaned against the
shut doors.

Those in the conference room were still puzzling over
the turn of events when a cry of alarm so desperate it
seemed barely human froze both souls and limbs.

Richard, who'd heard more screams than most people,
recovered first or at least moved fastest. But by the time he
reached the corridor there was no one in sight.

TEN

THEY FOUND LARRY in Sheelagh's room, sitting on the floor nursing his hand. Only relief, because like all of them she'd thought something dreadful had happened, kept Sheelagh from violence. Her lip curled. 'You?'

He realized what she was thinking, dismissed it irritably. 'Don't be silly.' He stood up and showed her his hand. Deep indentations pitted the skin below his thumb. 'The sod bit me.'

'The dog?' Tessa frowned. Different species produce different bite patterns and this one wasn't canine.

'Dog be damned.' Larry climbed to his feet. 'It was a boy.'

They were losing the capacity for surprise. As if explaining to a simpleton Joe said, 'It couldn't have been. How could there be a boy up here? It must have been the dog that startled Mrs Venables.'

Larry leaned forward, speaking into his face. 'Old man, I've been teaching tennis for fifteen years. There are those who'd tell you I'm better at the tennis than the teaching but I have worked out the difference between a boy and a dog. That'—he waved his hand under Joe's nose—'was a boy. Aged about sixteen. As for how he got up here, I presume the same way we did. A boy could at least operate the lift, which is more than a dog could.'

Tessa nodded. 'Those are human bite marks.'

'What happened?' asked Miriam.

Larry had waited impatiently for either the housekeeper to return or the lift to start up. After a moment it occurred to him that leaning on the doors probably wasn't a great idea: with the building unfinished the idiot-proofing of its systems might be incomplete too. He paced the corridor looking for somewhere to drum his fingers.

A movement in one of the women's rooms caught his eye. He assumed that someone else had had enough of this farce and was packing up. The door was open; he put his head inside to commend her common sense.

It was neither Sheelagh nor Tessa, nor anyone else he'd met. It was like nothing he'd ever seen. He had it in view for three or four seconds before it felt his scrutiny and rounded on him like a wild animal, and in that time he couldn't be quite sure he was looking at a human being.

His first impression was of something short and thickset, dwarfish, bent over the drawer whose contents it was examining with absorption. Larry got no immediate sense of age or sex; at that point he still half-believed it was an animal, an ape or a small bear, something covered in a dense mat of dark shaggy fur.

He wasn't sure what he did to draw its attention. But suddenly it whirled towards him, eyes wild in a moon-white face, and he saw what it was: a boy, an adolescent human male, wrapped in so many layers of old clothes that the ragged edges had frayed into a coarse pelt.

Larry closed the door behind him and turned the key. 'So what are you, sonny—a pervert or a thief?'

He advanced deliberately and the boy backed toward the window. But they were six hundred feet up. The windows didn't open and wouldn't break: he hadn't come in that way and he couldn't get out. The corner of the room stopped his retreat and Larry reached for him.

Despite having none of his own, Larry reckoned to know something about children. In particular, he had spent enough time with teenage boys to know they were stubborn, sullen, devious, deceitful and capable when provoked of real and sustained viciousness. He didn't expect this one to come quietly. He expected him to struggle, to punch and kick if he got the chance, and to use words not heard since McEnroe's last visit to Centre Court.

He didn't expect the boy to yell like an animal in a trap. Another man might have leapt back, spilling furniture in his surprise. But Larry fastened both hands in the boy's disreputable clothing and shook him. 'Stop that.'

The cry ended abruptly. The boy twisted like an eel inside his amorphous clothes and sank his teeth deep in the man's hand. Larry let out a few choice words of his own and lurched back, and the tangled knot of man and boy crashed to the floor.

The teeth, the fall or sheer surprise loosened Larry's grip. In a second the boy had thrown him off, bounded over the top of him, wrenched open the door and was gone.

'Didn't you see him? In the corridor?' Miriam shook her head. 'You must have! He was barely through the door before you arrived. Whichever way he turned you couldn't have missed seeing him.'

'Larry,' she said patiently, 'I'm telling you what we saw. Nothing. We heard the yell. We thought it was you—that you'd had an accident. It took us a second to react, then we rushed for the corridor. There was no sign of any boy then.'

Larry pushed through them, peered both ways. The corridor ran straight for thirty yards in each direction. 'He must have ducked into one of the rooms. Come on, before he gets away.'

But either they'd wasted too much time or the boy had moved faster than Larry thought possible. A search of the bedrooms, their own and the unfurnished ones beyond, was fruitless; nor had he sneaked past them into the conference room or the kitchen. The corridor ended in a blank wall to the east, in a locked door to the west. Larry scowled.

'There's nowhere else he could have gone. Unless the lift arrived?'

Mrs Venables was apologetic. 'I couldn't raise the builders. The phone was ringing but no one answered. You see the time? I think they've forgotten we're here. I think they've finished for the weekend and we'll not see them again until Monday morning.'

It was enough to evict the strange boy from their minds. Typically for people learning of a disaster second-hand, they couldn't quite believe the housekeeper had got it right. One by one they slipped away to the kitchen to try the phone for themselves. One by one they returned, looking chastened.

Joe spoke for them all. 'That's what they've done—gone home and forgotten us.' He looked disgustedly at his watch. 'Half past four on a Friday afternoon and there's nobody left on the bloody site. No wonder it takes them months to build a brick privy.'

'Can we phone for help?' suggested Tessa.

He shook his head. 'I tried that. It's not connected to the exchange. It's just an internal line.'

They regarded one another levelly, nine intelligent mature people trying not to panic in a situation that was the adult equivalent of getting locked in the cupboard under the stairs. They were trying to think if it mattered.

They'd come for the weekend. If the workmen returned at eight o'clock on Monday they'd be released twelve or fourteen hours late. Richard's wife would be puzzled but not alarmed: she was used to him misjudging when he'd be home. Tessa's husband, who worked in a hospital, was on nights and wouldn't expect to see her until Monday evening. No one else had anyone to go home to.

There was food to take them up to teatime on Sunday— it would stretch to an extra supper and breakfast. They had power, heat and light. It was an inconvenience, not a disaster.

They could have accepted the situation philosophically but for a growing sense of unease. Even before these new complications, they had made a disturbing discovery: that they'd been tricked into coming here by someone who knew private things about them, who had old and personal photographs of them. They couldn't imagine who he was or what his motive except that clearly it concerned Cathy Beacham. The puzzlement of a few minutes ago turned to anxiety with the discovery that they were no longer free to leave.

Nor was there much comfort in one another's company. They were not the random cross-section of humanity they were supposed to be. They traded suspicious glances as it occurred to them, one by one, that if someone had set them up the best place to observe the results was from their midst. They had been learning to trust each other; now they backed off fast. Someone was jerking their strings and, since they couldn't know who, everyone mistrusted everyone else. It was going to feel a very long weekend.

Even without some idiot boy poking through their belongings and howling like a banshee. Larry looked up as an idea struck him. 'He really isn't here, is he?'

'The boy?' Miriam shook her head. 'We've looked everywhere.'

The coach's lip curled. 'Don't you understand? If the lift's off and he's not here there must be some other way down.'

There was the locked door: the boy might have a key. But Larry didn't think so. 'There wasn't time for him to reach it without being seen. It was just seconds between him haring off and you people getting here. Linford Christie couldn't have got offside that quickly.'

Sheelagh hadn't seen any boy. Her tone was sceptical. 'Linford Christie was here too?'

Larry rounded on her, intimidating in his proximate strength. 'You don't believe me? You don't think there was a boy? You think I bit my own hand, screamed, then sat down in a corner? Have you got as far as thinking why?'

But Sheelagh was the last person he should have got ratty with. She thrived on discord. 'If that was the oddest thing that had happened it'd still make more sense than something that might be a boy and might be a dog stalking the penthouse of a forty-storey building and vanishing into thin air contrary to the laws of physics and common sense.'

Tariq distracted them with practicalities. 'Larry's right, there must be another way down. A fire-escape.'

Tessa looked at him as if he were mad. 'I am *not* climbing forty storeys down a ladder!'

'It'll be more substantial than that—a fireproof stairwell probably. The first thing they do in a fire is cut the power so the lifts go off. There has to be some way to evacuate the building.'

They'd all seen *Towering Inferno*. They liked him less for reminding them that they were trapped in a zone where the only passing traffic was weather balloons.

But they searched the corridor anyway, from the blank wall to the locked door, and there were bedrooms and domestic offices but no staircase. 'It must be beyond the locked door.'

Kneeling, Sheelagh put an eye to the keyhole. 'Then I hope we never need it. The corridor's full of stuff—piles of bricks, stacks of timber, plumbing. Even if we could open the door we couldn't get through.'

Miriam tried to inject a positive note. 'We could get on with what we came here for. At worst we're here till Monday morning; at best someone will remember the lift and come back.' She returned to the conference room, and after a moment an unenthusiastic trickle followed her. They had nothing else to do.

But they didn't pick up where they'd left off when the shade of Cathy Beacham joined them. They'd been led by the nose long enough: now they were going to set their own agenda.

'So this is about Cathy Beacham,' said Larry. 'Hands up those who knew her.'

Four hands went up immediately; after a moment he added his own. 'You're right about one thing,' he said coldly, looking at Will. 'I was her coach. Tessa?'

The doctor shrugged helplessly. 'Possibly. I'm not sure. I see a lot of patients in the course of a year. I don't remember the name. Where did she live?'

'The family lived in the Midlands,' said Sheelagh. 'I don't know where she lived in London—I had her number, that's all. Will, where was she when you knew her?'

The fury that had goaded him to pick a fight with a man he couldn't hope to beat had dissipated, leaving him subdued and a little sullen. 'She used to have a flat in Colliers Wood but she could have moved.'

'Then yes, it's possible I treated her at some point. I've never specialized in sports medicine but I could have seen her as a GP. I'm sorry I can't be more specific but I have a list of about two thousand patients at any given time and if I don't see somebody regularly...' Her voice tailed off apologetically.

Larry said, 'Five yesses and a maybe. Joe?'

He took time to answer. 'Yes, I met her too. My daughter played some tennis—most of her friends were other players. We met quite a few of them over the years.'

'She visited your home?'

'Yes.'

Larry spread his hand. 'That's it?'

Joe bristled. 'What were you expecting? It's normal enough for kids to bring their friends home, isn't it?'

'Joe, there's nothing normal about *any* of this,' Sheelagh exclaimed impatiently. 'Tell us again how you heard about this course.'

He looked faintly embarrassed. 'There was a postcard tucked into a business magazine I still get. Offering stressed-out executives a psychological MOT. I thought, Why not—what harm can it do?'

There was a lengthy pause while the others pondered that. Then Tariq said, 'So probably all of us have known Cathy to some extent at some time. But so what? What does anyone hope to gain by bringing us together like this?'

It had taken Will almost till now to start thinking clearly again. To learn, this long after, new shocking facts about the death of a girl he'd loved had swept the feet from under him. It had also been a shock to find himself among people he'd previously known only by ill repute. And losing control had shocked him to his foundations: Will Furney *never* lost his temper, whatever the provocation. So it had taken a little time for him to get his head together again; but now the answer to Tariq's question seemed obvious to him. 'Doesn't it rather smack of grudge?'

'Revenge? For what?'

Will stared at him. 'For the fact that Cathy's dead. She was twenty-six years old. She was beautiful and talented. She had everything to look forward to. But she drove her car—' His voice cracked on it; he had to swallow and try again. 'She committed suicide. Someone blames us for that. We don't know one another but someone knows us all. I think he blames us for her death. He wants—' He fell silent.

'What?' asked Tariq.

Blinking, Will returned from a moment's reverie. 'I don't know. But there's something he, or she, wants very much. And it occurs to me to wonder if the lift going off when it did was only a bit of forgetfulness after all.'

ELEVEN

You DON'T THINK this is getting a shade imaginative?' ventured Miriam. 'Isn't the obvious answer also the most likely—that the silly sods downstairs forgot? They're not used to having people up here.'

Will frowned. 'This is the first time you've held a course in the hotel?'

She didn't react as if she'd blundered. 'In this building, yes.'

'Who was the friend who fixed it up?'

'I told you, he's on the Lazaire's board.'

'His name?'

She smiled composedly. 'You wouldn't know him.'

'He went to a lot of trouble. They're still working down below, but up here we've got glass in the windows and doors that lock. We've got carpets, furniture, electricity and plumbing. Isn't that a rather odd way to build a hotel—from the top down?'

Miriam said nothing.

'And all for one weekend. Because you won't be back, will you?' The psychologist still didn't answer. 'This friend—was it his idea? He arranged it, got us here. All you had to do was turn up and put us through hoops. Not just any old hoops, though: friendship and betrayal. I think, if you told us his name, we might recognize it.'

For a moment she seemed to consider it. Then she shook her head. 'It would be a betrayal of trust.'

A smile bent Will's lips. He was still pale but this was a job he knew: extracting information from someone who didn't want to give it. 'Dr Graves, this whole thing is a betrayal of trust. We came to you for professional help with problems that have damn near torn some of us apart.'

A faint flush touched the psychologist's cheek and she nodded thoughtfully. 'I bet Wormwood Scrubs is full of people who underestimated you.'

Will shook his head. 'I don't do prosecutions. I defend.'

The others had followed with more or less facility depending on their intellectual equipment. Sapphire eyes snapping between the protagonists, Sheelagh demanded, 'Does she know what this is about?'

Will kept his gaze on Miriam. 'Yes.'

Larry shouldered his way between them. 'Then it's time she told us.' It wasn't necessarily a threat and he may not have intended violence. But the possibility sent ripples through the tense atmosphere.

Joe moved stoutly to the woman's side. 'Now then,' he rumbled, 'let's not get silly. It's a bit of a turn-up, but let's think what we're doing before we start throwing our weight around.'

'Old man,' gritted Larry, 'I know exactly what I'm doing. I'm going to find out what's going on here and who's behind it from the only person who knows—any way it takes.'

Joe's chest swelled and his voice, always gruff, dropped another note. 'In that case I know what I'm doing too. I'm stopping you.'

If they'd come to blows there could have been only one outcome, though the athlete was past his prime and the printer still a substantial figure. But there were too many disapproving onlookers for it to degenerate that far.

Larry backed down with a bad grace. 'She doesn't need your protection. Can't you see? She's making fools of us. We were brought here under false pretences, we're being kept here against our will, and we still don't know why. Someone's gone to a lot of trouble. He must want something. You're afraid *I* might get rough? Ask yourself what *he's* planning. Because we can't get away from here and we can't call for help.'

When Will had made the same point Richard had dismissed it as the anxiety of a naturally timid man. But Larry was a tough and pragmatic man who wouldn't feel threatened without good cause, and that shunted the situation across the shadow line into the realm of fear. The possibility couldn't safely be discounted that they had been betrayed into the hands of real malevolence. They'd been hunted down and their presence engineered by someone whose identity they didn't know, whose motives they didn't understand and whose intentions they couldn't begin to predict.

And Miriam still wasn't telling the truth. Tariq knew it too. 'I may have been talked into it but I booked my own place, and I didn't send that photograph. Where did it come from?'

Though it amused him to play a role, actually he was both intelligent and intuitive. In fact, none of these people was as they had been described to Miriam. She made a decision. 'Listen, everyone, this is getting out of hand. No one's in any danger, I promise. Nobody meant to keep you here by force—the lift going off really was an accident. I'll tell you what I can, all right?

'I haven't lied to you. My friend asked my help in bringing together some people he didn't think would accept an invitation. He used various personal and business contacts to get you here—Sheelagh's client, Tariq's colleague, Tessa's journal. He offered free places to Richard's station and Larry's club knowing that because of their current difficulties they'd be the obvious choice to send. He put a postcard in Joe's magazine and invented a competition for Will to win. You all knew Cathy. More than that, you're all people on whom at one time or another she depended—

her advisers, her friends, the man who almost saved her life.'

'*Why?*' rasped Larry. He seemed no happier now he was getting the answers he'd demanded. 'Does he blame *us* for her death?'

Miriam nodded. 'In a way. Cathy was a girl who had admirers all her life. She attracted people. They enjoyed being with her, partly because of who she was and partly because some of the glitter rubbed off. They enjoyed the benefits of her friendship. In spite of that she died alone. None of those who made personal or professional capital from knowing her during her best years were there when she needed them. My friend thinks that's why she died. Because she ended up alone.'

'But what does he *want?*' asked Richard, his voice reedy thin. 'Even if he's right and we let her down, we can't do anything about it now. We're all sorry for what happened to her, maybe we're all unhappy with our own performance, but we didn't kill her. It was suicide. Has he gone to all this trouble only to hear that?'

'He wants you to understand what you did,' Miriam said carefully. 'He's concerned that, precisely because you didn't push her in, you aren't aware of having contributed to her death. He believes that with better friends she'd still be alive.'

'Maybe he's right,' Tariq conceded quietly. 'Even if he is, what good can this do?'

'And maybe he's wrong,' snarled Larry. 'Cathy had as much going for her as anyone. What she lacked was the heart to ride out the difficult times. I taught her how to play tennis. I taught her to be a tennis-player, which isn't quite the same thing. But it wasn't my job to organize the rest of her life. When she stopped playing tennis there was nothing more I could do for her.'

Will said softly, 'It's her father, isn't it?'

There was a measured silence. Then Miriam said, 'What makes you think so?'

'The photographs. Most of them could have come from her effects—mine could hardly have come from anywhere else. Also, there's no one here from her family and if he was anyone else he'd blame them too. Home's the last refuge. When everything else goes wrong—your lover walks out and your friends laugh and your boss tells you to stop crying on his stationery—you pick up the phone and call home. Cathy loved her parents. When she sent me packing I told myself at least she had her family to fall back on if things worked out badly.

'Well, they did, worse than I ever imagined. But for some reason her family was no help. Maybe they'd drifted apart by then, or maybe they let her down too. Either way, whoever's behind this would blame them if he was anyone other than her father. Or maybe he does blame himself. Maybe we're here because he's desperate to share out the responsibility.'

Again it seemed a long time before Miriam spoke. 'You're a perceptive man, Will. Yes, we're here because of Cathy's father. Did you ever meet him?'

Will shook his head. 'Cathy visited them sometimes. Not often. It meant breaking her training schedule and her coach—' He stopped abruptly, his eyes meeting Larry's like a collision. All he'd known about Cathy's advisers had been second-hand. Now he had a face to put to what he'd been told and what he'd inferred. His voice dripped acid. 'Apparently Larry disapproved.'

Larry didn't like Will much more than Will liked Larry. He shrugged. 'It's tough at the top. You have to put everything else on hold for a while. I didn't mind her seeing them; I did mind her missing training. It would have been easier for them to come and see her but they wouldn't. Neither would you, as I recall.'

Will flushed angrily. 'Cathy didn't want me hanging round the courts. Tennis had taken over enough of her life. She needed somewhere she could retreat where it wasn't the only topic of conversation.'

'I was right about you,' sneered Larry, the twist of his lips sculpted in the hard musculature of his face. 'I knew you were no good for her. I didn't have to meet you—I knew your type. You think it's all frilly knickers and silver salvers, don't you, champagne and strawberries. You think it'd be a nice way for well-brought-up young ladies to make a living if it wasn't for the boring old men in the background taking it all so seriously.

'Let me tell you something. Cathy wasn't the girl you took her for. Tennis wasn't something pleasant to do on a sunny afternoon. It was her career. She worked at it. She pushed herself to the limits, then pushed some more. She shed sweat and tears for it, and if blood had been required she'd have bled too. And gladly, because being an athlete is a privilege. If God gives you the talent you owe Him ten years of your life in order to be as good as you can be. Not everyone makes the top, but if you give it all you've got for ten years you've paid your dues. Nothing that happens afterwards alters the fact that you were an athlete. No one can take that away.

'But she couldn't make you understand that, could she? You thought she should be working office hours, with five weeks' holiday a year. When she was too tired to hold in the tears, instead of saying, Cathy, you can do this, it's what you want and you're strong enough to take it, you wanted her to walk away. To give up all she'd worked to achieve. You're soft and you're ordinary, Will. You wanted a nice safe ordinary wife, and you couldn't take it that she wanted to fulfil her potential more than she wanted you.'

This was the woman Will had loved they were talking about, and today he'd learned that she killed herself because her glittering career was over and she was alone. Tears spilt from his eyes. 'I'd have done anything for her. But all she wanted was for me to leave her alone. So I did. I left her to your care. And you let her die.'

Larry had too much self-command to hit him again. But he crowded him until Will stepped backwards. His voice was thick with fury. 'You pygmy! *I* let her die? I'd have put my hand in the fire for Cathy Beacham. For five years, everything I did was designed to improve her chances, to get her to the top. You'd have done anything for her? Well, I *did* it. Everything in my life that wasn't helping Cathy I gave up. For five years she was my purpose for living.

'I let her die?' Again the threatening advance, the powerful body looming, before which Will had no choice but retreat. 'I loved that girl in a way you can't begin to comprehend. I understood her and felt for her. I knew what she was going through, and I knew where she was going to. I was closer to her than anyone she ever knew. How *dare* you say I let her die?'

Their slow two-step had taken them to the edge of the room. Larry reached for Will's shoulders. Will flinched, Richard started forward, but physical violence was not his intention. Larry turned the smaller man to the window, pressed his face against the glass. All the city spread below them, far down where the buses were like tiny preoccupied insects and the people were too small to see at all.

'See that?' Larry hissed in his ear. 'That's the view of eagles. That's how athletes see the world—from halfway to the sun. And it scares you shitless, doesn't it?'

Behind them the room stirred with indignation. But Larry ignored the angry remonstrance and held Will against the glass forty storeys above the street while his protests grew feeble and incoherent, his face went from pale to ashy and his eyes began to roll.

'Excuse me,' said Tariq, moving Miriam aside. He fisted one big hand in the neck of Larry's track suit and yanked.

TWELVE

'IF WE START PECKING at one another,' Tariq said levelly, 'there's going to be blood and feathers everywhere. We're likely to be here two more days and three nights. By then we'll be sick of the sight of each other. If we don't exercise a bit of restraint somebody's going to get hurt. That's the big danger—not what Cathy's father might do to us but what we might do to one another. Violence is a self-indulgence we can't afford.'

'Violence!' snorted Larry; but his derision somehow lacked conviction. He'd been as shocked as anyone at what he'd done. He was a physical man, a gladiator, and he didn't like to be reminded how close these manly virtues approached to vices. He wasn't a thug but he'd behaved like one and he was ashamed. He blamed the stress they were under. He blamed Will for provoking him. He blamed Cathy Beacham's father for bringing them here and the carelessness of the British workman for making them stay.

Will recovered his composure quicker than his colour. Once away from the window he had fewer qualms about looking at Larry than Larry had about looking at him. There was a glint of wry humour in his intelligent eyes. 'We should also try to avoid blaming each other. What I said was unfair. We're all pretty shocked—it's no wonder we're saying and doing stupid things. But we should remember we're not enemies. Our quarrel isn't with one another.'

'No.' Larry returned to the earlier theme with the relief of a man floundering out of a bog. He nodded at the psychologist. 'It's with her.'

'Yes,' agreed Will. He regarded Miriam coolly. 'Have you told us everything this time?'

She thought for a moment. 'Pretty well.'

'What are you expecting from us?'

'Nothing.'

'It doesn't matter to you that as soon as the lift comes on we're all going to leave?'

'Will, as soon as the lift comes on *I'm* going to leave. This hasn't exactly been a triumph for me, you know. I thought I could manage it better. It's true, I was using you, but I thought I could give you something in return. Self-knowledge, reconciliation, something. And then, you're not the people I was expecting. My friend—'

'Cathy's father.'

She acquiesced. 'Cathy's father has a rather jaundiced view of you. Naturally enough. He doesn't know you personally—all he knew was from Cathy and when things started going wrong she too was looking for people to blame. He saw you as callous exploitive people who'd taken his daughter for all she was worth then dumped her. I shouldn't have accepted that at face value. Maybe you could have done better but that's life, isn't it?—handling things badly and having regrets afterwards. As I'm doing now.

'So I suggest we tolerate one another till Monday, then part and hope not to meet again. Anyone who's out of pocket will of course be reimbursed. You have my apologies. You have my assurance that when I get him alone my friend will have some explaining to do. There's not much more I can say. As to how we spend the next sixty hours, I'm in your hands.'

The same idea came into everybody's head, and after a minute's resistance—it seemed crazy to do from choice what they'd been shanghaied into doing—Sheelagh voiced it. 'I'd like to hear more about Cathy. We were good friends once, I wish we'd kept in touch. You all knew her after I did—can you, I don't know, fill in the gaps? What happened to her? What went wrong?'

None of them was proud of their role in the short, brilliant, ultimately tragic career of Cathy Beacham. In other circumstances they would have avoided discussing it. But there was a lot of time to kill and no television, no radio, not even a pack of cards. And they all wondered what had gone wrong. None of them knew the dead woman throughout her career; Richard had known her for less than half an hour and hadn't exchanged an intelligible sentence with her in that time. Yet for these few days she would dominate all their lives. They wondered about her, what sort of a girl she had been, how her glittering career had turned to ashes. How she made the leap from tennis star to suicide.

'All right,' Larry said slowly, 'I'll start. I met her when she came to London. In the early eighties I was sidelined with injury. I did some coaching at the Fairfax School. I wasn't there long—I was twenty-six, at the top of my game between injuries—but long enough to see she had real promise. I knew I'd be seeing more of her.'

They'd sat down again, the neat ring of chairs relaxing into a more casual grouping. Larry crossed one leg over the other with the precision that marked his every act. 'I was right. Actually I didn't see a lot of her—unless you're playing mixed doubles you tend to hang out with the men you play with rather than the women—but she was always there, improving her placings with every tournament.

'Then I began losing ground. I couldn't stay fit long enough to keep my ranking. Finally I did my hamstring and never got back to match fitness.' The pain of that—not the physical injury but the more profound hurt—was still visible in the scar-deep creases around his eyes and audible in his voice.

'I fooled around at a less demanding level for a year or

two but there was no satisfaction in it. Not when I'd thought, I'd really thought, I could win Wimbledon. So I started coaching. If I couldn't be a winner maybe I could create winners. And I was good. I'd been there, and not so long before that I'd forgotten how it felt. I had some good players come to me. Cathy was one.'

He looked across the circle to Tariq. 'By then you knew her, didn't you?' He sniffed. 'She told me she had an agent as if I was meant to be impressed.'

The big man smiled. 'She told *me* her new coach ate barrow boys for breakfast.'

Larry laughed out loud. 'I remember saying that! I thought I was going to get advice on training as a form of earnings enhancement. I told her we'd get on fine as long as you never showed your face round the court.'

Tariq shrugged. 'I didn't need to see her play. I know nothing about tennis: my game is selling.

'We met at a party. She was only eighteen but already making her mark. The party was mostly sportsmen, artists, media people, and the conversation got on to sponsorship. I think I may have been holding forth, rather—at twenty years old I was a major pain in the bum. This tall black girl in a red dress came over afterwards and told me who she was. She said, If I was as good at selling as I thought I was, would I try selling her?'

He chuckled fondly. 'It was the sort of offer a cocky kid who thought the sun shone out of his own navel could hardly refuse. That was the start of a seven-year relationship.'

Sheelagh had an advantage over the others. She'd discussed this particular relationship with him before. 'How many of them were good ones?'

His eyes dipped an acknowledgement. 'Six. The last was a nightmare. She wasn't playing. Her private life was falling apart. She was strained, distracted, careless with her appearance, and when I did manage to get her an interview there was a good chance she wouldn't turn up. In the end I had to say, Look, Cathy, there's nothing more I can do for you. Sports stars don't go on being marketable too long after they stop playing—I don't think there's any mileage left in this.'

'What did she say?'

Tariq smiled and wiggled a false front tooth. 'She hit me.'

'What?!!' Cathy Beacham had been a tall, strong woman. But Tariq was a big man, and the idea of him being socked in the jaw by a girl in tennis whites was as engaging as it was improbable.

Will wasn't amused. He said stiffly, 'I find that hard to believe.'

Tariq tried to explain without adding to his hurt. So much of this was new to the man who'd loved her: he hadn't even known how she died. 'She changed, Will. After you parted. She was a different person. She used to be a nice kid—pushy but nice. Then one summer the niceness sort of dried up and blew away. She got—rough. Not tough, I don't mean that—she had to be tough to do the job. But that last year she got hard, mean. She'd do anything to get what she wanted. She was impossible to work with. I didn't know what to expect from one day to the next, almost from one hour to the next. I couldn't rely on her. And it wasn't just me she let down, it was clients and that reflected on my whole business. You reach a point where sentiment costs too much. When the stars cleared I told her we were finished.

'I wished her well—with blood dripping down my chin I genuinely wished her well. If she'd found someone else to represent her, cleaned up her act and made a packet just to spite me I'd have been delighted. But I didn't think it would happen and it didn't. The last I heard was about three months before her death, when she was arrested for being drunk and disorderly outside a Soho nightclub.'

THIRTEEN

WILL SAID, 'I don't believe you,' and his voice trembled.

Sheelagh reached over to touch his hand where it clenched the arm of his chair hard enough to blanch his knuckles. Unexpectedly gentle, she said, 'Will, it's true. It was about that time that she came to my office. I was shocked at the state of her.

'She wasn't there to gossip. She wanted a job. I'd have liked to help, because we were good friends once and she needed a friend. But there was nothing I could do. I couldn't have her meeting my clients—it was only midday but already she smelled of drink. I should have had the guts to tell her the truth, but it was easier to say I'd think about it, ask around, give her a call if anything came up. I took her number but I never meant to ring. If I couldn't use her I couldn't recommend her to anyone I knew.

'So I made an excuse and got rid of her. I told you I meant to keep in touch but that's not true. I hoped to God she wouldn't come back.' She folded her hands in her lap and stared down at them. Of the sharpness of word and manner that was her defining characteristic nothing remained. 'She didn't. And now I wish to God she had.'

The silence was broken at length by someone clearing a throat. It was the first contribution Tessa had made since things started getting serious. 'This is a medical opinion—though none of you are my patients so feel free to ignore it. But I'm not happy about what's going on here. You're flaying yourselves for failing to prevent something that was inevitable. If the girl's father can't accept that, maybe he needs a shrink, but I don't think the rest of you do. All this soul-searching—there's a price to be paid. Keep scratching a sore spot and you're going to bleed. If you want the damage to heal, stop playing with it.'

'I take it,' Miriam said softly, 'I'm not going to get unqualified approval from your journal.'

Tessa stared at her in frank astonishment. 'You expected to?'

Joe glared at them from under bushy eyebrows. 'Is this the best you two can do?' he demanded roughly, heavy head swinging from side to side like a bull's. 'For a poor dead girl and the people who cared about her? Bickering over who's got the best letters after her name? There are people here sweating blood trying to make sense of what happened, risking anger and ridicule and worse, and they could use a bit of help from the so-called experts.'

Having little to contribute to the process the former printer had seemed not much more than part of the furniture. Now the younger men and women who'd felt sorry for him and then forgotten about him eyed him with a respect that made the blood flush in his jowls. He backed off in embarrassment. 'I'm sorry, I know I'm less involved than some of you, but I want to know what happened too. I remember her as a bright girl in pigtails, a kid with all the world in front of her. How could someone like that, someone you all agree had talent to burn, end up killing herself? It can't just have been losing tennis matches. The world's full of people who can't play tennis—they don't all end up in the river.'

'When did she start losing?' asked Miriam quietly. She half-expected them to ignore her. But the thing had regained its momentum and now they were doing freely what Cathy's father had invested time and effort and money and deceit in: discussing the doomed girl who was the only link between them. In their various ways they had all cared for

Cathy Beacham. They all wanted to know what went wrong.

So Larry answered the question, accepting his share of their joint obligation, to the dead girl and to one another. 'You always lose matches. You can even hit a losing streak without it being the end of everything. But she started becoming a loser maybe eighteen months before her death.

'I became her personal coach when she was nineteen. She'd had a coach before, a good one, and she'd had some good results. But they both realized that if Cathy was to go as far as she could she needed something more—discipline, and technique, and someone stronger than herself not allowing her to fail. So she came to me.' Nothing that had happened since entirely destroyed his pride in that.

'For five years it was like training Pegasus for the Grand National. We could hardly lose. It didn't matter what the opposition was: if I got Cathy to the line sound in wind and limb she'd be the outstanding player. She didn't win every tournament she entered, but she won a lot of them and when she didn't win she fought like fury before she let anyone past her. If she got beaten she put us both through hell until she was back on form.

'I always knew she was good. The first time I saw her at Fairfax I knew, but I only realized how good when we started working together. At her best she made me think I'd never seen real talent before. She had the potential to be the best player in the world. For five years she got better and better.'

His eyes rolled to the ceiling. Tessa, who was closest, glimpsed tears. 'Then in the space of one season it fell apart. I don't know what went wrong. She'd never been stronger or looked better, and it wasn't her commitment that faltered. Some girls, once they reach their twenties, start wondering if the success is worth everything they've given up, but not Cathy. She wanted it more than ever.

Some days I thought she'd kill for it. But all the time she was losing control. At first I thought it was mental strain— she'd been in hard training since her mid-teens—but it wasn't. She could keep going all day.

'But something was badly wrong. All the ways that mattered she was going backwards. Her concentration started to slip and she got moody. Hell, it wasn't moods, it was instability. It got so if anything went wrong whoever was nearest got an earful. It was me, usually. Well, I could live with that, it was what she paid me for. It was harder to deal with when she started on other players and match officials.' His drawn face pinched tighter at the memory. The misery of watching her destroy herself in the one place he was helpless to protect her still stabbed like thorns. With all his imperfections he was a courageous man, and helplessness is worse for the brave.

'Then her coordination started to go. More than any other sport, coordination is what tennis is all about. Yes, you have to be able to cover the ground, and yes, you have to be able to power the racket, but if you can't hit that ball pretty well exactly where you want it you're wasting your time out there. Long before she had any technique to speak of she had superb hand-eye coordination. But it disappeared even as I watched. And there was no reason for it. She was in perfect physical shape: she was just playing crap tennis and losing her grip on her life.'

Sheelagh murmured, 'I suppose you considered drugs.'

He cast her a venomous look, but the anger faded almost before it reached her. He sighed. 'Of course. It's the first thing you think of, isn't it? I asked her; she denied it. I got rid of her on some pretext and searched her flat. I found nothing. She took urine tests from time to time like everyone else but nothing showed. Besides, I didn't see how she *could* be taking drugs. Feeding a habit is a time-consuming business and most of her time was spent with me. And steroids is a specialist area—I'd have heard if she was getting a supply through the usual channels.'

'What did you think was happening?'

Larry shrugged. Even this long afterwards there was an echo in his face of the agony of watching someone he was devoted to slide into the abyss. He'd seen himself as her rock, her strong foundations, but in the end she fell and he couldn't save her. He said softly, 'I didn't know. I took her to the doctor—under protest but by now I was desperate. I thought maybe she had a brain tumour or something. There was nothing on the scan. So I looked at the other possibilities. Maybe it was my fault: I was pushing her too hard. Maybe her boyfriend had been right and she needed more in her life than tennis.'

He looked at Will. 'I tried to contact you then. This was months after you split up. I wasn't sure if you'd want to know, but I had to do something—she was tearing herself apart. But I couldn't find you. She insisted she didn't want to see you again. She burned her address book in front of me so I couldn't call you, or her parents, or anyone else I thought might help. She'd done what I wanted—cut herself off from everything that might distract her from her task. I felt as if I'd sharpened the knife for her to cut her throat with.'

'We should have got together.' Tariq's velvet eyes were deep with regret. 'I felt the same way—I didn't know what to do with her. She'd had some good deals—sponsorships, endorsements, a bit of modelling, a TV ad. Then all at once she'd no more interest in it. It was something she'd fit in if she'd nothing better to do. She seemed to think the clients were lucky to get her. Worse than that, she let them see it.

'People who're spending good money won't stand for that. When she started losing matches as well as her manners they dropped her. I put off making a decision—hoping for a miracle I guess. Even if she never recovered her form

I could have done something for her if only she'd helped. She was an attractive girl and there was that spark of fire that meant you never forgot her. She could have been a property long after she was too slow to reach tennis-balls. But she'd dug herself a hole and wouldn't stop digging, and the time came that I had to let her go.'

'The time never came that I let her go,' Larry retorted fiercely. 'I coached her as long as she'd come. When she stopped coming I went and got her. She was still young, she could have got back. If I could have found out what the problem was I could have got her through it. But she quit. She wouldn't see me, wouldn't even talk on the phone. Dear God,' he laughed despairingly, 'I even wrote to her, but she never replied.

'By then she hadn't played in public for six months. She hadn't won anything worth having for more than a year. Maybe she was right and there was nothing left to salvage. But it shouldn't have ended like that—as if what she'd achieved, what I'd helped her do, was worth nothing. She was a great tennis-player, but the way she was that last year people couldn't wait to forget. She didn't deserve that. She didn't throw it away by choice. Maybe nothing showed up but I'll always believe she was ill.'

'Why did you stop coaching?' asked Miriam.

His eyes spat at her. 'I didn't. I still coach.'

'No,' she said patiently, 'you give lessons at a tennis club. I might call that coaching but until recently you wouldn't have done.'

Defeated, Larry bowed his head. 'It's a living. Why?— because I never want the responsibility for someone like Cathy again. She was a once-in-a-lifetime chance and I blew it. I don't know how but I blew it, and that failure cost her her life. I won't risk that happening ever again.'

Tessa broke the silence of respect, of remembrance, in

the crassest way imaginable. 'Any abnormalities in the brain would have been noted at the autopsy.'

'She drove into a river,' Larry said in his teeth. 'They wouldn't puzzle too long over the cause of death.'

'No,' she agreed, not realizing they were arguing. The intelligent hazel eyes were thoughtful. 'But they'd have spotted a brain tumour of any size. Were you at the inquest? Did they find anything interesting?'

'Stop it,' said Will.

'I have a copy of the post-mortem report,' Miriam said quietly. 'There was no tumour.'

Tessa nodded. 'Anyway, a lesion severe enough to cause personality changes a year earlier would probably have killed her.'

'Please, stop it.'

'Unless she had treatment and I presume you'd know if she had.' She twitched a little smile. 'I mean, it's hard not to notice when someone turns up with a row of stitches where their fringe used to be.'

'God damn you,' cried Will, coming to his feet, 'stop this! You've no right to talk about her like that. You don't even remember her! You've no right talking about her as if she was—dead meat.'

'But she is dead, isn't she?' Tessa said reasonably. 'That's why we're here—because Cathy Beacham is dead. Her life fell apart and she killed herself. Her father blames the people she knew but you all feel she was on self-destruct for more than a year. Larry suspects a neurological problem; I'm just saying it's unlikely. If there had been it wouldn't have gone undetected so long.'

'Why does it matter to you?' Sheelagh wasn't upset in the way Will was but she resented this clinical, even cynical intrusion into a grief Tessa clearly didn't share.

Tessa spread long-fingered hands, not understanding the hostility she'd provoked. 'It doesn't, except that it's why

I'm stuck here. I'm sorry I can't remember her. I agree, it's likely that I treated her, and maybe her father thinks I should have made a better job of it. Hell, maybe I should— maybe there were symptoms I missed, maybe I sent her away with a scrip for sleeping pills when what she needed was referring to a psychiatrist. I don't know. All I'm saying is, if it was a physical problem it would've shown up at the autopsy. What's your problem with that?'

Miriam said quietly, 'This is very personal to some of these people. Try to consider their feelings.' She asked Larry, 'Did she start drinking because she stopped winning or vice versa?'

'She never drank when I knew her,' the coach said emphatically. 'Not even socially, not even when the trouble began. It wasn't a cause. It wasn't even a direct result. Maybe it was a last resort, after everything was gone.'

'Then what *was* the beginning?' demanded Tariq. 'She went into the nineties in sparkling form. She was playing well, she was playing the sponsors like a violin, she was still heading for the stars. What changed? What happened to alter her whole attitude?'

'You think I haven't asked myself that?' snarled Larry. 'Or that something could turn her inside out and I wouldn't notice? I noticed when she missed an hour's sleep, when she got a tax demand, when she ran out of coffee for God's sake! For five years I lived for that girl. I knew her better than she knew herself. I knew what she was capable of, and what she needed.

'Then suddenly I didn't know her any more. I don't know what happened. It was as if someone had stolen my golden girl and left a changeling in her place: a coarse replica, aggression instead of drive, temperament instead of talent. She was almost literally a different girl. I don't know where my Cathy went. Try as I did, and I tried till my heart was broken, I never found her.'

Miriam stood up, just touching his shoulder in mute sympathy as she passed behind him. She sighed. 'It's getting late. It's been a funny old day but maybe not a wasted one. Even if it took deceit to get you here, you all had reason to come and it seems to me that dealing with what happened to Cathy has been good for you. Maybe we'll talk some more in the morning.' She smiled. 'Unless we get up and find the lift's back on, in which case I don't expect I'll see you for dust.'

No one argued. They were exhausted, in the brain and in the bone, heads and bodies aching with the effort of exploring their own and one another's psyches. The fact that the day had taken an unexpected turn actually added little to that burden. It was the searching that had worn them out, not what they had found.

Mrs Venables laid out supper on the dining table, but most people took a drink and some biscuits to the privacy of their rooms where they could be alone with their own thoughts and not bludgeoned by each other's.

Tessa was sitting on the edge of her bed sipping cocoa when she heard Sheelagh's voice, sharp with concern, from next door: '*Now* what?'

'What's the matter?'

'My key's gone.' Tessa's door was ajar and Sheelagh came in, her face scrubbed, her dark hair spread out in a cloud from brushing. 'The key's gone from my door—I can't lock the damn thing.'

Tessa looked at her own door. 'I haven't one either. Don't let it worry you. I doubt anyone's got the energy for a midnight ramble.'

Sheelagh scowled. Without the warpaint she looked like a well-developed adolescent, until you saw her eyes. They were a soldier's eyes, crystal hard. She wasn't afraid of anyone sleepwalking in her direction: that she could deal with. She was worried by the implications. 'That's not the point. It was there earlier—Larry locked my door to keep that boy inside—and now it's gone. Somebody took it. I imagine the same person took yours.'

Tessa refused to share her concern. 'Perhaps the boy grabbed it as he ran.'

'So not only can I not lock the little bleeder out but he *can* lock me in!' snorted Sheelagh. 'Terrif.'

Tiredness made the other woman irritable. 'Wedge a chair under the handle if it bothers you.'

'Damn right it bothers me,' snapped Sheelagh, tossing the black hair fiercely. 'It'd bother you if you'd take the time to think about it. Yes, my key could have been grabbed in blind panic—he'd just enough wit to turn it and not enough to let it go. But yours makes it deliberate. He's been back while we were in the conference room and made sure we can't protect ourselves while we sleep. Tessa, that's terrifying! He must mean to come back tonight. How the hell can we sleep knowing that?'

'Speaking personally,' yawned Tessa, 'like a log. I'm dead beat—it'll take more than an idiot boy who's scared of his own shadow to keep me awake. Look, there are nine of us within earshot. What can happen? If you have a bad dream you'll wake up to find eight people peering under your bed.'

Sheelagh was only a little reassured. 'Maybe I should tell Miriam.'

'What's she going to do—sit up with you? Be your age, Sheelagh. It's odd, it's not a disaster.'

'Say that tomorrow,' muttered Sheelagh darkly, returning to her room, 'when you wake up and find you've been murdered in your sleep.'

Tessa was not murdered in her sleep that night. Neither was Sheelagh; but if she'd followed her instincts and reported her discovery Miriam might not have got her head beaten in with a rolling-pin.

FOURTEEN

RICHARD DREAMED. In the core of himself where he knew he was dreaming he felt a pang of disappointment. Extraordinary things had happened during the long day past, and some were good and some bad but together they'd changed his view of the last fifteen months; not just the events but his role in them. Whatever her reasons, whether she was only the instrument of a bitter man's vendetta or had become committed to the group as individuals, Miriam had identified the source of his dysfunction and set him on the path to resolving it. Finding himself back in the old nightmare was a cruel blow.

It was a Bosnian village, its name unpronounceable for lack of vowels. That much was true. But the nightmare sent him driving up the road from Brcko an hour early so instead of discovering the aftermath of atrocity he stumbled on the slaughter in progress. The trench scratched in the dirt of the main street. The last dozen inhabitants, too old, too young, too sick or too stubborn to run, lying face down over it, bound like rolls of carpet. Two young soldiers working steadily along the line, lifting each head by a handful of hair, slitting throats. The trench running with bright blood that an hour later would be congealed to a black paste.

In reality he'd been sick, his heart raging at the inhumanity but his more pragmatic stomach rebelling at the smell. In his dream he wasn't sick so much as bewildered. He found the soldiers' commander and asked why.

The man misunderstood. 'This is how we kill sheep. It is an efficient way to kill many sheep.'

Richard shook his head. 'Not why this way. Why kill them at all?'

'They are different to us.'

'So?'

The officer shrugged. 'If God had meant us to live together He would not have invented hatred.'

Richard never found the man who killed old women like sheep but he'd conducted enough interviews to know what he'd have said; what they'd both have said. They would have been professional about it, the soldier talking about orders and the need to achieve objectives, the reporter swallowing his outrage long enough to do his job.

But in the dream he was bound by neither propriety nor fear of the consequences. There was a gun on the desk. He picked it up. 'And if He'd meant you to butcher each other and the rest of the world not to care, He'd never have invented television.' Then he shot the officer in the heart. Not once, but again and again until the gun was empty.

The shots echoed in his head long after the scene had faded. Just as he realized the noise was real, someone hammering at his door, it stopped. The door flew open, his light was snapped on and Tariq was shaking the sleep out of him. 'Get dressed and come with me.'

'What's happening?'

'Quickly.'

He pulled on his clothes and followed the big man—the dove-grey suit replaced by charcoal denims with the label prominently displayed—along the corridor. Tariq tapped softly on one of the women's doors and it opened.

Miriam Graves lay supine in the middle of her carpet, bulky and still as a beached whale, her round face white in the electric light. Tessa was bent over her, stethoscope applied to the broad bosom where the jacket and shirt were unbuttoned.

Richard's breath whistled in his throat. 'Is she dead?'

The doctor straightened up. 'No. But she is concussed. Lift her on to the bed for me.'

Joe was there too, ashen, a tartan dressing-gown over his pyjamas. He went to help but Tariq moved him aside. She was a big woman; lifting her was a young man's job.

While Tessa continued her examination Richard asked, 'What happened? Did she fall?'

Tariq directed his attention to an object on the floor. 'Sure. She was just contemplating a little late-night baking when she tripped and fell head first on her rolling-pin.'

Richard stared. 'You mean—someone *hit* her?'

'It didn't go off while she was cleaning it.'

'Who? When? *Why?*'

'Don't know who,' Tariq said laconically. 'Or when, except that it was probably some time ago—it's after three, everyone else was in bed but she's still dressed. Why depends on who.'

'Who found her?'

'I did.' Joe had sat down and some of his colour was returning. 'I couldn't sleep, I was hungry—I went to the kitchen to see how we were fixed for biscuits. When I saw the light under her door I stuck my head in to say it was only me prowling about, and saw her—' He jerked his head at where the carpet was spotted with blood. 'When I couldn't rouse her I went for Tessa.'

'How is she?'

Tessa let the injured woman's eyelids close. 'It's a bad knock. She won't wake up for a while, but I think she'll be all right. If there's a fracture it's not depressed. There are worse things you can be hit with than a wooden rolling-pin—harder things, things with corners. I think she'll wake up with a headache later today and feel a good bit better tomorrow.'

Richard was trying to think through the cloying mists of

the nightmare. 'I suppose we'd better wake everyone up, ask them—'

'What?' asked Tariq, one eyebrow arching. 'If they brained anyone tonight? They'll say no. Most of them, maybe all of them, will be telling the truth. If it was one of us, there's been plenty of time for him or her to calm down and wash their hands. Someone might confess in a fit of remorse, but if she's been lying there for three hours the urge has probably passed by now.'

'We have to do something!'

'We are doing,' said Tessa calmly. 'We're caring for her. And in fact Mrs Venables is getting everyone up. Until we know what happened we ought to be awake.'

As she spoke the others began arriving at the open door, in silence, faces pale and drawn. They looked into the room, saw the doctor tending the woman on the bed, didn't come in. Tariq repeated what he knew.

'So someone finally voted with their fists,' said Larry. 'Well, it wasn't me.'

Tariq's gaze was level. 'No one said it was.'

'No. But it's me keeps losing his temper, me who wanted to leave and couldn't, me who threatened her in front of everyone. I want it on record that it was someone else who laid her out with a blunt instrument.'

The note of flippancy in his voice grated but it may only have been his reaction to stress. Tariq nodded. 'She'll tell us what happened when she wakes up.'

'She'll be all right then?'

'Oh, I think so,' said Tessa from the bed. 'Concussion is never trivial but her vital signs are pretty good. I think she'll wake up when she's ready.'

'Thank God for that,' said Tariq fervently. 'I don't know how we'd set about getting help for her.'

They had worried about their isolation before, but Miriam had promised no one would get hurt and by and large they'd believed her. But she'd been wrong; and if they couldn't get out when they wanted to, they also couldn't get out if they needed to.

Sheelagh pushed through the gathering in the corridor and felt behind the door. Her voice was barbed with meaning. 'There's no key.' Seeing their puzzlement she spelt it out. 'They've all gone. When we first arrived there were keys in the bedroom doors; now there aren't. Miriam was hurt because somebody took her key.'

'Who?'

Fear as much as impatience made her snap. 'That crazy bloody boy, of course! The one who was fooling around in my underwear and Tariq's briefcase. And the kitchen. I presume that's where the rolling-pin came from?'

Mrs Venables nodded. 'He could have taken it. I hadn't missed it, but then I wasn't looking for it.'

'How's he getting up here?' wondered Richard.

'Maybe he was here all along,' said Tariq.

They'd searched carefully after Larry's encounter; now they wondered if they'd missed something. Sheelagh walked the length of the corridor again in case they'd overlooked a cupboard he could have used but they hadn't. The locked door was still locked.

'There's nowhere he could have been.' She'd pulled on not her sharp suit but a powder-pink track suit; her hair, tangled from sleep, was tied loosely in the nape of her neck. 'There's also nowhere he could have come from. Make sense of that.'

'Did you try the lift?' asked Joe.

Resigned to the fact that it was inoperative, she hadn't. She went to try it now and Will went with her.

No lights came on and no sound whispered in the shaft at the press of Sheelagh's finger, its crimson point chipped. 'Someone would have heard it anyway.'

Will chewed pensively on his lip. 'Even without a lift

there's still a shaft. Could there be another way up it—a ladder fixed to the wall, something like that?'

'But you can't open the doors if the lift isn't there. For obvious reasons.'

'They can be forced. The Fire Brigade would have it open in a moment.'

She pursed her lips, half-amused, half-annoyed. 'Got a handy fireman, have you?'

'No.' He put his hand to the seal on the doors. 'But neither has this boy. If he's coming and going quickly and quietly it isn't so much a hatchet job as a five-finger exercise. Maybe there's a weak spot that—'

He never finished the sentence. His hand went through the rubber seal to the depth of his elbow; off balance he stumbled against the door, and the door opened.

JOE SAID, 'Until we get out of here on Monday we have to protect ourselves. We should double up on the rooms.'

Though he still had teeth marks in his hand Larry was having trouble equating the terrified boy he'd cornered with Miriam's injuries. 'Is that necessary?'

The older man waved an unsteady hand at the bed. 'That happened because we had a room each. Do you want to wait till somebody else gets their head stove in? Is your privacy that important?'

'He's a boy,' said Larry calmly, 'only a boy. Maybe if he was scared enough, but—'

'How old do you need to be to break someone's head with a rolling-pin? Look, this isn't a normal kid. He's not much more than a wild animal, and he's got some way of getting in here that we don't understand. Sheelagh's right— there isn't a key left in the place. We're stuck here for the rest of tonight and tomorrow, all tomorrow night and the next day, and all the night after that. If we double up we can look out for one another.'

Larry shrugged, not troubling to hide his scorn. He was a physical man, considered himself equal to any physical threat. 'If it makes you happy. Though you may have noticed we're an odd number.'

Tariq said, 'No problem. Will you stay with Miriam, Tessa? I'll stay too—until she wakes up she's not going to be much use to you if the kid comes back.'

'If you like,' Tessa said, without much enthusiasm. 'Joe's right, it's silly to take chances. We don't want this happening again.'

There was a muttered chorus of agreement from the gathering around the door. But then quiet fell and they moved aside for Sheelagh who, chalk-faced, was walking with one hand on the wall as if she couldn't feel the floor. Richard reached for her but she brushed him off. She was concentrating on what she had to do, couldn't afford to be distracted.

Once in the room, with every eye on her and into a waiting silence she said, 'Will's dead.' Her voice was low and empty; shock had stretched her eyes to huge cobalt pools in the parchment pallor of her face.

For long seconds they could only stare at her. Will? Will was fine. They'd seen him a minute ago when he went to check the lift just down the corridor. If anything had happened to him they'd have known.

Joe pressed her into the chair. 'Sheelagh, what's happened?'

'The lift,' she said. Her voice remained an aching monotone. 'It wasn't working, but he thought there might be a ladder inside. He felt for a weak place in the seal.' She barked a little gruff laugh, cut it short when she felt it getting away from her. 'He was right: there was one. When he found it the doors opened and he—and he—and—'

Tariq said briefly, 'I'll go see.' He left at a run.

Sheelagh began to weep, without reserve or dignity, her

mouth open and ragged, spit coming out with the words she couldn't now stop. 'He fell. He was terrified of heights, and he died falling forty storeys down a goddamned lift shaft. Six hundred feet falling in the dark. It must have felt like for ever.'

Larry put an arm round her, clumsily, a man unpractised at gentleness, but she wouldn't be comforted. 'I could have saved him. I could have pulled him back. I grabbed for him as the doors opened. I touched his clothes. But I couldn't— And then he was gone. He didn't even shout. He fell into the darkness, and it was as if he'd never been here.'

'It happened too fast,' the coach explained, as if she'd missed a return. 'Nobody reacts instantly. It takes a moment to work out what's happening, what you have to do. By then it was already too late. You couldn't have saved him, Sheelagh. No one could.'

But as the shock faded her distress grew, great racking sobs bursting from her. There was no point talking any more. He pulled her into the curve of his body, stifled her crying against his shoulder.

Richard was grey. He'd liked Will but that wasn't the only reason. What had happened, what Sheelagh was feeling now—the grief and the guilt of being nearly and not quite able to save a life—was something he knew in the deepest fibres of him.

Joe looked as if he'd been kicked in the face. For him too the thing had a personal dimension. It wasn't just a tragic accident: Will's death resonated in him as if he'd loosened the doors and given him a shove to make sure.

There was nothing to learn at the lift. The doors had opened because of an obstruction between them and closed when it was gone. They looked like any pair of lift doors, except that the triangles that indicated where the gondola was were dark. Tariq dragged a couple of chairs from the conference room and made a barrier of them, not expecting anyone to repeat Will's mistake but needing to do something. Then he returned to the sickroom.

He was just in time to see Joe sway and his eyes roll. He grabbed him but there was nowhere left to sit him down. He steered him into the next room and into a chair, tipping him forward to get the blood back into his head.

The older man moaned, 'This is my fault.'

'That's nonsense,' Tariq said firmly. 'It's nobody's fault—not even the boy's. He couldn't know that by continually forcing the seal he was weakening it to the point where someone was going to fall. It was an accident. If you hadn't suggested checking the lift someone else would have.'

'You don't understand.' He pushed aside Tariq's steadying hands. 'I have to talk to—everyone.'

Tariq watched with concern and wouldn't let him up for fear he would fall. But as the seconds ticked by, the ghost of an intuition solidified into understanding. Eyes wide, he backed away and straightened up. 'All right.' His voice was hollow.

When they saw the two men coming back and took in their expressions—Tariq's watchful and controlled, Joe's harrowed and defensive—they thought something else had happened. Tessa traded a quick, troubled glance with Richard, and Larry muttered, 'Now what?'

Joe cleared his throat and looked round. 'Is everyone here?' They were, including Mrs Venables, standing by the bedhead as if on sentry duty. 'I have some things to say. I owe you—explanations, apologies—more than that, but— Oh God, what a mess. I didn't want this. I didn't want anything *like* this. I never intended anyone to get hurt. I just—

'God,' he groaned again, 'I'm doing this so badly. I wanted to meet you, to talk to you, mostly to listen. None of the rest of it—' The half-formed sentences broke down in an incomprehensible jumble of words.

Tariq sighed. 'In case anybody didn't get that,' he said, 'Joe is Cathy's father.'

FIFTEEN

SHEELAGH CRIED OUT and flew at him, claws out like a cat. She actually reached his face, leaving a bloody trail down his cheek. Then Tariq swept her up in one arm and held her against him. But he shared her feelings, saw no reason to protect Joe from a verbal assault.

'You bastard!' she screeched. 'Will's dead because of you. He needed a psychologist like God needs pockets. Now he's all smashed up on the floor of the atrium. Are you satisfied? You wanted revenge, didn't you? You wanted to make us pay. Will that do? Or won't you rest till you've smashed us all?'

Joe looked like an old, old man. He wasn't surprised by her reaction. When he had decided to tell them, he'd known how they'd respond—had to: he was the author of great misfortune for reasons which seemed increasingly bizarre even to him. He'd planned this before he met them. If he'd been right about them the consequences would still have been appalling but he could have justified what he did. Now even that consolation was denied him. His misjudgment had led to the death of a decent young man and a murderous attack on a woman who was his friend. He didn't blame Sheelagh for swiping at him with her nails. He'd expected Larry to knock him down.

But he needed to put the record straight, for his sake and theirs. He couldn't maintain the deceit any longer. If in their fury they decided to chuck him down the lift shaft too he would hardly have resisted.

'I don't expect you to understand.' His voice was a gravelly murmur, thick with emotion. 'But I swear to you I never wanted *anything* like this. Miriam explained what I was trying to do. It doesn't make much sense, I know—by the time we'd talked a little I knew it was a mistake. But I never imagined anyone could get hurt.'

'Hurt?!' echoed Richard, and his voice cracked. He looked as if he wanted to say more but nothing more came.

Larry said flatly, 'You're lying. You may have set this up but you're not Cathy's father. She was black all the way through—she'd none of your blood in her.'

'Neither mine nor Martha's,' agreed Joe, 'but she was our child legally and every way that matters. We fostered her as a toddler, adopted her when her mum died. She chose to keep her own name. Since no one was ever going to take her for our natural child we thought it best too. As far as I can remember, that was the only problem we had adopting a black child. Twenty-odd years ago there weren't the same ideological hoops to jump through. They reckoned if you wanted a kid and could look after it, and you were a nice couple, she was better off with you than in care. Political correctness hadn't been thought of then. They still reckoned you were doing a child a favour by taking it in.'

'Only a grown woman with a mind of her own wasn't just as cute as a little black kid in pigtails. Was that when you lost interest?' Larry was keeping his hands off the older man but the effort showed in his face. 'I never coached anyone else whose parents didn't want to see them play. I never met you, never even spoke to you on the phone. *I* knew I was taking care of her but you didn't!'

'That's a monstrous thing to say!' Joe literally spluttered with anger. 'Cathy was our girl for most of her life. We loved her, wanted the best for her. When she asked us not to come to matches, reluctantly we agreed. Except sometimes we'd buy our tickets like anybody else and watch from the grandstand. A couple of times she spotted us but mostly she didn't. Why didn't she want us there? Like Will said, she wanted a private life, a place where she wasn't anybody's rising star. And it was easier not having to explain us. The racial awareness lobby made her feel a freak for having white parents.'

Tessa was puzzled by practicalities. 'You did all this? The hotel, everything? You said you were a printer. But this took serious money.'

'I was a printer. Cartwright's was a family firm—it ended up mine. I sold up when Martha became ill. One of the things I put the money into was Lazaire's Hotels, and it bought me a favour when I needed it. Miriam explained how I got you all here. It began as a crusade—I wanted you to *know* the harm you'd done. After I'd listened to you for a while, found you weren't what I was expecting, it wasn't that clear-cut any more. But by then I had other reasons to keep going. I was learning things about Cathy— not all of them good. But she was my daughter, I wanted to know everything. Just hearing her name was like having her back for a little while. If I'd confessed you'd have left and I'd have lost her for good.'

'So you marooned us up here,' gritted Larry. 'You had them fix the lift so we couldn't leave before you'd gorged on all our sad little memories. What kind of a man would do that—pick over the bones of his dead child?'

A little earlier, staggering under a burden of remorse, Joe had come to bare his soul before these people, willing to accept almost any expression of their fury. But he was not a victim by nature and as he recovered from the initial shock of Will's death the urge towards martyrdom diminished. Fisting big artisan's hands in the front of Larry's sweatshirt he slammed the startled athlete against the wall.

'How dare you say that to me? This is my girl we're talking about—of course I want to know what happened to her. One minute everything was fine; then she says she's going through a sticky patch but she's got her fingers crossed; then she's given it all up and she's making drunken scenes at nightclubs, and before I've got over that they're dragging her car out of the Thames. And I don't know how it happened. I was the only father she ever knew. I nursed her through mumps, I taught her to swim, I held her hand in the sad bits of *Bambi*. I loved her. I thought I knew her.'

He swallowed hard. 'Then there's people on the doorstep telling me she's killed herself. Cathy? She was a fighter, I'd have said suicide was nowhere in her nature. Something happened to change her profoundly that last year. Maybe if I hadn't been so preoccupied with Martha's illness I'd have seen it coming. But I didn't, and none of those who did picked up the phone to tell me. You didn't. He didn't'—a jerk of his head at Tariq. 'You both knew she was coming apart but you never thought to discuss it with her parents. So don't you dare criticize me. If I'd known she was in trouble when you did she'd be alive today.'

But the coach had loved her too. Neither man could face the idea that he might have done something more, or something different, to save her. They were ready to fight rather than share the responsibility.

Tessa interrupted icily. 'If you're going to scrap, don't do it in my sickroom.'

Trading killer looks, the men backed off. Joe cleared his throat. 'For the record, I didn't tell the builders to put the lift out of commission.'

'Why should we believe that,' demanded Sheelagh, 'when you've done nothing but lie to us since before we met?'

'I think it's true.' It was Mrs Venables, still on sentry-go at the bedhead. 'I'm Dr Graves' housekeeper, when we're not doing this I look after her at home. I was involved from early on. I knew what Mr Lockhead had in mind and how he meant to do it, but the first I knew of the lifts going off was when the builders called up.'

Sheelagh tossed her dark mane angrily. 'Anyway, it doesn't matter. The man responsible for Will being here is responsible for his death.'

Joe's voice was low. 'I didn't say I wasn't.'

They weren't getting anywhere now, just piling on the hurts. Tariq broke it up. 'We'll have to talk some more about this. But Tessa's right, this isn't the place. Let's make some coffee and plan the sleeping arrangements.'

The rooms were all of a size: they moved bedding and belongings into those nearest the lift. It took a sweaty hour to arrange things to everyone's satisfaction but no one complained. It was what they needed: something to occupy their hands and leave their minds free to consider developments. It wasn't just the death of Will Furney, or meeting their tormentor. It was the way fear had crept up all around, barely noticed, like a mist rising out of the earth at evening.

They'd been puzzled; they'd been angry; they'd been horrified by the lightning strikes of mayhem. But somewhere in the recent past all that had been swallowed up by fear. They were afraid of the dark. They were afraid of the emptiness of the great building under them. They were afraid of the boy, afraid of each other, afraid to be alone. Trapped between a bitter man's vendetta and the random violence of a mad child, the millennia peeled away like sunburn and left them craving the comfort of caves, spaces they could fill with their own bodies leaving no dark corners to be colonized by phantoms, narrow entrances they could shut against the unknown and the danger of attack.

But the human mind cannot sustain an unrelenting level of either joy or fear. By the time the last bag had found a home under the last bed the intensity of their feelings had eased. Still afraid, they were learning to handle the fear. Joe remained unforgiven but recriminations would have to wait. A time would come when they would be rehearsed in detail but for now there was a broad acceptance that, whoever was to blame for the situation, they were in it together. Somehow they had to get through the next few difficult days, and putting their grievances on hold made that possible.

The most volatile among them, Sheelagh was also about the most resilient. She locked up deep within her the terrible memory of what she'd witnessed and threw herself into the furniture removals with a passion, even managing a small joke. Lowering the foot of a bed that had Tariq at its head, she grunted, 'The name of this place—they spelt it wrong.'

He didn't follow. 'What should it be?'

'The Lazarus Hotel,' she said, kneading a kink out of her back. 'Take up your bed and walk.'

Larry put his head round the door, looking for Tariq. 'Those chairs in front of the lift. Did you put them there?'

Tariq nodded. 'Just to remind us.' His eyes dropped at how foolish that sounded.

'Then this is probably a silly question,' said Larry. 'But you didn't put one of them on its side for some reason?'

SIXTEEN

'MAYBE ONE OF US knocked it over,' Tariq offered lamely. 'There's not much room in the corridor for shifting furniture.'

'Nobody's been shifting furniture past the lift,' said Larry. 'We've moved it from the outside rooms to the inside ones. Besides, any of us knocking a chair over would have picked it up again.'

'He's here, isn't he? That murderous bloody boy.' Sheelagh was not a timorous woman. Both professionally and personally she was an aggressive, even ruthless competitor who never shirked a fight. Friends who had known her for years and come through hard times with her had not heard that icy thread of fear lacing her voice.

It was not to be wondered at. Too many things were happening too quickly, all of them bad. Being marooned six hundred feet above the city, surrounded by people they knew nothing good about while a vicious child haunted the corridors waiting a chance to do them harm, chiselled at her nerves as any number of enemies attacking in plain sight would not have done. 'He's come up the lift shaft into the penthouse, and even though we're awake this time we neither saw nor heard him. How can we stop him if we can't see him? It's like fighting a ghost!'

'How long is it since you put those chairs out?' Larry asked Tariq. 'Half an hour? Maybe he's still here. We could look for him.'

'Damn right we look for him!' snapped Sheelagh. 'One of us is dead and another badly hurt because of him. You want to leave him at large till there's nobody left?'

'So we look,' agreed Larry. 'Only try and remember it's a kid we're looking for, not a division of panzers.'

'And you try and remember,' she said fiercely, 'it's a killer we're looking for.'

Tessa and Mrs Venables stayed with Miriam. While the others made a cordon in the corridor, Larry and Tariq set about flushing him out. They began at the dead end beyond the women's quarters and worked towards the lift, searching every room and every cupboard.

It wasn't hard except on the nerves. The searchers couldn't know, each time they opened a door, if only dust or a homicidal boy armed with a kitchen implement would fly out. It made them jumpy, and also slow. The more cupboards they searched, the more they expected to find him in the next one. The odds rose with every door they opened.

But they reached the lift without sight of him. 'Do we do the conference room now or later?'

'Now,' decided Tariq. 'Get it out of the way.'

He wasn't there either: not under the table, behind either of the big sofas or in the shuttered alcove that would in the fullness of time become a bar. 'Kitchen?'

'Kitchen.'

Sheelagh watched in shivery fascination. If there was anything innately absurd about grown men storming a kitchen like Green Berets entering a Vietnamese village it didn't show in their faces. The cost of carelessness fresh in their minds, they proceeded in deadly earnest, each keenly aware of where the other was and how quickly he could react. They heard each other's breathing rasp as they snatched open the doors, soft curses when one more cupboard proved bare. No one said, If anything moves, blast it, but that was how they felt.

When they were sure the boy wasn't there the cordon moved up past the kitchen door. If he was in the penthouse he was in one of the men's rooms; if he got past the searchers into the corridor it was important to deny him access to knives and forks and skewers.

Joe's room was empty. Larry's room was empty. Tariq's room was empty and so was Richard's. So, finally, was Will Furney's.

They looked at each other in disbelief. Tariq said, 'He isn't here. He's done it again.' His voice was breathy with the release of pent-up tension.

'I don't *get* this,' Larry said tersely. 'I really don't. Where does he go to? And why does he keep coming back?'

'He's travelling through the lift shaft, that's obvious,' said Tariq. 'I don't know what he wants from us. To steal—food, clothes? To scare us off? If he thinks of this place as home, maybe he just wants rid of us.'

'Enough to brain one of us with a rolling-pin and shove another down the lift shaft?'

Tariq scowled. 'Nobody pushed Will—that was an accident. Don't for pity's sake make things out to be worse than they already are.'

'All right, it was an accident. But it wouldn't have happened if that boy hadn't been making free with the place. What in hell's a kid like that doing here at all?'

From the corridor Sheelagh said, 'Tariq?'

He raised his voice. 'No, no sign of him here either. He's given us the slip again.'

'*Tariq!*'

Her tone brought both of them quickly to the door. The little cordon was still stretched across the corridor but now it had turned its back on them. Through a gap between Sheelagh and Joe, Tariq glimpsed a dark, stocky figure in front of the lift. Very softly, advancing a step at a time, he said, 'Don't anybody move. Don't frighten him off.'

'Frighten *him*?' echoed Sheelagh faintly.

As Tariq edged through the cordon he saw the boy

clearly for the first time, and his initial reaction was more pity than anger. He understood now, as he had not before, how Mrs Venables—taken by surprise and seeing only its swift departure—could have thought it was a dog. It was certainly shaggy, but under the pelt of disintegrating woollies there was, as Larry had insisted, a boy of sixteen or seventeen years.

The cocoon of clothing—how did he take it off without it falling apart? *Did* he ever take it off?—gave an impression of bulk reinforced by the well-developed muscles in his hands and forearms. Of course, Tariq thought inanely; all that climbing. But the pale skin and hollow eyes told of hunger and cold and damp places out of the sun. It was like chancing on some subterranean creature and feeling the squirm of primordial distaste; and then seeing the terror in its eyes that said, however little you liked the look of it, it liked the look of you even less.

Tariq saw panic rip through the boy's eyes and, because he was essentially a kind man, for a moment forgot about the damage the boy had done and tried to reassure him. He spread his hands and said quietly, 'Nobody's going to hurt you. What's your name?'

The answer came in a voice deeper than any of them expected, barred with a fear that trembled. 'Will.'

Resentment rose like bile in Sheelagh's throat. She didn't believe him. He'd taken the man's life, and now he was stealing his name. Her lip curled in disgust. 'Liar.'

The same instinctive revulsion kicked Larry over the edge of fury. He saw the boy standing, sullen and defiant, in front of the shaft that he'd used as a weapon, and rage burgeoned in him. 'You bloody little ghoul!' He flung himself through the cordon like Agassi after a wide ball.

For twenty-five years his reactions had been an intrinsic part of how Larry Ford made his living. But for wild creatures their reactions are how they stay alive, which is an even higher imperative. Fear is faster than hunger, or anger, or anything else. The boy slipped under Larry's closing hands and fled up the corridor.

That corridor ended in a blank wall beyond the last of the women's rooms. 'We've got him now!' yelled Larry in triumph, leading the pursuit. 'He'll try to come back this way. Don't let him past!'

With Larry on his tail the boy ran until the wall stopped him. He gave a desperate little grunt, as if he'd forgotten it was there. For a second he pressed himself against it as if he could melt through, then reality intervened and he turned. Beneath the grime his face was white in the harsh glare of the naked bulbs, his eyes great with fear.

Larry braked, waiting for the boy to try and pass him. In his breast was the tight satisfaction of knowing he controlled the court. Twice the youngster had outplayed him, but not this time. This time he could take his beating. In Larry's mind and in his eyes was an ambivalence as to whether that was a sporting metaphor or not.

The boy saw and let it decide him. He wasn't sure he could evade the man again but he knew he had to try: he'd as soon throw himself from the roof as on the mercy of a man with those eyes. But as he went to make his move Tariq came to join them. A moment later Richard did, then Sheelagh, then Joe. The boy stumbled back against the end wall; his shoulders dropped and he swallowed.

Suddenly Tariq felt ashamed of himself, of all of them. They'd chased a half-witted child to the end of his strength, cornered him like an animal, and now they were crowding him as if they intended to beat the crap out of him. Five of them: four strong men and a terribly angry woman.

Tariq shut his eyes an instant to organize his head. 'Now, just hold everything while we think this through. Once we've got him, what are we going to do with him?'

Sheelagh threw him an incredulous glance. She was literally panting, not just with exertion. 'What do you *think?*'

'No, Sheelagh,' the big man said quietly, manoeuvring his body between her and the boy, 'what do *you* think? What I told him back there—I meant it. Nobody's going to hurt him.'

'We'll tie him up,' decided Larry. 'There's bound to be some rope or cord or something. He won't give us much trouble trussed up like a chicken.'

'Jesus, Larry,' Tariq sighed despairingly, 'he's just a kid. He's terrified already. You're going to throw him on the floor and hog-tie him, and throw him in a room, and open the door at intervals and throw him a bit of something to eat—not much because we haven't got enough for ourselves. If he's a sandwich short of a picnic now, he's going to be a gibbering idiot by the time we get out of here. You really think we have the right to do that?'

Joe was a stout man in his mid-fifties who hadn't so much as trotted after a bus in years. His barrel chest was going like a bellows so he had trouble getting the words out. 'It may not be right, but it's necessary. He's too dangerous to turn loose.'

Tariq wasn't blind to that. But he didn't know how to restrain a wild creature except by brute force. 'How about this? We don't tie him but I'll stay in the room with him. I'll park my bum against the door—the only way he can get out is through me.'

'And if he brains you too?' demanded Sheelagh.

'Then you were right and I was wrong.'

'It's more than your neck, though, isn't it?' she snapped. 'If that happens there's one more casualty to look after and one less of us to fend him off next time. I say now we've got him we make sure.'

'But what does that *mean?*' Tariq asked again. 'You

want to tie him up, like Larry? Or do you want to open the lift doors and push him down after Will?'

She raised her hand to slap him for that. The truth was that she didn't know what she wanted, except that she wanted to feel safe. But at the crucial moment, with Sheelagh's hand swinging up and back and her eyes spitting fire in Tariq's face, the boy said, 'No! Don't fight—help. Will.' His voice was rusty, the words just the closest he could get hold of at short notice.

Sheelagh stared at him and her arm dropped slowly. Tariq turned, searching the parchment face for signs of intelligence. 'Help? Help who? You?'

The boy shook his shaggy head insistently. 'Will! In—in—the hole. Falling. On the—the— Needs—' His residual command of language defeated, he gave a giant tremulous shrug and recalled a final imprecation. 'Oh, buggery!'

Richard felt the blood drain from his face, taking all expression with it. He didn't dare look at the others just yet. He spent seconds analysing the words, considering what else they might mean. But finally he risked putting what he was thinking into words of his own. 'Is he saying what I think he's saying?'

SEVENTEEN

IT WAS HARD to be sure, depended on things they couldn't know—like, how firm a grasp on reality the boy had. It was no use attempting to deal with a feral boy as if he were an intelligent adult.

On the other hand, what he was saying seemed to make sense. The hole was the lift shaft, and he knew Will had fallen. He knew his name. That didn't prove the man was alive, but no one who'd fallen six hundred feet got up to introduce himself afterwards. He was on something, the boy said. But there couldn't be any kind of a ledge or the lift wouldn't run...

The lift. 'A torch,' Tariq said tersely, heading for the lift at a purposeful jog. 'Quickly! Mrs Venables, can you find me—?' She was on her way before he finished the sentence. A couple of small torches for emergency use were stowed among her kitchen equipment.

Sheelagh stared after him, wide-eyed. 'You think he's on top of the lift? Dear God, we didn't even check! I knew he'd fallen—I never looked to see how far!'

'Don't get your hopes too high,' cautioned Richard. 'It must be at a lower level or he wouldn't have fallen, he'd have walked into it. If it's more than one or maybe two levels down, it won't make very much difference.'

'But he's alive! Isn't he?' She turned to the boy, her cobalt eyes aflame with possibilities. 'Isn't he?'

Richard thought she was going to shake him. He put a hand on her wrist. 'Tariq's got the doors open. Let's see what the situation is before we get too excited.' He beckoned the boy. 'You come too.' Whatever they found in the shaft, he didn't want that boy disappearing again; and he didn't much want him at his back. 'What's your name, anyway?'

The reply was slow coming. Richard suspected he was having trouble remembering. Then, 'Midge.' Which seemed unlikely, but if it was what the boy called himself it would do. Warily he allowed Richard to usher him back up the corridor.

Tariq had levered the doors open and Joe held them with a solid shoulder. 'Larry, your hand.' Thus anchored Tariq leaned carefully into the dizzying space.

For a moment the sense of distance threatened to swamp him. The beam of the torch magnified the unsteadiness of his hand and bounced around the smooth oval of the shaft, fragmenting and repeating until he could make no sense of what he was seeing. He blinked and wiped his eyes on his sleeve, then he tried again.

The shaft did not end at the penthouse, but continued up perhaps another couple of levels. The domestic offices, he supposed—the water tanks, the winding gear for the lift, maybe the boilers—all the esoteric superstructure for a building the size of a town. Somewhere up there the boy must have a bolt-hole for when people were working, or in this case living, in the penthouse. In the other direction the shaft plummeted six hundred feet straight down.

Of those six hundred feet, the first forty were the only ones that counted. If the top of the gondola had stopped Will's fall inside a couple of seconds there was a chance he was alive. The gondola all but filled the shaft. He could hardly have slipped past and kept falling. Of course, he could have broken something vital—you could do that if you were unlucky enough falling off a stepladder. But there was a chance. Tariq took a deep breath and held it, trying to steady his hand.

As the beam stopped oscillating he began to pick out, at

the extreme limit of its range, something blocking the shaft. It had to be the gondola, there was nothing else it could be, but for a tantalizing minute longer he couldn't be sure whether it was just the top of the car he was seeing, complete with its cable mechanism, or if there was something more.

'Richard, have a look—I can't make this out.'

Richard lay full length on the floor, his head and shoulders projecting into the shaft. He too had to wait a moment for what he was seeing to start making sense. But when it did he had no doubt. 'He's there all right, on top of the gondola. He isn't moving. Will? Will!' But there was no response.

'How far down?' Tessa had reached the same conclusion as Tariq, that mathematics were the best guide.

'I don't know. Twenty feet? Thirty?'

'Looking down, it's never as far as you think,' said Richard. 'I don't think that would even be twenty feet. And twenty, even twenty-five feet—that's not a killing fall. Not necessarily.' He wriggled back from the brink and stood up. 'We have to get him back.'

Tariq nodded. 'Yes. How?'

Richard shrugged. 'I don't know, but we have to. We can't leave him there. When the builders remember us the first thing they'll do is send the lift on up. If Will's still there he could get sucked in between the car and the shaft. It could literally tear him apart.'

In the second before she could get rid of it that image kicked Sheelagh hard under the heart. It was unendurable, that Will might have survived the fall only to die screaming when the lift started up.

She found herself looking at Midge, her cheeks growing hot. 'This is your fault. What are you going to do about it?'

'Give the kid a break,' growled Tariq.

But Richard agreed with Sheelagh. 'You want to help Will, Midge? Good, you can. You use this shaft all the time. It's how you come and go. Well, *how?* Show us how we can get to him.'

Under the disreputable clothes Midge's shoulders, broad with climbing, heaved once. ''S what Midge is trying to *tell* you,' he sighed heavily. ''S why he came. But—' He gestured with a thumb up the corridor where they'd chased him. Then he shook his head, impatient with the uncooperative words. The more he tried, though, the more they came back to him. 'Will's——OK. Pretty much. Hurt'—he tapped his head—'but OK. Only, scared. Too scared to move.'

'He's afraid of heights,' nodded Tariq. 'Midge, could you take a rope down to him?'

'Sure,' agreed Midge immediately. 'What rope?'

That was the problem. Even fully operational hotels are not a natural source of long lengths of strong rope. Joe scavenged through the rooms for anything that would serve and came back with several lengths of Terylene cord from the blinds. 'Best I can do.'

It wasn't good enough. It might be strong enough, but it might not. It would have to be joined in several places, and then it would be impossible to grip tightly enough to haul a man's weight twenty feet up a shaft.

Richard shook his head. 'I've done a bit of climbing— nothing too demanding but enough to know what you can and can't do. That's asking for trouble.'

'More trouble than Will's in now?' demanded Sheelagh incredulously.

'Oh yes,' Richard said with certainty. 'He's fallen once, he doesn't need to fall again. Midge, *how* do you climb in the shaft? Can I do it? Can I go down to him and bring him up?'

For answer the boy leaned casually into the shaft and directed the torch into the narrow end of the oval.

Will had been looking for a ladder when he fell. This wasn't one but it was designed to serve as one for short distances, so that an engineer in a harness might reach a problem from the level immediately above. Even Jacob's angels would have thought twice about using it for any other purpose.

Fretted tracks either side of the shaft guided the gondola and provided an emergency braking system. The frets were just wide and deep enough to support someone who knew what he was doing.

They all looked where Midge indicated. They reached the same conclusion. Tessa put it into words. 'You're crazy even thinking about it. Even if you get down to him without falling, how do you get Will to climb back up? He wouldn't do it for Midge—why should he do it for you?'

'Because he's bloody *got* to,' Richard grunted. It wasn't much of an argument but it was all he had.

Tariq was at least prepared to think about it. 'Seriously— do you reckon you could climb down that? And back up again, without falling?'

Richard took another moment to be sure. 'Yes. Hell, I can't guarantee it, but I don't think I'll have too much trouble.'

The bigger man nodded. 'You realize the builders might have remembered us already—that you could be halfway down to the lift when the damn thing starts up to meet you?'

Richard hadn't. He blinked. 'Tariq, I know it's risky. But if we leave Will where he is he's going to die. Don't talk me out of this. Help me work out how to do it.'

Improbably enough, Tariq was smiling. 'Aren't you the guy who came here because he'd lost his nerve in danger- ous situations?'

That brought Richard up short. He barked a little edgy laugh. 'Me? No. That's my twin brother. I'm the one who goes bungee-jumping and runs the Pamplona bulls. Stop asking stupid bloody questions and help me here. So I get down to him—what do I do then?'

'OK. You take the cords with you. You fashion a safety rope that'll steady him if he starts to wobble. Maybe you could belay it round the cable? If he actually falls you won't be able to hold him, but if he thinks you can, maybe that'll do. Get him climbing up the track ahead of you, and don't follow him till he's damn near out of reach. By then he'll be halfway to where we can grab him.'

Richard was visualizing it. It sounded reasonable enough, but experience told him that putting it into practice would reveal unexpected difficulties. 'What if the worst happens and we both fall? Will the lift hold us?'

There wasn't a lift engineer among them. But Tariq had the sort of mind that absorbed useless information, and he'd once seen a television programme on the subject. 'Should do. It's designed to fail safe—it can only move if the cable's taking the strain. If the weight goes above a certain level the brakes lock automatically.'

'Do do,' said Richard, 'or should do?'

'Do do,' Tariq said with more confidence than he felt. 'It must be safe or they wouldn't have let us use it.'

'What about the gondola itself? That acrylic or perspex or whatever it is—we're not likely to go straight through it?'

Tariq had never seen a programme on thermoplastic resins. All he could do was shrug. 'Will didn't and he fell twenty feet. Of course, he could have loosened something...'

The point had come for Richard to do it or not. The longer he thought about it now, the less likely it was to happen. 'OK,' he gritted, 'give me the cords and I'll see what I can do.'

Midge said, 'Midge too.'

Richard paused a moment, scanning the boy's eyes, thought what he saw there was an earnest desire to help and nodded. 'Yes. Thanks.'

A small hand gripped his wrist tightly, and he turned to meet Sheelagh's urgent gaze. 'No. Richard, don't take him. You'll be safer on your own.'

Tariq was watching Midge, saw him recoil as if she'd slapped his face. He said nothing, but plainly he understood what was being said. Blood flushed sullenly in his sun-starved cheeks.

Richard scowled, offended on the boy's behalf. 'He wants to help. He's only here because he thought he could help.'

'Yes?' she retorted, hard and fast. 'And he thought he was helping Miriam, did he, with a rolling-pin behind the ear? Richard, you're proposing to do something desperately dangerous on the word of a crazy boy who's notched up two victims already. All right, you can judge for yourself whether you can climb the track and whether you can get Will to. But you don't need a juvenile psychopath on your back while you're doing it.'

The speed of the exchange, and the long words, left Midge floundering. He knew he was being accused of something, wasn't sure what. His forget-me-not eyes went from one to the other of them. 'What?'

Tariq would have liked to dismiss it as paranoia. But that was too easy, and the consequences could be too expensive. 'She has a point, you know. He's at home in there—you're not. Let's at least try and find out why he hit Miriam, if only so you can avoid annoying him the same way.'

After a moment Richard nodded. 'But make it quick. Before my brother gets back.' He flashed Tariq a tight grin that Fran, had she been there, would have recognized with joy and wonder.

'Midge, can you help us with this? Can you tell us what happened to Miriam? You know, the fat lady? She got hurt. Can you tell us how?'

He understood that well enough. His eyes widened with indignation. 'No!'

'Did she startle you—did you hit out before you realized who she was?'

'Midge never hit anyone!'

'Midge sure as hell bit someone,' grunted Larry sourly.

'You frightened me!' The boy's skill with language was developing even as he spoke, Tariq noted. Personal pronouns now. Maybe there wasn't as much wrong with him as they'd assumed.

'Miriam could have frightened you,' he suggested. 'It was late, it was dark—I thought maybe she surprised you and you struck out in self-defence. Is that what happened, Midge? Tell us, we won't be angry.' That probably wasn't true, he thought, but necessity justified a fib or two.

But still Midge shook his head, long tangles of fairish hair flicking across his face. 'No.'

'OK,' said Tariq then, casually, as if it didn't matter; and when Sheelagh opened her mouth to protest he shook his head. 'Leave it. There's no point everybody getting angry when we can't prove anything. Richard, it's up to you— do you want his help?'

Richard too had accepted the obvious explanation of Miriam's misfortune. Now, though, it seemed less clear. For a boy set on mayhem, Will's accident would have come as manna from heaven: why on earth would Midge have brought them the news of his survival? Assuming that's what he was doing. Assuming it wasn't just the first thing that came into his mind when they caught him by the lift.

In the end, there was no way of knowing. In the end he

had to guess. But since it was him going down the shaft no one had a better right to. He nodded slowly. 'Yes. I'll be glad of his help.'

Sheelagh blew out her cheeks in explosive disbelief. No one else said anything.

Richard pocketed one of the torches, passed Larry the other. 'Shine it down on top of us. It'll be steadier than mine.' He turned to Midge. 'You want to show me how to do this? Bearing in mind that I won't be as good at it as you?'

The boy nodded. Then he stepped into space.

EIGHTEEN

WHEN THE LIFT DOORS opened so abruptly, caught off balance Will fell into his worst nightmare. The blackness wheeled beneath him: six hundred feet of it, the chill air sliding aside for him, stroking his face and running icy lover's fingers through his hair. Six hundred feet of falling through nothing, so bathed in gravity he seemed weightless, accelerating earthwards at a rate of thirty-two feet per second per second; at least until his spinning body started to ricochet, bones breaking and organs rupturing with every impact, dying even as he fell.

Though he had no time even to yell, all this raced through his mind in the less than a second, much less than thirty-two feet, that he fell before the acrylic dome of the gondola came up like a piston to hit him in the ribs.

The blow drove all the air out of him; he thought it had broken him in half. Nor did he come to rest where he landed. The smooth curved dome, designed to shed the dust and other detritus that would inevitably fall into the shaft, shed him just as easily and he found himself swallow-diving for the crack between the car and the wall. If there'd been anything in his lungs to do it with, then he'd have yelled.

His hands, clawing at the acrylic and failing to slow him in any measurable degree, were not there to buffer him; so he hit the wall head first, hard enough to stun himself. His body went limp, sprawling over the curve of the dome, his feet higher than his head, one arm sliding into the abyss, just too big a piece of detritus to follow.

For some minutes he lay in a kind of limbo. He wasn't

even afraid any more. Despite the distant hot ache in his ribs it occurred to him he was already dead. If not, he couldn't imagine why not: in the darkness of the shaft, unable to see what he was lying on, he failed to piece together the circumstances which saved him.

He'd assumed that the lift was down below when power was cut. The alternative, that it was still at penthouse level, evaporated when the doors slid apart and instead of merely squashing his nose against the glass he fell. But the last person to use it was not Larry Ford arriving but an apprentice electrician fetching the builders' afternoon tea. He came up in the lift and went down later in the cradle, leaving the gondola parked immediately below the gallery.

But in the dark and with his head swimming Will could fathom none of this. He came gradually to understand that he was still alive, but the return of his fluttering wits like tardy pigeons to the loft warned him that was the only good news. He wasn't safe; perhaps he'd merely delayed the inevitable. If there was some way of using this shaft as a thoroughfare his hopes of finding it in the dark were vanishingly small. He tried shouting but knew from the frailty of his voice that it would never carry outside the shaft. He didn't think there was anything else he could do.

So when somebody said, 'Help?' his first thought was that it was him, his second that he might as well save his breath. He pressed his cheek flat against the cool dome, spread his arms for the meagre stability they gave him, and indulged a tear of sheer self-pity. He wasn't ready to die but he thought it was going to happen anyway.

But—was that rusty voice his? He was willing to believe that almost any pathetic little squeak might be him. Even in court he couldn't produce the sort of clarion delivery that moved mean old magistrates to mercy. He won, when he won, on logic rather than personality. But he didn't smoke and he didn't sleep in damp sheets, and if his voice had been getting rusty his secretary would have made an appointment with his doctor.

And if it wasn't him it was someone else, not seeking help but offering it. 'Who—what—?'

'Here.' In the darkness the shock of the touch made him jerk and gasp aloud, and his head cannoned off the wall again. Instantly the touch on his arm firmed to a grip and the rusty disembodied voice by his ear promised salvation. "S all right. Midge got you.'

Afterwards Will was ashamed of how he reacted. He knew full well the danger he was in, that without help he was probably going to die in his own personal worst-case scenario. But when he realized who was holding his wrist he didn't think of rescue: he thought of Miriam Graves with blood in her hair, felled by a maniac with a rolling-pin. He snatched his arm away, even though it set his body sliding on the smooth surface. A soft wail of pure terror escaped him.

Midge could no more see Will than Will could see Midge. But he knew his way around in here, was used to relying on touch alone. Even the top of the gondola was an unexpected luxury: mostly he scampered between the levels on the tracks, his fingers grown strong as an ape's.

He didn't have to see to know where the noise was coming from. One grimy hard-padded hand clamped over Will's mouth, the fingers gripping his jaw. 'Stop,' he said sternly. "S no help. Midge'll get you out of here. But you gotta do what he says.'

If there was anything essentially ludicrous in the idea of a teenage squatter of dubious mental capacity and an apparent propensity for violence taking responsibility for an intelligent grown man in this way, neither of them acknowledged it. Will needed help, Midge was able and seemed willing to give it.

Will allowed himself to be half-guided, half-towed to the

top of the gondola, where he fell on the cable like a lost child on his mother's hand and knelt clutching it to him. By a judicious combination of cajoling and bullying, Midge got him to his feet—groaning as he stretched the damaged muscles in his side—and even persuaded him to release the cable with one hand and reach for the track with the other.

But try as he might he couldn't get Will to forsake the cable and start to climb. ''S not far,' he promised. Lacking a conventional mental geometry he described it as 'One man on top of another on top of another.'

Will felt the narrow frets with outstretched fingers. 'I can't do that,' he murmured in quiet conviction.

'Easy,' insisted Midge; but Will didn't dare try and when Midge, despairing of success any other way, yanked his hand off the cable and slapped it beside the other on the frets, Will gave a terrified little howl and dropped to his knees, groping in panic for his lifeline.

Finally Midge admitted defeat. 'Midge'll go get help.' Unseen in the darkness he smiled. 'Don't go away.'

Will had lost his self-command and his dignity but not the last vestiges of his sense of humour. 'Believe it.' He clung to the cable, shuddering, as Midge climbed away from him.

RICHARD HAD TACKLED harder climbs than this. He was reminding himself of the fact all the time he was watching how Midge did it—exactly how he did it, where he put each hand and foot.

Getting on to the track was the worst part. Midge chose the left-hand route so Richard did the same, stepping out over the abyss to reach for it. He had the cords looped out of his way over his shoulder. Tariq kept hold of one end to jerk him to safety if he missed. It was the last help he could expect from the people in the penthouse until he climbed back up.

The next hardest part was keeping steady. The frets were barely the width of a boot, could accommodate only one hand or foot at a time, and as he started his descent Richard's body swung from side to side, threatening to tear him off the track. 'Slowly,' he said aloud, and it wasn't an instruction to Midge so much as a reminder to himself. He crept down the thread like an infinitely cautious spider, and though the distance was a scant twenty feet he took minutes to do it and felt he'd taken hours.

At last Midge said, 'Here.' Looking between his feet Richard saw a change in the quality of the darkness where some other light source was beginning to compete with the torch now far above his head. The night outside was just starting to lift, the rumour of sunrise entering the shaft by the clear tube through the open gallery.

Will was huddled against the cable, didn't let go even as Richard stepped carefully off the track on to the dome beside him. The gondola didn't move. 'Who...?'

'Richard. Jesus, Will, it's good to see you.' He took out his own torch. So close, after so long in the dark, the beam made Will screw his eyes up and raise his arm defensively. 'How're you doing? Midge said you hurt your head.'

'I banged my head. I gave my ribs quite a thump too. I'm all right. But Richard'—finally he looked round, white-faced in the beam—'I don't know how the hell I'm going to get out of here.'

'Same way I got in,' Richard said briskly. 'Up the track.' He took the cords off his shoulder, began laying them out across the dome.

Will watched in horror. 'I hope you're not thinking—' His teeth chattered uncontrollably.

'Listen, Will.' Richard straightened up, eyeing him levelly. 'You can't stay here. We're taking you back upstairs. There's heat and food, and Tessa can check out your head and your ribs, and you'll be OK. You'll be safe enough.

Midge'll go first—he's better at this than I am—and you'll
be roped to him. I'll be right behind. If you freeze, or if
you slip, I'll hold you. A few minutes is all it takes. It's
not difficult. If you can climb a ladder you can do this.
OK,' he hurried on, 'I know you'd rather not climb a ladder. But with your neck at stake you'll be surprised what
you can do.'

'I can't do that,' said Will with certainty.

'You got no choice. I mean it, Will—you're going up
there if I have to carry you.'

In the end Will allowed himself to be manoeuvred to the
track, his hands to be placed on the frets. Midge led, trailing
the makeshift rope like an umbilical. When the cord tight-
ened about his waist Will obeyed its summons. Richard's
hand in the small of his back both held him safe and left
him no room to retreat. After only a brief pause he started
to climb.

The idea that time is a constant is patently absurd.
Midge, accustomed to using the shaft as other people use
staircases, climbed up to and then past the open door in the
space of a few minutes, throwing the safety cord to Larry.
But at the other end of the same cord, his hands raw, his
muscles cracking with tension, his eyes stretched with a
terror he could control but not contain, Will hung in the
void almost for ever before Tariq gripping one wrist and
Larry the other hauled him bodily into the corridor.

He said, inanely, 'Hello.' Then his knees folded under
him and he sat down with the surprised expression of a
puppet breaking a string. The laughter of sheer relief rip-
pled through the anxious gathering.

Richard came next, twisting awkwardly, extending his
left hand to Tariq, gripping the edge of the door with the
other.

In a fraction of a second everything changed. Richard's
right hand skidded wildly; instead of guiding him to safety

Tariq was left carrying his whole weight, his hand Richard's only contact with reality. Richard let out a startled squawk as his feet swung in space. His flailing right hand found the track again but grease on his fingers ruined his grip. Whatever he touched took the slippery contagion and would not support him.

A moment later Larry realized what had happened. 'Hold him!' He hauled Will to his feet and stripped the cord off him like undressing a child. There was nowhere to tie it so he knotted swift loops in both ends and tossed one to Joe. 'And you hold that, tight!' Full length on the floor with his head and shoulders in the void, he fished for Richard's foot.

Time warped again. It took Larry maybe a minute to make his catch and join Joe on the rope. But Tariq was holding Richard much longer than that. He had all the time in the world for two perfectly coherent thoughts. The first was that Richard was heavier than he looked: he couldn't hold this thin cord much longer without it cutting through his flesh. And the other was that if that was what it took that was how it would have to be, because he'd rather die than turn his back on another desperate human being.

Then small strong hands—Sheelagh's—joined his on the cord. Her support may have been more moral than practical, but it kept him going until Joe and Larry were able to share the strain, pulling Richard to safety over the lip, landing him like a gasping, exhausted fish. The doors closed on the void with a faintly disappointed hiss.

For a long time no one spoke. They sprawled in the corridor recovering breath and nerve. One hand after another patted Will's arm or shoulder as if to confirm that he was alive. But no one spoke. Even when Richard realized Midge wasn't with them, had vanished again into the empty carcass of the building, he managed only a pant of regret.

Joe was the first to find a voice, and it climbed in a

gravelly plaint at how near to disaster they had come. 'What the hell *happened?*'

'Grease.' Richard held up his right hand, palm out. 'Must have been left over from when they installed the lift. Mustn't have expected people to be climbing up and down the shaft. No imagination.' He had to break the sentences in half to get them out a breath at a time.

The older man peered at his hand with an intensity no one else understood. Then he cleared his throat. 'If that was left by the men installing the lift, this must have been where they ate their sandwiches. That isn't grease. I think it's butter.'

NINETEEN

RICHARD STARED at the pale oily residue in amazement. 'Where the hell did I pick that up?'

Tariq hauled himself up, padded over to the lift. The doors were closed now; there was an oily smear to the left of the join. 'Here, by the looks of things.' He exhaled in a silent whistle. 'Thank God you didn't touch it on the way down. You'd never have made it.'

On her knees beside him Tessa peered into Will's eyes, felt along his ribs till he winced. 'Come into the cottage hospital. I'll see if I can make you a bit more comfortable.' With Joe to help, Will made it to his feet and, shakily, into the room where Miriam Graves still slept impervious to all the drama.

A frown creased Richard's freckled brow. 'I don't get this. If that's where it came from, how *did* I miss it on the way down? But there was nothing wrong with my grip right up to the moment when I had no grip at all.' He stood at the door making t'ai chi movements, trying to remember exactly where he put his hands as he climbed into the shaft. Still he could make no sense of it. He must have held the side of the door, couldn't have reached the track without. Defeated, he shook his head. 'It couldn't have been there earlier.'

'It must have been,' Tariq said reasonably. 'How could it have got there in the fifteen minutes you were down below? You think maybe Larry got bored holding the door open and sent out for a sandwich?' He meant it as a joke. When Richard failed even to smile his eyes widened and his voice stumbled. 'In God's name, what are you thinking?

That it wasn't an accident? You're crazy. Why would Larry want you to fall? Why would anyone?'

Sheelagh was standing beside them, following their exchange intently. She said quietly, 'I know who might want you to fall, and it isn't Larry.'

They stared at her. 'Who?'

'That crazy boy. No, *don't* look at me like that,' she said, fielding Tariq's dismissive glance. 'Think about it. We've already had two incidents he was responsible for. Doesn't that alone make him prime suspect for a third?'

'We don't know that he hit Miriam. And though you could blame him for Will's fall it wasn't deliberate. And he helped us to get him back when we couldn't have managed alone.'

'We gave him no choice! Larry was about to beat the crap out of him and he knew it—he'd have said and done anything then. Yes, he helped Richard get to Will. But if he greased the handholds he never intended them to get back. It was only good luck that saved them. He made damn sure he wasn't there to, didn't he? Isn't that a little suggestive too?'

'But—why?'

'Because he resents us and he's scared of us. Because this is his home and his adventure playground, and it was all his every night when the builders went home. When we moved in he felt invaded. God knows how he expected to get away with murder. He may be just crazy enough to think that if he got rid of us no one else would come.'

Richard was slowly shaking his head. 'It doesn't work. No, listen.' Sheelagh swallowed her interruption and listened. 'Midge went down the shaft ahead of me and when we came up he kept going. He never touched that door again. How did he grease it so that I missed it going down but met it coming up?'

Tariq shrugged. 'Maybe it was there all along and you

were luckier where you put your hand first time. Maybe it really does date back to the builders' sandwiches.'

'And maybe you'll keep making excuses for that boy until he finally kills someone,' snapped Sheelagh in exasperation. 'I'm not suggesting that we lynch him on the basis of what I suspect. I'm suggesting we take precautions in case I'm right, and if we get another opportunity we hold on to him and never mind how little he likes it.'

Tessa joined them, drying her hands on a towel. 'I agree. Too many odd and dangerous things are happening. There are only two choices—either Midge is behind them or someone else is. Who do we consider more likely to be rifling through our belongings, stealing keys and attacking us? Do we really think there's another Care in the Community case wandering round up here?'

'All right,' conceded Richard, 'some of it was obviously him. It was him knocked over Mrs Venables' tray, and it was him rooting round in Sheelagh's belongings. I don't think he meant any harm—he's like a child, he likes pretty things. But he swears he didn't hit Miriam, and if he wanted to harm us why did he help rescue Will?'

Tessa shrugged. 'You're talking as if he's normal. He's not. He may not be able to form and carry through coherent plans the way you and I can. He may not be capable of sustained logic. Anyway, what's the alternative? If it wasn't him it was one of us.'

'Don't let's get silly.' Tariq fetched a cloth from the kitchen, scrubbed the grease off the lift door. Feeling their eyes, a little bashfully he explained. 'If he didn't put it here it's more of a danger to Midge than to anyone. You don't really want him to fall.'

Sheelagh shook her head in wonder. 'God forbid.'

By then it was full day. Because it was Saturday the streets below were not filling at the customary rate with jostling, blaring traffic but there were signs of life that made their isolation atop a pinnacle of glass and masonry more pointed somehow, more offensive. Six hundred feet away, which is nothing measured in strides along the ground, there were people who could help them: turn on the power, send up the lift, summon the police to investigate the violence they had suffered.

But the people below, delivering milk and papers, hurrying to their high-powered breakfast meetings or Saturday morning exercise classes, didn't know there were others marooned in the empty building, and those in the penthouse didn't know how to tell them. They might have dropped messages—a hundred might have blown away but eventually one would have been found and read—if they could have opened a window. But it was a modern air-conditioned building, its toughened windows impervious to all but light. They could have launched their paper planes from the roof, but wherever the access was it wasn't in the small block of rooms between the blank wall and the locked door. Anything they dropped down past the lift would only be found when the builders returned on Monday morning.

'It's incredible,' said Larry, shaking his head in savage amusement. 'Here we are in the heart of one of the great cities of the world, with thousands of people inside a half-mile radius, and we could die up here before we could attract their attention.'

'I've got an idea about that,' murmured Will. There was a purpling bruise on his temple and he moved stiffly, his ribs bound up beneath his shirt. 'But it'll have to wait till tonight—it won't work in daylight.'

'Go on.'

'We've got lights, haven't we? This high up we must be visible for miles. If we start flashing an SOS somebody's bound to notice.'

'They'd just think we were having trouble with the power,' objected Sheelagh.

'Maybe most of them would. But as Larry says, there are thousands, maybe millions of people who can see this building. All it needs is for one of them to be looking, to recognize the most identifiable piece of Morse code in the world and to pick up the phone. It might take a couple of hours but it could save us a day and a half.'

Richard was nodding with growing conviction. 'He's right. Something like that, somebody would notice. Why did nobody think of it last night?'

'Stupidity?' hazarded Tariq, and they grinned. 'At least somebody's thought of it now. Another twelve hours and it'll be dark again. What shall we do till then?'

'Come and eat your breakfast,' said Mrs Venables firmly, coming in with a tray. Joe carried another and together they set the table. 'It's a bit skimpy, I'm afraid—I don't want to run out of things if we're not sure how long we're going to be here. Incidentally,' she added, gazing round with a certain censure, 'it would be easier to judge what we're going to need if people would stop raiding the pantry. Somebody must be eating butter with a spoon!'

There was a sharp intake of breath around the table. 'So much for the builders' sandwiches,' murmured Tariq, his eyes low. Against all the odds he'd still hoped it was an accident. It was impossible to go on believing that now.

'*Why?*' whispered Richard, appalled.

Tariq shook his head. 'The question is *who?*'

'You do know what you're saying?' Sheelagh's small, strong body was taut. 'That while Richard was hand-over-handing it down the lift shaft in the hope there was enough left of Will to be worth rescuing, one of us was greasing the door so they'd both fall, and this time maybe they'd die. Is that what you believe? Honestly?'

Tariq would have given anything to be able to deny it. But the situation was too serious for good manners. His eyes were steady. 'Yes.'

Larry said tightly, 'I was there from when Richard went down until he came up. I never left the door—if I had it would've closed. You're saying either I did it or I stood by and let someone else do it.'

'I'm not accusing anyone,' Tariq insisted. But in the circumstances the words lacked conviction.

Will had been present more in body than in spirit, so his mind was uncluttered by recollections. 'Which side of the door were you standing?'

'On the right. They climbed down on the left so I stood on the right to shine the torch past them.'

'And the grease was on the left?' Richard nodded. 'How much was there?'

'Enough. It wasn't plastered on but it was well spread about.'

'It could have been done without Larry knowing. Say it was me. I put some on my left hand, then I go and ask Larry what's happening. He looks down the shaft and says, Nothing much. He isn't going to notice that I'm resting my hand on the side of the door. I could have run it up and down a dozen times and he still wouldn't have seen.' It was a modest enough demonstration of logic, but they were impressed enough to embarrass him. He lifted narrow shoulders self-deprecatingly. 'Just because it could have been done that way doesn't mean it was.'

'No,' Larry said slowly. 'It could still have been me. But I know it wasn't.'

'Before we go any further,' Tariq said, 'has anyone got an innocent explanation? I mean, we all do daft things. If somebody dropped the butter and got it on their hands, now's the time to say so.' He waited but no one said anything. 'Then who was standing by the lift while all this was going on? We know about Larry. Who else?'

After a moment the hands started going up. Only the housekeeper's remained in her lap. Larry nodded ruefully.

'That's my recollection—just about everybody had a look at some point.'

'I don't know how relevant this is,' said Tariq. 'But when Richard slipped and I was holding him, Larry and Sheelagh were right there to help. If either of them wanted him dead they could have got themselves offside.'

'If we're trading alibis,' offered Tessa, 'I can vouch for Mrs Venables. She never left Miriam's side while all this was going on.'

Some at once and some more slowly, some with a tactful hesitancy and others quite frankly, the gaze of all present swivelled round to Joe. He'd put his tray on the dining table and sat down heavily behind it. The lines of his face were set, his expression hard to read. It could have been hurt at what they were thinking, or the soul-clenching anger of a man with enough hatred to want people dead, or a kind of defensive carapace against their accusations because he couldn't disprove them.

Sheelagh said softly, 'Joe?'

He looked at her then. 'What? Did I try to kill Miriam and Will and Richard? No, I didn't.'

'But you did ask someone to check the lift,' she remembered.

'Check it,' he agreed shortly. 'Not force it open and dive through.'

Richard was remembering too. 'Yesterday evening I was talking to Miriam and she went to have a word with Joe. Then we heard Midge yell and we all made for the corridor.'

'So?'

'If she caught up with him later, Joe could have been the last person she saw before she was attacked.'

Tariq was watching the older man. 'Did she talk to you, Joe?'

For a moment it seemed he would refuse to answer,

hunch down behind the redoubt of his craggy impervious face and take the tentative artillery of their questions. Then he softened. 'Yes, she did. She came to my room after supper. She thought it was time I explained. I argued. She said she wasn't going to stand by and let me perform emotional vivisection on you.' He looked at Richard. 'She said you, for one, had had just about as much as you could take.' Richard flushed but didn't deny it. 'She said if I wouldn't make a clean breast of it she would.'

'And you were angry,' Tariq suggested. 'You'd gone to all this trouble and she was going to let you down. You followed her to her room and . . .' He tailed off.

'And picking up a handy rolling-pin I hit her over the head?' offered Joe, heavily ironic. 'That wasn't snatched up in the heat of an argument. The rolling-pin equals premeditation. Is that what you're saying—that I meant to murder her? She's my friend. If she wasn't none of this would have been possible. Maybe I do hate you, and him, and him'—his eyes stabbed round the circle—'and all of you. Maybe I've hated you so long I want to see you dead. So I could have tried to kill any or all of you. I didn't, but it's possible. But do you really think I argued with Miriam, went to the kitchen for a rolling-pin, went to her room and beat her head in?'

There was a long silence. No one ventured an opinion. Probability wasn't the issue: everything that had happened since Friday morning had surprised them. Joe Lockhead could have attacked the psychologist and tried to kill the climbers; so, on the basis of strict possibility, could others. Actions that seemed to clear them of suspicion might have been performed for that purpose.

Tariq sighed. 'Tell you one thing. We'll have to move the beds again.'

'What?!!'

He had the grace to look embarrassed. 'One of us is

dangerous. If we sleep two to a room someone's going to be alone with that person. I suggest Tessa and I stay with Miriam and the rest of you move in here. All right with you, Tessa?' He smiled gently. 'I can't prove I'm not the mad axeman, but if I'd meant Richard to fall I wouldn't have sweated blood hanging on to him.'

She smiled back. 'I'll take your word for it. Hell, I feel safer already.'

TWENTY

NO ONE USED THE WORDS Prime Suspect but the feeling was unmistakable, hanging in the air. When they carried the mattresses into the conference room, Joe's ended up nearest to the door; without a word of comment Richard's was moved from the corner and put in its place.

Joe lowered both brows in a scowl. 'You want me to carry a bell as well?' But no one smiled. It was only funny if he were innocent.

To make room for the mattresses and personal effects the dining table was pushed into the middle of the long room, the sofas were pushed against the walls and the ring of chairs Miriam had set out were stacked roughly out of the way. As if there'd been a party, thought Richard, the drunks had ended up dossing on the floor, but now it was time to start tidying up.

Mrs Venables, who had hardly left Miriam's side, returned to the sickroom. The others sat at the table. It was noticeable how everyone checked that everyone else was accounted for: anxious for one another's safety or else concerned that no one had sneaked away to lay more traps. They sat at the table rather than on the couches so as to have something between themselves and people of whom they were no longer sure. They took their seats, spacing them out warily, and watched Tariq with expectant eyes.

The big man didn't know quite how he'd found himself chairman. He didn't remember an election, wouldn't have stood if there'd been one. But somewhere along the line he'd had that dubious piece of greatness thrust upon him and it was easier to fill the role than pass it on.

He took a deep breath. 'The situation is, we're stuck here till Monday morning unless we can raise the alarm. Will's got an idea about that but it means waiting for dark, Even then it's not foolproof. We could be here another two days, which wouldn't be a problem if one of us wasn't trying to kill the rest.'

There were outraged mutterings at that but he wouldn't withdraw it. 'I'm sorry, there's no other way to read it. Everything we do now has to take account of that. Since we don't know who's responsible we can best protect ourselves by staying together. All the time.

'Whoever it is doesn't seem to be armed, thank God. So far the attacks have been opportunistic—there's no reason to suppose he or she will suddenly produce a Kalashnikov.' A couple of bleak chuckles rewarded his attempt at humour. 'So if we stick together maybe we can prevent any more incidents.'

'There's one other thing we should do,' said Will, 'but nobody's going to like it. We ought to check each other's things. Probably there's nothing to find, but we'd feel so silly if someone really did have a gun.'

He'd misjudged them. The brief humiliation of turning out their bags was easily outweighed by the reassurance that everyone else had done the same. But the search revealed nothing.

'Good, fine,' said Tariq. 'Er—anybody any idea what we do next?'

'As a matter of fact, I have.' Sheelagh produced a pair of long-bladed kitchen scissors.

It spoke volumes for their state of mind that half of them thought she was about to continue with the scissors a task she'd begun with the rolling-pin and butter. Chairs scraped as a couple of them recoiled physically.

At the shock on their faces Sheelagh gave a cackle of derisive laughter. 'Don't panic, I'm not planning to cut throats, only a sheet.' She spread it on the table, cut out a pair of enormous letters H. 'Will gave me the idea with his SOS. Only this way we don't have to wait for dark. We hang one in the window in here and one in the window of the sickroom which faces the other way. It might not be seen but you never know. There are other high buildings, and helicopters. If anyone spots it they'll know what it means.'

But as morning turned to afternoon and wore on towards evening it became clear that the giant Hs which so dominated the rooms where they were hung were invisible in the real world where ordinary people were doing ordinary things and anyone facing unexpected danger had only to shout loud enough for a man in a pointed hat to come along and help. Up here they were in mortal peril and a day after being cut off they still hadn't found a way of telling anyone.

'We might as well be on a spaceship,' Richard said, gazing out across the city in wonder and despair. 'Even then we'd have a radio—we could tell *someone*.'

'The Starship *Lazarus*,' mulled Larry. 'It has a ring to it.'

They chuckled darkly, deriving some crumbs of ease from a companionship neither would have chosen. Then reality supervened. Richard thought, It could be *him*—I could be standing here joking with a man who tried to kill me, who'll try again.

Or was it not Richard but Will who was the target? Or not Larry but one of the others who was the attacker? His head rang with the permutations. Whoever it was, he was shut in here with someone with murder in their heart. Even fifteen months ago, before half an hour in an icy river introduced him to the concept of mortal fear, he'd have worried about that.

Long legs crossed in an attitude of professional calm

betrayed by the tapping of one foot on the floor, Tessa had a cup of tea on the table beside her and her bag under her chair. She never ventured far from it now, nor did she have to explain why. It contained sharp things and poisonous things, and the fact that they were designed to save lives would not stop someone bent on mayhem from turning them to other ends. She said to Tariq, 'When do we try out Will's idea?'

'Once it's dark. It won't be seen before then and I don't want to risk fusing the lights for nothing.'

The sparkle was gone from Tessa's hazel eyes, making room for a deep unease. 'The last thing we want is to be left in the dark. Are you sure it's worth the risk?'

Tariq shrugged. 'The lights didn't stop someone beating Miriam's skull in or greasing the lift. Our best chance is getting the hell out of here as soon as we can.'

'What about the boy?'

'Midge? I don't know where he went. Up into the roof-space, I guess.'

'I meant, why are you so sure it isn't him? Many mentally handicapped people have no impulse to violence but those who have can be triggered by very little. God knows how long he's been living like this—he may have had minimal contact with other people for years, be so emotionally isolated that he panics if he's approached. When Larry cornered him he bit him. Why are you so sure Miriam didn't startle him into attacking her?'

'I can't be sure he didn't hit Miriam. But someone else greased the lift, and it seems more likely there'd be one homicidal maniac in the building than two.'

'At least we can imagine how the boy might feel moved to violence. I can't think why any of us should.'

'Me neither,' Tariq said apologetically, 'but that doesn't mean there isn't a reason. Until last night we didn't know we had anything in common. Maybe there's still something we don't know.'

'Or maybe it's something we do know,' murmured Tessa, glancing significantly across the room.

'Joe? It's hard to forget he brought us here, isn't it? We only have his word that he meant no harm. If Miriam found out different and threatened to tell us he'd have had to shut her up. Then he could start on the rest of us.'

She was watching him closely. 'Is that what you believe?'

'Tessa, I don't know what to believe. But if it happened that way, at least we'd know why.'

She made a determined effort to rise above it. 'Well, the sun's down now. Let's hope there are people in this city with nothing better to do of a Saturday night than watch the lights come on. If any of them can also read Morse code we'll be out of here in an hour.'

'If the electrics hold,' said Tariq, crossing every finger he owned.

When the last oyster gleam had faded from the sky, leaving a dark screen on which the city projected the glow of its activities, they turned off every light and power point in the penthouse and—excepting Mrs Venables—gathered in the conference room. Since it had been Will's idea, Tariq asked him to do the honours and Will made a little curtsey like a lady mayoress turning on the Christmas illuminations. It was a mistake, as his ribs quickly reminded him. Still half-bent, he groped for the switch in the dark. 'Three short, three long, three short?'

He could have keyed it faster, deliberately went slow enough for the flashes to separate into distinct pulses. He didn't want to transmit the notion that someone had left a light flickering in the half-finished building. So he keyed the letters slowly and rhythmically, and the twin chandeliers each mounting a cluster of six bulbs blasted solid

chunks of light out into the darkness: …— — —… … —
— —… … — — —

'Dot dot dot,' Richard supplied helpfully.

Will's voice was flat with disappointment. 'It's dead.
Fused, I suppose. God damn!'

'Don't panic,' said Tariq. 'There'll be a fuse-box somewhere. If there's any wire I can fix it.'

He'd armed himself with the torch against this eventu-
ality. It produced a pathetic worm of light compared with
the great slashes that had belted from the chandeliers, but
it was enough for him to find the fuse-box tucked away in
the pantry and he opened the front. 'What the hell—?'

Richard was looking over his shoulder. 'That's pretty
dramatic as blown fuses go.'

The inside of the box was running with a whitish fluid
that dripped from fuse to fuse and finally to the floor where
it formed a greasy, pungent pool.

'It's bleach,' said Sheelagh in wonder, sniffing it. Her
tone altered. 'Kitchen bleach. Mrs Venables?'

'She's with Miriam. Has been since teatime.'

'Do we actually know that?'

Tariq squinted at her. 'No-o. But there are no padlocks
on the kitchen cupboards. Anyone could have taken the
stuff.'

'Same with the rolling-pin,' murmured Will. 'And the
butter.'

'I know it sounds a bit suggestive,' admitted Tariq, 'but
that's because kitchens *are* full of lethal implements. What
did you bring here—paper, pens, a calculator, same as me?
You can't have a reign of terror with those. But the
kitchen's stocked with knives and forks, and yes, a rolling-
pin, butter and bleach. Sure Mrs Venables could have done
this. But so could any of the rest of us.'

'Apart from Mrs V and Miriam, we were all in the conference room when we turned the lights out.' It wasn't a

guess: Sheelagh had counted. 'But after that anyone could have left. Except Will, who was on the switch. And I heard both Richard and Tariq within seconds of the fuse going.'

'You think that's an alibi for all four of you?' Larry said tightly. 'Well, we know Richard and Will are in the clear— they were down the lift shaft during one of these incidents. But you weren't. It wouldn't be too difficult to throw bleach in the fuse-box and hurry back in time to hear us wondering what the hell happened.'

'Hear *us?*' she echoed spikily. 'Larry, I didn't hear a word out of you until right now. Where were *you* when the lights went out?'

'OK, OK,' interrupted Tariq wearily, 'don't let's bicker. Is everyone here now?' He raised the torch and looked round the kitchen, identifying the faces it picked up. 'Where's Joe?'

They filed back to the conference room. Tariq shone the torch in all the corners but he wasn't there. 'Stay put, everyone. I won't be long.' When he'd gone, taking the torch, they were left in darkness.

He checked Miriam's room: Mrs Venables, sitting by the bed, looked up at the intrusion. 'When can we have the lights on again?'

'Lord knows,' he grunted despairingly. 'How's she doing?'

The injured woman was still unconscious but there was a little more animation in her face and the rhythm of her breathing suggested Tessa was right and she'd wake before long. 'No worse,' said Mrs Venables.

'Somebody sabotaged the fuse-box. Did you hear anything?'

She shook her head, failing to dislodge the cement curls. 'I had the door shut. Anyway, you were all closer to the kitchen than me.'

Tariq nodded. 'Just a thought. Have you seen Joe?'

She stared. 'Is he missing?'

The big man shrugged. 'Maybe the excitement got to him and he's just gone to the loo.' He bit his lip. 'Er—wouldn't you be better off with the others in the conference room? I don't like leaving you here on your own.'

'And I'm not leaving Dr Graves on *her* own,' said the housekeeper stoutly. 'Not with weird stuff happening again.'

He took her point. 'When I've found Joe I'll come and keep you company. Till then, yell if you need me.'

Her torchlit smile was both coy and tough. 'Aye, Mr Straker, and you do the same.'

He searched the newly vacated bedrooms, started on the empty ones. At first he called Joe's name as he went, swinging the beam ahead of him like a blind man's cane, poking it in all the corners. But the further from the conference room he moved the less he liked advertising himself quite so plainly, the desire to find Joe tempered by a reluctance to let Joe find him. His footsteps grew softer, his caution more pronounced; he moved through the dark rooms not so much like a forest animal, which at least knows if it is hunter or hunted, as like a soldier in enemy territory who may find himself playing either part at a moment's notice. He dropped into an unconscious crouch and the hairs along his arms and at the nape of his neck stood up.

At the last room before the dead end Tariq hesitated a moment, drew a breath to steady his nerve, then punched the door open and followed the torch inside in one swift movement that he'd learned from watching cop shows on TV.

Inside he found what he was seeking. Joe was sitting on the floor under the window, his head sunk on his arms. Releasing his breath in a sigh, Tariq said weakly, 'What are you doing here?'

Joe didn't look up. After a moment, frowning, Tariq crossed the room and shone the torch in his face. 'Joe?' It was half a minute before he realized the older man wasn't going to answer.

Richard heard running feet in the corridor and his heart lurched. He kept his shoulder against the door until he was sure that the voice, though breathless, was indeed Tariq's. 'For Christ's sake let me in!'

TWENTY-ONE

TESSA COULDN'T ADD MUCH to Tariq's first impression: that Joe was far from well, hovering on the brink of consciousness. He seemed vaguely aware of her ministrations, pawed weakly at her hands as if a mosquito were disturbing his sleep. His own hands were clammy and twitched loosely; sweat dewed the creases of his face.

'Someone did this to him?' Tariq voiced the thought uppermost in everyone's mind. If Joe had become a victim they needed another suspect.

The doctor shook her head. 'He's ill.'

'Heart attack?'

'Maybe, but…' Her forehead knit and she continued her examination. Joe muttered complainingly as she took his pulse—her eyebrows elevating momentarily—and shone the light in his eyes, but most of what he was saying was unclear and the rest made no sense. Tariq made out the word 'needle'.

Tessa looked up in sudden understanding. 'When you searched his things, was there a hypodermic?'

'Not that I found.' Then Tariq's smooth deep voice soared. 'You think he's a junkie?'

'A diabetic. Sniff his breath—can you smell the sweetness?'

But Tariq's nose was less well trained than hers. 'If we can't find his insulin will he die?'

'No,' she said quickly. 'I carry insulin. I can keep him ticking over till we can get him to a hospital.'

Larry searched Joe's bag again, still without success. Tessa turned out his pockets but didn't find what she was looking for. 'Maybe till now he was able to control it by diet. If he's not insulin-dependent he wouldn't have a syringe.'

'Will you inject him?' asked Tariq.

'Yes. I'll have to estimate the dose but I can refine it when I see how he responds. Don't worry,' she said, shining the torch into her bag and selecting what she needed, 'he'll be all right. Thank God you found him when you did.'

Though barely conscious Joe seemed to recognize the syringe and tried to take it from her. 'No, let me do it,' she said; but he went on fumbling for it. 'Tariq, would you hold him still?' So he did.

He was still holding him when the convulsion hit, the man going suddenly rigid in his grasp. Alarmed, Tariq looked for guidance, but before Tessa could speak the rigidity turned to violent spasm, the sturdy body arching as if the spine would double back on itself. His arms and legs jerked so that Tariq fought to hold him, like holding a frantic animal. The muscles each side of the heavy jaw clenched, and strange sounds and saliva bubbled from the corners of his mouth.

Tessa's voice cut across the alarm in the room. 'Don't be frightened. It's a reaction to the insulin. I've probably overestimated the dose a little. He'll soon stabilize. Are you all right, Tariq?'

Tariq had been shocked to the core. He'd held on only because he couldn't think what else to do. 'Er—fine,' he managed. Already Joe's struggles were weakening; after a minute Tariq tried easing his grip. The older man lay against his chest as if exhausted. 'Is *he?*'

'He will be,' Tessa assured him. 'He'll sleep now. We'll put him in with Miriam. At least there was some heat on in there till the power went.'

They'd overlooked that: that when the power fused they

lost not only the lights but the heating and the cooker as well. In their favour they had bedding, extra clothes and outdoor wear suitable for a wet, blustery March. But it was going to be a long cold night.

When Joe's bed had been carried round to the sickroom Tariq brought a couple of chairs. 'One for you so you can look after him, one for me so I can look after you.'

Tessa smiled. 'Who's going to look after you?'

Immediately they met Tariq had been aware of the powerful alloy of strength, intellect and understated sexuality that made up Tessa McNaught. He was used to professional women, women who wielded authority, women who made full use of their own magnetism; but there was something different at work here and he still hadn't worked out quite what it was. The sway of self-possession, perhaps. That cool, calm exterior hid only a cool, calm interior on which the views of others hardly impinged. She'd mentioned a husband, which surprised Tariq a little until he remembered that he worked nights and she worked days.

The same inborn autonomy also explained some less appealing traits: her habit of speaking her mind unfettered by discretion, of distancing herself from the group when it suited her. She gave scant consideration to her effect on other people, to an extent that was both a strength and a weakness. She was not reliant, nor did she invite reliance. It all made her easier to admire than to like; but Tariq was a man for whom admiring women was easy, and usually enough. He found her deeply impressive.

He would have died rather than say any of that. Instead he chewed his lip reflectively. 'I'll get another chair.'

Tessa laughed out loud, the first time anyone had done so for some time, and the hazel eyes danced. 'Are you always such a clown?'

'Um—probably.'

'Well, go and be a comfortable clown in your own bed.

I don't need watching over. Anyway, I think Mrs Venables is going to sit with Miriam so we can keep one another company. We'll call if we need you.'

'No,' he said, serious now, 'it's too risky. Too much has happened already. I'm not leaving two women to cope with him alone. Mrs Venables, why don't you get some rest in the other room? You could give Tessa a break halfway through the night if they're still both OK.'

The wrinkles on Mrs Venables' brow reflected the grey corrugations of her perm. Though plainly unwilling to leave her employer with strangers, she'd been on watch for eighteen hours with hardly a break; if she didn't take the chance to sleep now she'd nod off at her post, a poor guardian for the helpless woman. 'You'll both stay here? You'll call me if either of you's going to leave?'

'Promise,' said Tariq.

'And if she wakes up?'

'And if she wakes up. Go on, get a break while you can.'

The housekeeper nodded, reluctantly conceding the wisdom of it. In the doorway she turned back. 'And if—'

'Mrs Venables, if she snores, sneezes, rolls over or starts whistling "Dixie" I'll call you. I promise. Now go!' She went.

Tessa examined the big woman by torchlight, Tariq watching from a respectful distance. 'I think she'll wake up before long.'

'Then maybe we can find out once and for all who hit her.'

'If she remembers. People often don't after concussion. Or they think they remember but it's wrong, they dreamt it.'

'So even if she says it was Joe we still can't be sure?'

'Not beyond reasonable doubt,' Tessa said wryly. She turned then to her newest patient, played the torch over his stolid sleeping countenance. 'He's not going to hurt anyone else, you know. Not in this state. You should get some sleep while everything's quiet.'

He shrugged broad shoulders. 'I know, I worry too much. But I promised Mrs V. Besides, Joe waking up isn't the only danger. If it was him who hit Miriam you're probably safe enough. But if it wasn't, neither of them will be much help if the real culprit comes back.'

They were alone with the sleepers. Tessa spoke her mind. 'I can only express a medical opinion. I didn't know any of you before we came here, I certainly don't know anything about Joe that you don't. But pathologically it makes sense. He's been under a lot of stress—he's been through a double grieving, and before he found his feet he was planning this. Stress is a major factor in maturity-onset diabetes.

'We know he was behind a lot of what's happened. He launched a hate campaign against the people he blamed for his daughter's suicide. Then at the last minute someone he needed to carry it through let him down. He was already wavering between sanity and the other thing. Suppose fury tipped him over and he hit her? The emotional stress of that would send his need for insulin soaring. A healthy pancreas responds, a fragile one loses control.' Her gaze was steady. 'I'm not saying that going into a diabetic coma proves Joe attacked Miriam. I'm saying it would be consistent medically.'

It was the least unpalatable of the options before them. Joe had a motive, he'd had time to plan his actions and enough freedom to carry them out. He and Miriam were friends; she'd have lowered her guard with him in a way she wouldn't with the others. He could have booby-trapped the lift as easily as anyone else. But carrying so much anger in his heart brought on a disease that betrayed him into the hands of his victims. As well as medical consistency there was a kind of justice to that which almost compelled belief.

Tariq would have been satisfied but for the sheer convenience of it. If Joe was responsible for all that had happened and now he'd collapsed, they were safe. It didn't matter if the lights were out; it didn't matter if they had to survive another day and night on cold baked beans and mineral water. They were safe. Even when he came round they wouldn't let him threaten them again. If they watched Joe they wouldn't have to watch each other.

If Joe were the attacker. If not, the fact that they believed themselves safe was the most dangerous thing of all.

This wasn't Tariq's world. He put together deals. He wooed clients, charmed money out of sponsors. He'd walked a lot of tightropes in his time but they all had nets beneath: nobody suffered, except financially, from wearing the wrong logo on their shirt. He'd never made decisions that lives could depend on. He didn't want that responsibility.

But somehow it had come his way and no one wanted to take it back. So he made the best decisions he could, but any mistakes would be on the side of caution. Maybe Joe did attack Miriam Graves; maybe he wanted to kill them all; but Tariq wasn't going to stake anyone's life on it.

'So I'm fussing. But let's make sure, OK? We'll both stay. If only to save me from Mrs Venables' wrath if she finds out I fibbed.'

TWENTY-TWO

IN THE CONFERENCE ROOM they prepared for the night ahead with a strange ambivalence. They very much wanted to believe it was over. They'd been anxious, even afraid, even those who would never admit it; but if things were as they seemed this time there was no more cause for concern. They would still be cold, they might be hungry, they would ache for rescue by Monday morning, but they had nothing more to fear in the way of violence. No one had to worry that he was turning his back on a would-be murderer.

If the jigsaw pieces were giving the true picture this time, and the sick man across the corridor had done all they believed. But they'd had a suspect before: they'd blamed Midge. It seemed they'd been wrong. Or they were wrong this time, in which case they were warming their hands at the hearth of relief altogether too soon.

So although it was late, and they'd been awake since early morning, and all the light they had was one small torch—Tessa having claimed the other for the sickroom—they were less keen to sleep than they might have been. With the mattresses pushed together in a corner of the room, with their warmest clothes on under the duvets and their coats spread on top, they looked for some other way to pass the time.

They began by talking about what they'd do when they got out on Monday morning. But that was like discussing Christmas: it was too far away to seem real. After this long cold night there would be another, with a long cold day between. And when they left here, after they'd told their story to an incredulous constabulary—'You're saying you couldn't find any way of letting us know what was happening in *nearly three days?'*—they would have nothing in common any more. They would go back to their divers lives, to families who would listen raptly to the first and second tellings, dutifully to the third, then go and feed the cat. It was a future they yearned for, but here and now reality was one another, people they hadn't known before Friday.

So the conversation drifted back to the one thing they had in common: Cathy Beacham, who had the world at her feet and somehow kicked it over the fence and past recovery.

'The bit I have trouble with,' said Sheelagh, 'is that it ended in suicide. I'd never have believed that. Cathy was a born survivor. I'd have said nothing could happen to her that she couldn't hammer into some sort of viable compromise. She was the last person in the world to take a dive because things didn't work out.' She meant it as a figure of speech, winced at its aptness.

'She didn't lose her grip because things went wrong,' remembered Larry. 'It was the other way round.'

'Then why? What made her change?'

He shrugged. 'I never found out. There are always ups and downs, you have good games and bad ones, times when the run of the court seems against you and others when you'd win playing with a biscuit-tin lid instead of a racket. But Cathy knew that. She'd been through rough spots before. She knew the answer because it's always the same— work. If you're playing badly work not only improves your game, it makes you feel positive about it and that gets you winning again. And if you're cruising work keeps you sharp. Nobody's at their peak all the time. You have to be philosophical about the odd defeat. But not so philosophical that it becomes easier to lose than to fight.'

The others who knew her had seen the change taking

place, had tried to help and had their efforts repulsed, had finally accepted they were powerless to reverse the process and make the girl who she had been before. Even Sheelagh, who hadn't seen her for years, met Cathy shortly before her death and knew that her childhood friend was long gone.

But the last time Will saw the girl he'd wanted to marry she was riding her success, high on achievement and ambition, sure where she was going and willing to make whatever sacrifices were necessary. As one of those sacrifices he had not shared her enthusiasm, but he hadn't thought she was on the brink of disaster either. He had worried that those around her would let her down, never imagined she'd let them down.

They'd had two good years together, had made each other happy. Cathy's decision to separate came out of nowhere, devastatingly sudden, irrevocable. She'd said (or had he assumed?—so long after it was hard to be sure) that it was forced on her, that her agent or coach had thought him a poor consort for their golden girl. It was a comfortable notion in a way because it relieved him of responsibility for what followed. But meeting the two men, confronting the gap between perception and reality—Tariq an amiable guru, even Larry with his iron dedication no thug—challenged his memory of events. Carefully not looking at the man he murmured, 'Larry, did you tell her to finish with me?'

Larry was plainly startled. 'Me? No.'

'Advise her, then.'

The coach shook his head. 'It was none of my business. I told her how to play tennis. I told her how to eat, how to exercise, how to train and how to win. But her personal life was just that—personal, and hers. You think she'd have *let* me tell her who she could and couldn't see? A couple of times I warned her the late nights were damaging her game. But what she was doing when she should have been sleeping, and who she was doing it with, were her concern. I didn't expect her to be a nun. All I cared was that her extramural activities didn't spoil her game. Tell her to elbow you? I didn't know you from a hole in the wall.'

'But she *said*—' Will heard the plaintive whine in his voice and stopped.

Larry's tone softened. 'Maybe she was trying to let you down lightly.'

'There was someone else?' He sounded surprised.

'After you? Of course there was. She didn't go into purdah just because you left the scene.'

'Who?'

Larry shrugged. 'I never met him either. He wasn't a tennis-player, that's all I know. Harry something—or was it Jerry? I only remember that because of some joke she made about his name and mine.' What she'd said was that it was enough to have one of them riding her all night without having the other on her back all day, but some impulse of decency stopped him sharing that with Will. The man was hurting enough.

But Will was also thinking. 'Then where's he?'

Larry didn't understand. But Sheelagh did and her eyes sharpened. 'That's right. We're here because Joe reckoned we let her down, yes? But if she left Will for this other guy, why isn't he here instead?'

'Maybe he couldn't find him,' Richard suggested.

'So he roped in the guy Cathy dumped for him? Is it likely?'

Richard's sandy eyebrows climbed. If logic was any criterion none of them would be here. But he took her point. 'Then maybe he didn't know about Harry. He didn't see much of Cathy that last year, remember—maybe she never told him she had someone new.'

'He knew about me,' said Sheelagh. 'Not just that Cathy

and I used to be friends—he knew she'd come to me for a job and I turned her down. She must have talked pretty freely that last time he saw her. So *why* didn't he know about Harry?'

Richard puzzled over it but came up with no answer. If she'd poured out her heart in enough detail to include the fact that she'd been refused a job by an old schoolfriend, why had she made no mention of the man in her life? Perhaps by then he was the ex-man in her life. But her father thought it was Will who let her down. Why did she let him think that?

'Maybe he was married,' offered Larry. 'Maybe she knew there was no future in it.'

'So she didn't tell her people she'd finished with Will? She let them go on asking after him, wondering when she was going to bring him home? You wouldn't,' said Sheelagh, shaking her head with the certainty of someone who'd been there. 'You'd say, It wasn't getting anywhere, I gave him the push. And to stop them asking if there was anyone else you'd say, I'm too busy, I haven't time for men right now.'

'But for nearly a year,' Will said slowly, 'she let her people believe it was still her and me. Maybe there wasn't much risk of them hearing different, but why pretend? We'd never met—why would they care if she threw me over? Why not just say, You know Thingy the solicitor?— he's old news. Isn't that what she said to you?' Larry nodded without comment. 'Then why not to her parents?'

Sheelagh knew. 'Because Larry was only interested in her tennis but her parents were interested in her life. They'd have asked questions she didn't want to answer: why, why now, when she'd been happy with you for two years and you were planning to marry and then suddenly it's over? Larry didn't ask any of that, and she knew he wouldn't. She was safe telling him.'

The coach bristled. 'It was none of my business. She had to have some life I'd no say in, for God's sake!

'Coach and athlete, that's a relationship that's too close for comfort a lot of the time. It has to be. You have to know a person inside out to get the best out of them, but there's a price to pay. There's no privacy, not even in your head. Your thoughts, feelings, desires, fears—you have to be ready to share all that, and have it picked over and pulled apart in case there's a bit of extra performance to be got out of it. Most athletes hate their coaches most of the time. For a day or two after a good win they love us dearly, but most of the time they hate our guts. It's not a bad thing. When you're too damn tired to remember why you're doing this you can keep going on hate.

'But you need someone else to talk to. Friends, family, lovers, even casual acquaintances and pets—anyone who hasn't seen you doubled up and crying with cramp and frustration. You need someone who won't try to use what you say, because you know that sooner or later your coach will. That's his job.'

'Would Tariq have known about this—Harry?' Will fought the urge to spit the name out and then wipe his mouth on his sleeve. After all, it wasn't Harry who owed him better: it was Cathy, that he'd loved, that he'd been engaged to, who lied to him.

'Ask him.'

Will pushed the quilt aside and stood up, wincing at the tug on his side. Tessa had found no broken ribs. There had been just enough give in the acrylic to absorb the first massive impact of his fall, not quite enough for it to collapse and let him through. Despite the fact that he felt bruised in every muscle, and would feel worse before he felt better, he knew he'd been lucky. 'Talk among yourselves till I get back.' He gave a quick grin. 'About me, if you like.' He closed the door behind him to conserve the heat.

Only as he felt his way up the black corridor did he remember that they were supposed to be seeking safety in numbers. But that was before Joe's seizure, and even if the man was feeling better now he was under constant supervision. How much danger could he be? And indeed, Will reached the bedroom without incident and tapped on the door. 'Can I have a word?'

No one answered. That should have alerted him: two responsible people watching over a psychopath were unlikely to take forty winks at the same time. But that's what he thought: that it was late, everything was quiet, both patients were asleep and Tessa and Tariq were dozing. He opened the door and put his head round. 'Everything OK?'

There was no light in the room; probably they'd turned the torch off to save the batteries. But the blinds were gone, their cords sacrificed to his rescue, and the sky above a major city is never entirely dark. There was enough pinkish backwash to show him—well, nothing. No one in the chair beside the door. No one in the chair beside the nearest bed. No one in the bed.

'Oh shit,' he said, very softly and with utter foreboding.

TWENTY-THREE

THE BED UNDER THE WINDOW was still occupied: he could see the mound that was Miriam Graves, slumbering undisturbed through another crisis. At least, he assumed she was sleeping. In sudden horrid premonition he leaned over the bed, peering in the near darkness for signs of life. For an awful moment he thought there were none—that what had been started with a rolling-pin had been finished with a pillow, or a pair of strong hands, or another blow. But then Miriam gave a little mumble that was half a snore and shifted under the duvet, and Will exhaled in relief.

He turned his mind to the question of the three other people who should have been in that room and weren't. He tried the bathroom, though he couldn't imagine the circumstances in which they would all have piled in there together. With no window the place was dark enough to develop photographs: Will made sure it was empty by the simple if nerve-racking expedient of groping round until he was sure he'd have found anyone in there, alive or dead.

Leaving the bathroom his foot came down in glass. Already broken, it splintered under his weight. He shuddered. It was only as an afterthought that he'd put his shoes on: he'd been going to pad across the corridor in his socks.

He had to get some light. Until he could see better than this Will was doing nothing more. He stepped gingerly over the glass, reached for the door.

Someone moaned. Will froze. Under his shirt the hairs along his arm lifted to the sound like antennae. Fear licked at the back of his neck. For a moment he tried to tell himself it was Miriam, returning from the velvet abyss to the pain of a broken head; but if she was on her way back the psychologist was comfortable enough to be at peace and anyway that wasn't a woman's voice. Joe or Tariq. Either Joe had woken and resumed his career of mayhem or—what? Something unforeseen that had thrown the whole bloody mess back in the melting-pot again.

The most sensible thing would be to call for help. Whoever made that sound was hurt, another victim. But the attacker could be there too, hidden in the same dark, and that thought clamped Will's throat. Leaving would have been the second most sensible thing, but he was loath to abandon two injured people to their assailant. So he did the third most sensible thing: listened intently for several seconds and did nothing. Then he drew a deep breath and moved towards the sound, one cautious step at a time.

As he skirted the empty bed something grabbed his legs. He stumbled wildly and crashed along the carpet, the impact like a blowtorch on his side. He kicked frantically at the hands clawing him before he realized that what he was fighting was an upturned chair. With a sob of relief he subsided against the footboard.

What crawled over the carpet then, and over his hand to fasten on his wrist, could by no stretch of the imagination have been furniture. In the marginal light his horrified eyes registered only a pale gleam but his skin reported a flaccid touch like a dead hand. Will yelled and snatched his arm away in terror, and kicked at whatever was groping for him.

His feet found a target and something heavy rolled away from him. A whine of agony stabbed him with guilt like knives: in fear and darkness he'd found not the assailant but the victim who'd come crawling to him for help. Will got his knees under him and scrambled in pursuit, and immediately his hands brushed the twisted bulk of a man's body. His fingers found a face, olive smooth rather than craggy; long straight hair spilling over the cheek confirmed it. His fingertips came away wet and sticky. He had no way of knowing if the blood was his doing or not.

The door banged open and light stabbed into the room. It wasn't that bright—hearing his cry Richard had grabbed the torch and dived for the door with the others on his heels—but Will's eyes had dilated in the darkness. When they cleared he found himself crouched over Tariq's head as the man lay, half-conscious and mumbling, under the window. Blood had washed down his left cheek and bore the unmistakable imprint of a shoe.

'What *happened?*' demanded Richard, quartering the room with the weak beam. 'Where's Tessa? And Joe?'

'I don't know,' stumbled Will. 'Jesus, you don't think *I* did this? I mean, yes, I kicked him. Somebody grabbed me. I didn't know who. It was dark. I kicked out.' He heard himself babbling, made an effort to calm down. 'I knocked on the door but no one answered. There was no light. Then I heard someone groan. When I went to investigate I fell over a chair. Then someone grabbed my arm.'

'So you kicked him in the face?' Larry's tone was incredulous.

'I didn't know what was happening! I thought someone had jumped me.'

'Him?' Sheelagh was on her knees by the injured man, easing a pillow under his head. The blood came from a jagged wound above his ear.

Mrs Venables picked her rapid way through the now crowded room, bent over the woman in the bed. 'Dr Graves? Dr Graves, are you all right? I should never have left you. I *knew* I shouldn't have.' She righted a chair and sat down beside the bed as if nothing less than dynamite would move her again.

Will shook his head impatiently. 'Sheelagh, I didn't have the benefit of a damn great arc light to work by. I didn't know it was Tariq, and I didn't know he was hurt. Somebody grabbed me and I lashed out. After all that's happened, that surprises you? I was scared and I lashed out at the wrong person. But I didn't do—this.' He gestured unsteadily at Tariq. 'You do *know* that, don't you? You know that whoever's doing this, it isn't me.'

There was a pause as people tried to remember what they knew and what they only surmised. 'Yes, of course we do,' Richard said wearily. 'Sorry. It looked—bad.'

'It *is* bad.' Will accepted his proffered hand: he'd have had trouble getting up without it. 'We're being decimated here.'

With Tessa missing and Mrs Venables preoccupied, Larry turned his hand to first aid, fashioning a passable bandage from the hem of a sheet. When he'd finished Tariq looked like a maharaja after a night on the tiles.

He was surfacing by then. His eyes still rolled under heavy lids and his hands moved vaguely as if he didn't quite know where they were, but slowly what he was saying began to make sense.

'I was asleep,' he said. 'Near as damn it. In the chair by the door. It was dark. Somebody…' He was losing it. He stopped a moment, bit his lip and tried to concentrate. 'Someone was moving around. Tessa had the torch and I wondered why she wasn't using it. I said—something. Then the beam hit me full in the eyes. I started to my feet but the roof fell on me.' Tariq braved a tiny smile. 'I went out like a light.'

Will didn't smile. His focus on the big man was absolute. 'Someone hit you. Who?'

Tariq didn't understand. 'Well—Joe, I suppose.'

'You didn't see him?'

'I couldn't *see* anything. But I had my back to the door. No one could have come in without moving me.'

Will accepted that. 'I found broken glass by the bathroom door. Could he have hit you with a bottle?'

Tariq thought for a moment, nodded. The movement dislodged lumps of pain that tumbled through his head making him wince. 'There was a lemonade bottle. Would that do?'

'Oh yes. With that he could have taken your stupid head off.'

Tariq's eyes dropped at the rebuke. 'I couldn't stay awake. It'd been a long day, and I thought it was over—I thought the guy responsible was out for the count and all we had to do was wait to be rescued. When Tessa switched off the torch I nodded off.' Then his eyes flew wide. 'Dear God, Tessa! Miriam! What—where—?'

'Miriam's all right,' Sheelagh reassured him. She put a blanket off the vacated bed around his shoulders. 'She seems to be coming round. I don't think he's touched her. Tessa's missing.'

Tariq moaned as if the hurt was physical. 'It's my fault. I was supposed to protect her. All I had to do was stay awake. Now he's loose and she's missing, and it's all my fault!'

'Yes,' agreed Will coldly. 'It is.'

'All right,' said Sheelagh sharply, looking up with angry eyes and tight lips, 'you've made your point. He cocked up. And he got his head beat in for it. Now, do you want to rub it in a bit more or can we start looking for Tessa?'

Chastened, Will nodded. 'Yes, of course.' She was right; he'd been wrong to concentrate on what happened anything up to an hour ago when a madman and the woman tending him were both unaccounted for.

The little torch was growing weak; once he was sure neither of the missing people was secreted anywhere in the room Richard switched it off.

'We've got to have light,' growled Larry. 'We can't manage without.'

'If we don't save it while we can we'll have to manage without.'

They had thought the horror was behind them, that all they had to worry about was the cold and the boredom until rescue came on Monday. Discovering their mistake so dramatically shocked them to the core. Nervous and apprehensive, the last thing they wanted now was to split up, but there was no alternative. Tariq was too shaky to take part in the search that must be made. They helped him on to the bed, and Will and Mrs Venables stayed with the casualties.

Will didn't like being classed along with the injured man, the unconscious woman and the elderly one, but the state of his ribs made him no asset to the search. In the oppressive dark of the sickroom, tracking the progress of the searchers with one ear, he used the time to do what he did best, better than anyone else present. He thought.

Using the torch as sparingly as they dared, the search-party moved through the penthouse checking bedrooms, bathrooms, wardrobes—anywhere that could accommodate a big man or the body of a tall woman. No one admitted that was what they were looking for, but if she was alive Tessa would be shouting her head off and there was nowhere she could be that they wouldn't have heard her.

Sheelagh took the torch to leave the men's hands free. When they'd finished in the eastern corridor Richard tapped on the sickroom door. 'Nothing yet.'

Even as he spoke he became aware that Sheelagh had stopped, that the faint beam was no longer moving ahead of them but had veered off and stopped. He peered, trying to make out what she was looking at.

She was looking at the lift doors. Unable to see what had stopped her in mid-stride and was continuing to absorb her attention, he stepped closer. So, on the other side of her, did Larry. Then they saw what Sheelagh had seen.

'Dear God.'

A few, perhaps no more than half a dozen, longish red-brown hairs were held in the closed jaws. Richard wondered how Sheelagh had spotted them, until the fractional air current caused by their passing made the hairs lift and dance slightly, catching the light.

'Quickly,' snapped Larry, 'get these doors open!' He punched at the rubber seal until it gave and the doors opened. Richard pointed the torch down the shaft.

The battery was weakening steadily so that less light than before reached the stranded lift. It would have been harder to make out Tessa sprawled across the domed top than it had been to see Will. But as Richard's eyes adjusted he realized something was different, though it took him another moment to be sure what.

Will's body had appeared as a roughly man-shaped obscurity failing to reflect the torch beam as the polished acrylic did. Richard looked for the same sort of thing again; but what he saw was half an acrylic dome, the glitter ending abruptly where the other half should have been and was not.

His voice sounded as hollow as the shaft. 'I think the lift's broken up.'

'What?!' Larry leaned over as far as he dared. 'My God! You were standing on that—you and Will both.'

Richard lifted one shoulder helplessly. 'It felt firm enough then. I don't know, maybe it didn't just break up. Maybe something hit it.'

For a couple of minutes they kept looking, as if something might change. But even by failing torchlight there was no doubt what they were seeing. Half the dome had been torn away, taking with it the clear panel that formed one side of the gondola. Anything that had hit it had gone straight through. What had been a bung in the neck of the bottle was now half a bung at best.

Sheelagh's voice was flat, scoured of emotion, as if caring about one another was a weakness they could no longer afford. 'I don't think we're going to find Tessa however hard we look.'

TWENTY-FOUR

THEY COMPLETED THE SEARCH because even if Tessa was gone none of them believed that Joe, overtaken by remorse, had followed her into the forty-storey abyss. But they found no sign of him.

'Could he have climbed down the shaft?' Sheelagh asked doubtfully.

Richard shrugged. 'I wouldn't have thought so, but...' He had managed, with some help; Midge did it without; but a bulky retired printer whose strength-to-weight ratio had been going downhill for thirty years even before illness left him weak and witless? On the other hand, single-minded obsession gets people through all manner of things that no rational assessment of their capabilities would predict. 'I think he must have done, otherwise we'd have found him.'

'He might have fallen,' hazarded Larry. 'While he was...' He gestured with his head towards the lift, reluctant to say it.

'He might,' agreed Richard sceptically. 'But I don't think we should count on it.'

They returned to the sickroom and broke the news. Mrs Venables turned away. Tariq shook his sore head in wonder. 'So he really means to kill us all. In spite of what he said, he blames us for Cathy's death and he wants to kill us for it. He doesn't care about getting away with it. He just wants us dead.'

'Why Tessa?' asked Will. 'She hardly knew Cathy.'

'Why any of us?' countered Richard. 'Nobody killed his daughter. She committed suicide. Maybe in a perfect world we could have saved her, but God help us, we did our best! Joe knows that. If he still wants us dead it's because he's crazy. We'd better accept that we're dealing with a madman.'

A tremor vibrated in Sheelagh's voice. 'He daren't leave anyone alive. On Monday morning the builders are going to find bodies and call the police. If there's anyone left to say what happened Joe'll end his days in Broadmoor. But if we're all dead, maybe he thinks he can just slip away. Maybe no one else knows he was here.'

'Of course somebody knows he was here,' growled Larry impatiently. 'It was him set this up, remember? However casual it was, even if there's nothing on paper, somebody must have given him the OK, the keys, even the goddamned furniture. Lazaire's won't cover for him when the police ask why their building's full of corpses.'

'He must have known that,' mused Richard, 'and decided it didn't matter. So if getting away isn't a priority, why *did* he kill Tessa?' He looked at Will as if it were a puzzle to which Will had the solution.

That wasn't quite true. Will hadn't worked out the answers yet but he was getting good at identifying the questions. 'Because she didn't tell us the whole truth. She knew Cathy as well as the rest of us. Think about it. Joe wouldn't have wasted his time and money getting hold of a GP who might have treated Cathy but not often enough to remember her. Hundreds of people must have known her better than that, and any one of them would have had as good a chance of saving her. But Joe wanted Tessa here, and he paid a medical journal to commission the article that would bring her. He *must* have had a good reason for that.'

No one spoke. But the quality of the silence changed as they acknowledged the possibility.

'We began by thinking we were a random cross-section of everyday neurotics on a regular course and there was nothing odd about an independent observer. Even when we stumbled on the hidden agenda, it seemed enough that Tessa agreed she could have treated Cathy. But if Joe brought us here not to confront us but to kill us, there had to be more than that. Whatever she said, Tessa knew Cathy too.'

'She might have made a mistake, like she said,' suggested Richard. 'Maybe Joe thought that was the beginning of the end—that if she'd been treated appropriately then none of the rest need have followed.'

It sounded feasible. But Larry shook his head. 'I can't say Cathy never consulted Tessa, but she wasn't her regular doctor. I knew him—he worked with a lot of tennis-players. He was experienced and pragmatic and we both trusted his judgement. That was important.'

'What about when she stopped playing? Could she have gone to Tessa precisely because you didn't know her?'

'She stopped seeing my man, I know that. I asked him to look out for her when she wouldn't see me any more, and he said she hadn't been near him for months.'

'That's it, then,' said Richard. 'She was Cathy's doctor. Joe blamed her for not seeing the state she was in.'

'But by then Cathy's problems were already well established,' said Will. 'Joe couldn't have blamed them on Tessa.'

'He couldn't blame you, either,' Tariq said reasonably, 'but he did.'

'I know where Tessa fits in.' There was a note of certainty in Sheelagh's voice that made everyone look at her, and she nodded. 'She may have treated Cathy professionally, but that's not why Joe brought her here or why he killed her. Tessa was the missing link, the one who should have been here and wasn't. She was Cathy's last lover.'

Whatever they were expecting it wasn't that. Silence fell: the sort of lumpen silence that falls from a height and kicks

up dust and rocks people with its tremors. None of those
closest to her had guessed: not her coach, her agent or her
fiancé.

They thought about it now, eyes flickering in the skimpy
light. It solved some of the puzzles. Neither Larry nor
Tariq, familiar with the untrumpeted side of professional
sport, was surprised or disconcerted when friendships
among women who worked, travelled, stayed and social-
ized together turned to something more. It was a coach's
job to make sure it didn't affect performance and an agent's
to see it didn't affect income, that was all. If Cathy Beacham had told them she had a mistress they'd have advised discretion then wished her luck.

But Will Furney had wanted to marry her, and the idea
that he'd been thrown over not for her career, not for another man but for a woman jolted him to his foundations.
He didn't believe it; wouldn't believe it. Partly it was a
streak of prudery running through him—solicitors are natural conservatives: such things happen to clients but he'd
never expected to meet them in his own life—but mainly
because it made a mockery of his time with Cathy. She'd
slept with him, and to Will that meant commitment, but if
she preferred women what was it about? He'd thought it
was love. But how could she have loved both him *and*
Tessa? If Sheelagh was right the sweetest nights of his life
had been a sham. He couldn't begin to deal with that so he
denied it. White-faced, he mumbled, 'That's not possible.'

'It *is* possible,' Sheelagh said gently, understanding his
distress, 'and the evidence is there. Who's missing from
this route march down memory lane?—the famous Harry.
Or it might have been Jerry. Suppose, though, it was Terry.
Tessa's short for Teresa, isn't it?'

'Coincidence,' muttered Will, but there was no conviction in it.

Sheelagh shook her head. 'It wasn't the first time, Will.

It's no big deal, all right? Lots of girls go for other girls. It doesn't mean they're life-long lesbians. For some it's a phase you grow through. I didn't know about Cathy, I hardly saw her after we grew up, she could have changed. But she had the hots for me when we were fifteen. It didn't go anywhere because it wasn't my idea of fun, but she made it pretty clear it was hers.'

'Then—what about *me?*'

'Will, I don't know. But you could be the only man she ever loved. Maybe that's something to be proud of.'

'If you're right,' Richard said pensively, 'other things start to make sense. The state she was in that last year. Larry ruled out drugs because she wasn't getting them from him, she wasn't getting them in the locker-room and he trusted her doctor. But Tessa could have got them for her.'

'She must have taken urine tests,' said Tariq, chewing the inside of his cheek. 'If she was on steroids it would have shown up.'

But Larry knew two answers to that. 'You can use a blocking agent if you understand the chemistry well enough. I dare say a doctor could have helped her with that too. And sometimes you can fix it so that it's not your sample they test. The procedures aren't foolproof. Everyone's heard of samples being switched or interfered with. And by this time Cathy was no longer winning. She could have got someone to help her out, especially when there was nothing at stake. People would have felt sorry for her when she was losing who wouldn't have helped her win that way.'

'Steroids?' asked Tariq.

'Going off how she was. They build bulk, strength and aggression. She certainly got bigger—I thought it was the work she was putting in—and she was strong. It was her judgement that was the problem, on court and off. You must have seen how angry she got, how trivial irritations sent her into orbit. That was new. I never had a problem with her temper till then. I put it down to frustration, but only because I didn't think it could be steroids.'

Richard said slowly, 'If Joe knew this—if he knew *half* of this—he'd think it motive enough for murder. His daughter's lover supplied her with stuff that wrecked her head and her career, then left her to fall apart alone. I'd want to kill someone who treated my child like that.'

Will hadn't come to terms with this, was dealing with it by shifting into a kind of professional detachment so that he could consider the facts stripped of their emotional burden. 'So when Joe woke up he saw Tariq dozing in the chair by the door and Tessa by the bed. He got up, took the lemonade bottle and the torch, and hit Tariq because he was the biggest danger. The noise woke Tessa so he hit her too—not with the bottle, that was in pieces. He's a big man, his fists would do.

'Then he waited and listened. But we'd heard nothing and no one left the conference room. So he hauled Tariq out of his way, dragged Tessa to the lift, opened the doors and pushed her through. She didn't scream so maybe she was already dead. She hit the gondola so hard the whole side broke away.' A tic flickered under his eye. It could as easily have broken up the last time something hit it.

'Probably he intended to go back for Tariq and Miriam. But he heard me opening the conference-room door so he hid in the shaft. He didn't have to climb. All he had to do was get on to the track and the lift doors closed to hide him. He stayed there while we searched. Hell, he may still be there. Or maybe he climbed out as soon as we came in here.'

There was a long silence. Nobody challenged his hypothesis. Nobody offered to check it by looking round outside. Eventually Sheelagh said, 'What do we do now?'

'We go back to the conference room, we take Miriam with us, and we stay together. We barricade the door, and we don't answer it for any reason whatsoever.'

TWENTY-FIVE

CARRYING HER ACROSS to the conference room finally edged Miriam into a kind of rudimentary wakefulness. She asked in a weak voice what was going on; she asked for Esme Venables, who held her hand and made reassuring noises while they got her settled. She complained that her head hurt; but with her hand halfway to showing where, forgot what she was doing and, frowning, remarked critically on the state of the conference room.

'Ask who hit her.' The thought was in everyone's mind but they waited for Sheelagh to voice it. The group had become a gestalt, Richard thought, a single entity comprised of multiple individuals each fulfilling a particular function. Will was its brain, Sheelagh its voice, Tariq its conscience. He himself seemed to have been cast as the group's man of action, which was hilarious when you remembered why he came here in the first place. But then, they'd all plumbed reserves they didn't know they had to cope with this. It was as if Joe, or fate, had deliberately created situations in which they could redeem their betrayal of Cathy Beacham by pulling out all the stops for one another.

Mrs Venables hesitated. 'I don't want to upset her. She's been unconscious twenty-four hours. I'm sure we shouldn't be bothering her with that.'

'I think we have to,' said Tariq. 'It's important to know what we're dealing with. Ask her. If it upsets her we'll back off.'

But it was already too late. While they were discussing it Miriam gave a sigh like a sounding grampus, turned on her side and went back to sleep. Tariq shrugged. 'Oh well, just a thought.'

Though there were hours of darkness ahead no one wanted to sleep; nor were they in the mood for small talk. They huddled under the duvets for warmth, thought of the furniture they'd piled behind the door for comfort, then they just sat. An hour dragged by.

Without preamble, but with something startling about the way she dropped the remark into what had seemed a compact of silence, Mrs Venables said, 'I once worked for a family whose son was diabetic.'

The people around her stirred from the dreary repose into which they had sunk. Richard straightened so abruptly he bumped his head on the wall behind him. For some seconds no one knew how or whether to respond. Then Larry let out a gust of laughter that, if not quite a spontaneous expression of joyous camaraderie, was better than nothing. 'Did you?' he chuckled. 'Did you really?'

She gave an offended little sniff. 'I'm sorry, did I wake you?'

'No—no,' said Larry airily, 'I was just sitting here in the dark wishing someone'd start telling anecdotes.'

For a moment it seemed she'd been embarrassed into silence again. But Esme Venables was not easily intimidated. She said stiffly, 'I mention it for a reason.'

'You were thinking of Joe,' said Sheelagh.

'There's something awry about that. I'm no expert, you mind, but I do remember how it was with Simon. Now, he was a teenager and I know the disease is different in older people. Even so, I don't see how...'

'What's bothering you?' Will asked patiently.

There was a pause while she ordered her thoughts. Then: 'Simon was about fifteen when I first went there. He was sensible about his insulin, could judge for himself when he was going to need more or less. The odd time he got it

wrong he knew what was happening and took the appro-
priate measures. Most of the time he was like any other
teenage boy.

'But there was always the risk of an incident so everyone
in the house had to know what to watch for. The main thing
to know was, there are two kinds of coma. You get one
when you haven't had enough insulin—you missed a shot,
maybe, or you need more because you're poorly. That's a
diabetic coma. And you get another kind if you take too
much insulin, or you don't eat enough sugars and carbo-
hydrates to balance it. Or maybe you've been busy and used
up more that way. That's hypoglycaemia—sugar-lack
coma.

'You have to know the difference because insulin will
cure the first but make the second worse. You could kill a
hypoglycaemic diabetic by assuming all he needed was his
insulin.'

They had listened to humour her. Now she could feel
their interest sharpening. Will said, 'How do you tell them
apart?'

'It isn't difficult if you know what to look for. A diabetic
coma comes on slowly, starting with nausea. Then the patient gets drowsy, his breathing slows down and he loses
consciousness. His breath smells sweet and his skin's dry
and flushed. With too little sugar the situation's more dramatic. It comes on quickly. He's sweaty, shaky and agi-
tated. If the situation isn't resolved he becomes confused
and drowsy. Then he starts convulsing.' She waited for
someone to comment but no one did. It was a text-book
description of Joe's condition when they found him.

The housekeeper sighed, clearly thinking them very dim.
She explained as if to a class of six-year-olds. 'If Mr Lock-
head was suffering from hypoglycaemia, why did Dr
McNaught give him insulin?'

The silence quickened with serious thinking. There were

little grunts as people started to say something and then stopped. Will's was the first intelligent response. 'How sure are you about this?'

'About the symptoms of diabetic and hypoglycaemic comas? I am sure. When a child's life depends on it you have to be. Besides, there's a mnemonic—the first letters. Dry skin means Diabetic coma, Sweaty skin means it's Sugarlack. Mr Lockhead was sweating. Why would a doctor give him more of what was making him ill?'

'Why did you wait till now to mention this?' Larry's voice was harsh and combative.

'There's been so much going on,' Mrs Venables said apologetically. 'It was only now, thinking about it, that it struck me as odd. I tried to tell myself I misunderstood but I didn't. Mr Lockhead *was* sweating. And Dr McNaught said she was giving him insulin.'

'It sounds such an elementary mistake,' said Sheelagh, puzzled. '*Would* a doctor get that wrong?'

'I wouldn't have thought so,' said Mrs Venables.

'Then what *are* you saying? Tessa wasn't a GP?'

'Oh, she was a GP all right. I've been with Dr Graves for ten years and most of her friends are medical people. You can spot a doctor at ten paces in a coal-hole. Mrs McNaught couldn't have been anything else. And she diagnosed the diabetes, which was the hard bit. It's not something a layman would guess from sweating and confusion.'

'If it wasn't a mistake,' Tariq said slowly, not wanting to consider it and not daring not to, 'what was it?'

But Mrs Venables had said all she intended to. She didn't know what it meant and wasn't prepared to speculate. But it had struck her as odd, and if they'd shared their misgivings from the start they might not have been in their current situation.

'Could she have intended to disable him?' ventured Richard. 'We were pretty desperate. Maybe she thought it was the only way we'd be safe till he could be locked up.'

'Then why not say so?' Tariq pushed the wreckage of his pony-tail off his face with rough fingers. 'It wasn't unreasonable in the circumstances. He was dangerous. We were entitled to do anything necessary to protect ourselves. Why pretend she was treating him?'

'Maybe she thought we'd object,' suggested Richard. 'It was a pretty extreme way to keep the guy out of action. I mean, people *die* of diabetes. If she had insulin in her bag, surely to God she'd some sort of sedative?'

Larry was the first to reach, or at least to put into words, the conclusion they were all trying to avoid. 'Perhaps she wanted to do more than sedate him. Perhaps she wanted him dead.'

'Jesus!' exclaimed Tariq in disgust.

'Think about it. Mrs V knows that giving insulin to a diabetic who's short of sugar would be life-threatening and she only worked in a family with diabetes. Tessa was a doctor: she must have known. She didn't say anything because, with Miriam unconscious, she didn't expect anyone to notice. It's a fluke that someone did.'

'Why would she want to kill him?'

'Because she knew what we've just worked out—that he had a bloody good reason to want to kill her!'

'Because she was his daughter's lover?'

'Because she got Cathy started on the crap that finished her career and then walked out on her,' snarled Larry. 'Maybe none of us has much reason to feel proud of ourselves, but Tessa really did fuck her up and chuck her out. If anyone's to blame for Cathy's suicide it was Tessa.'

Will had the scent of his natural quarry, the significant line of inquiry. 'If we're right about this, or even most of it, Joe would be a danger to her as long as he lived. If he was arrested for what he'd done he'd tell the police why he did it, all the details would come out, and that would mean the end of Tessa's career, maybe her marriage, maybe criminal charges. It could be motive enough for murder.'

'*Attempted* murder, anyway.' Sheelagh's voice was brittle. 'She didn't succeed, did she? Even if that's what she intended, what happened is that Joe woke up, brained Tariq and chucked her down the lift shaft.' She seemed to hear herself then because she stopped with a sharp intake of breath. When she began again her tone was sober. 'Whatever she intended, whatever she did, she paid for it.'

Will murmured, 'Do we in fact know that?'

In the darkness everyone stared at where his voice was coming from. 'What do you mean? Of course we do.'

'No,' he explained carefully. 'What we know is that we've got one broken bottle, one dizzy guard, two missing persons and some long hairs in the lift doors. We've put a certain interpretation on that and we may very well be right. But is it the only possible interpretation?'

Richard glimpsed the ghost of what he was proposing but saw no reason to make it easy for him. 'Isn't it?'

Will sighed. He suspected Richard knew exactly; maybe the others did too. He felt he was being used as a kind of mental Rottweiler, someone to do their dirty thinking for them. 'Going off the bare facts, Tessa did something extraordinary and professionally indefensible. And she did it without the knowledge or consent of anyone else.

'So why assume that Joe killed Tessa? That in the middle of the night while the watchman slept'—Tariq shuffled uncomfortably, the whisper of his clothes the only commentary—'everything changed. The unconscious man woke. But not vague, mumbling and wondering which end of the sky fell on him, like Miriam just did. Oh no, he came to in perfect control of mind and body. He knew where the torch and the bottle were, he knew what to do with them, and he slipped out of bed and disabled two fit people before they could defend themselves. We really think that's what happened?'

Larry this time, softly, also aware by now where this was leading: 'What's the alternative?'

They were determined to make him say it so Will did. 'That a woman who'd already made one lethal attack now made another. She knew we were in no danger. Joe wasn't going to wake up—not then, possibly not ever. But to be safe she had to get rid of both him and Miriam, and all that stood—or slept—in her way was Tariq. That may have been her doing too. Did she give you some of that lemonade?'

Tariq nodded; then, realizing that wouldn't serve, said doubtfully, 'Yes.'

'And soon afterwards you started nodding off? So the answer to Richard's question is, She did indeed have a sedative in her bag.'

'It was Tessa behind the torch?' Tariq's voice rose incredulously.

'Look, I don't know,' admitted Will. 'I wasn't there. But it makes more sense than the alternative. She drugged you, then she hit you—by the state of the bottle, hard enough to put you to sleep for good. When we found you we were meant to think that Joe had come to swinging. It's just her bad luck that Mama Straker didn't raise no weaklings.'

More than the note of levity, the syntax shocked Will a little: he shook his head in disbelief. 'Then she hauled you away from the door and dragged Joe out of bed and down the corridor to the lift. He was heavy but she's no weakling either and it's only a few yards. That's when her hair got caught in the door. Not when Joe was disposing of her body. When she was disposing of his.'

TWENTY-SIX

THERE WAS A LONG PAUSE as they considered it: a speculative quiet from those who thought Will could be right, the silence of disgust from those who thought he was wrong. After a moment the torch flashed on, the beam wavering slightly before finding the pale oval of his face. Its strength was waning but they'd been sitting in the dark long enough that it made him flinch. With his eyes screwed up and his face half-averted he looked shifty and unreliable, making it easy to dismiss his words as spite.

Sheelagh sniffed her disdain. 'That's the sickest thing I've ever heard.'

But Richard had spent a lot of time listening to lies and listening to the truth, and staking his reputation on which was which. He judged Will an intelligent, perceptive and decent man, so his opinion was worth something even if unexpected light made him squint. But he didn't switch the torch off. 'Is that what you believe?'

'On the balance of probabilities,' said Will, resorting to legal formulae. 'Perhaps not beyond reasonable doubt.' The missing woman would lose a civil action based on the evidence but win a criminal one. She might have to pay damages but she wouldn't do time.

Such niceties were lost on Larry. He believed in what he knew, and the one thing they were sure of was who brought them here. The rest followed from that. 'Next you'll be telling us it was her hit Miriam and greased the lift door!'

Will thought about it, grey eyes blinking in the torchlight. 'Perhaps it was.'

Larry's tone was derisory. 'Why would she?'

'Why would he?'

'Because— You *know* why!'

'I know why he brought us here—to give us a hard time for failing Cathy. But there's no proof he meant to kill us. Nothing seriously unpleasant happened while Joe and Miriam were the only ones who knew what was going on. Somebody rifled Tariq's briefcase, probably to find out just who he was. Well, Joe knew already. It was only after that, when we all knew what it was about, that people started getting hurt.'

'The lift going off?'

'Could have been accidental. Or Joe could have done it to stop us walking out at half-time. Either way, it doesn't compare with a violent attack.'

Richard again. 'Why would Tessa attack Miriam?'

Will found this end of a cross-examination less familiar than the other. He would have been happier if he'd known anything, but he didn't. It was a matter of conjecture, of looking beyond the obvious answers to where others, less convenient but possibly more illuminating, might lie. He'd hoped the group could pursue the exercise on that basis. But they weren't interested in semantics, they wanted facts. They were afraid and needed to know where the danger lay. Until he started this driverless train rolling they had at least had that consolation, and they resented him for shaking it.

But the train was rolling now and the only alternative to staying with it was jumping off. He improvised. 'She came here like the rest of us, in good faith. But when she realized what was going on she knew how serious it could be for her. She needed to find out just how much Miriam knew and what she intended to do with it. Remember, none of us knew about Joe at that point. Tessa thought Miriam was the one she had to deal with.

'She must have meant to kill her—she'd gain nothing by

knocking her out. But ask any mugger—it's difficult to judge how much force it takes. The same blow that'll kill one person will put another in hospital and make a third angry enough to grab your blackjack and wallop you with it. Even when Miriam was found alive it didn't seem a major problem. She was deeply unconscious. She wasn't going to wake up for hours or maybe days. In the meantime she'd be at the mercy of the only doctor present.

'Except that Mrs Venables hardly let her out of her sight. The odd time she was alone Tessa was occupied and couldn't get away without people noticing. When Tariq persuaded Mrs V to get some sleep it was the only chance Tessa would get. By morning Miriam could be awake and talking. It was now or never, and with Joe unconscious and Tariq unsuspecting it wasn't difficult. She set about disposing of the people who knew enough to ruin her.'

Tariq was following the discussion now though his head still sang. 'What about the lift? What interest had she in making you fall?'

'My fall was nothing to do with her—Midge forced those doors so often that they gave at a touch. I can't imagine why she'd want either me or Richard dead,' he added honestly. 'Miriam and Joe, yes, but she'd nothing to fear from the rest of us. We didn't even know she was hiding something.'

'No, but we'd have found out,' Richard said slowly. '*You'd* have found out. Maybe your fall was an accident but she knew an opportunity when she saw one. It wasn't me she was after with the butter—it was you.'

Having Richard take up the theory, no longer having to carry the full weight of it in the teeth of blanket disapproval, was like shedding a physical burden. Will's face lifted in almost comic relief. On the tail of that came amazement at what Richard had actually said. '*Me?* Why me? I don't know any more about her than you do.'

'No, but you think better than we do. Before we'd been here half a day that was obvious. When she decided what she had to do she must have worried about you. She could fool the rest of us but you were always going to see that bit deeper. When she decided to dispose of everyone who threatened her, you had to go too.

'For a while it must have seemed fate had done the job for her. We thought you were dead. Then Midge said you were OK and we organized a rescue, so she had to think fast. To be safe she needed the three of you out of her way. The survivors could leave on Monday and never know that one of us was a murderer.'

'We don't *know* it now!' Sheelagh said fiercely. When the torch flicked her way her face was flushed. She'd liked Tessa, was not persuaded by an imaginative fiction dreamt up by people with too much time to kill. To the best of her belief Tessa was another victim of the man who, crazed with grief, wanted to punish them all. She despised the way these clever, articulate men were twisting the facts to serve their argument. 'You think it—there's a difference. I'm not even sure you think it so much as like the idea. Neat, hey?—let's have the broad do it this time!

'Well, this isn't Hollywood, it's the real world. Death here isn't a dramatic device. It's tangible and it's permanent. It's people getting their skulls caved in. It's people being thrown down forty-storey shafts. It's messy and it's scary, and it isn't a suitable topic for you two to play boy detectives on. If you've got some evidence let's hear it. If not, keep your mouths off a woman who'd be here to defend herself if she hadn't made two honest mistakes. She tried to help a man who was sick, and she assumed that the guy who volunteered to protect her would stay awake long enough to do it.'

The silence in the dim room was complete enough for them to hear the breath hiss in Tariq's teeth. As a judge-

ment it was harsh; as a fact it was unarguable. He preferred
Will's theory that he'd been slipped a Mickey Finn, because that way he wasn't to blame for what followed. But
he didn't know. He might just have nodded off long enough
for the sick man to resume his campaign of terror. If Sheelagh was right about Tessa and Will was wrong, Tariq was
more to blame for her death than the madman who killed
her.

Larry had no vested interest. He thought Sheelagh was
probably right about Cathy and Tessa; he thought she could
have given the girl steroids. But it was too big a leap from
there to murder. The stakes weren't high enough. A lesbian
affaire might have caused Tessa some embarrassment but
nothing more; and supplying banned substances was easy
to condemn, harder to deal with. Everyone in sport knew
it happened; there were occasional scandals that ended the
careers of athletes and their advisers. But the proof was
hard to come by when all those involved had too much to
lose by talking. It would have been difficult to make a case
when Cathy was alive, almost impossible now. Tessa must
have known that. She didn't have to kill anyone. She just
had to deny it.

'It all sounds pretty far-fetched to me too,' he grumbled.
'It might have been awkward having her name linked with
Cathy's, but it's like the drugs, isn't it?—easier to say than
to prove when the other party can't confirm it. Do people
commit murder to avoid innuendo? You wouldn't. It would
always be safer to do nothing. A week later the gossips
would be dissecting somebody else.'

For a man with few intellectual pretensions he'd hit precisely the flaw in Will's reasoning. Tessa had had both
means and opportunity, but her motive was too modest for
what it was supposed to have driven her to. The same argument could be applied to Joe: what he'd done, if he'd
done it, was out of all proportion to the reason for it. But

Joe was a man pushed to the edge of sanity by an accumulation of grief. He hadn't hidden the enmity he felt for the strangers he blamed for his daughter's lonely death. It was much less of a leap from there to violence.

'Actually,' murmured Mrs Venables, 'it doesn't matter what we decide. We'll know the truth soon enough.'

Before he found her with the torch Richard realized what she meant. 'Oh. Yes.'

'Yeah,' drawled Larry, uninhibited by tact. 'On Monday morning we'll see who's splattered all over the concourse. The murderer's the other one.'

But it was a long time to Monday morning: the sun had yet to rise on Sunday. Richard switched off the torch and an uneasy quiet fell, weariness gaining the upper hand over fear until one by one they yielded to a kind of torpor, resting their bodies and letting their minds slip out of focus. It wasn't peace so much as disengagement.

The quiet and the illusion of peace were shattered in the blink of a light-starved eye by a shriek of horror reverberating in the corridor only the thickness of a partition wall away.

TWENTY-SEVEN

RICHARD, who hadn't realized he'd been asleep, woke in the grip of icy terror; as if someone had drilled a hole in his skull while he drowsed and filled it with meltwater that poured over the folds of his brain and percolated down through his spinal cord. His first half-coherent thought was that he'd dreamed himself back in the Thames, trying to hang on to a woman who must have changed her mind about dying seconds after her car left the dock. She begged for her life—'Don't kill me, don't let me go'—but in the end he did. If he could have held on for another ten minutes none of them would have been here now.

But she never screamed. She never vented anything like that cry of immediate and mortal terror, the shriek of a hunted animal taken by the heels. He hadn't dreamed that, it was real, and the one thing worse than a nightmare is one that doesn't go away when you wake up.

He threw off the quilt, groping frantically for the little torch, his limbs colliding with those of the men and women around him who were also reacting confusedly to what they'd heard.

'What the hell—?'

'Tessa—it had to be.'

'Then why—?'

'Where's that light?'

'Get the frigging door open!'

'No!' yelled Will. There was a tramping of feet and a bumping of bodies as he struggled clear of the sleep-befuddled litter. When the weak bulb finally lit it found him with his back to the barricade, clutching his battered ribs.

Larry skidded to a halt in front of him, hands knotted. 'Shift yourself, sonny.'

The smaller man stood his ground but his voice soared. 'It's Tessa. We can't let her in.'

The door thundered to a volley of blows. 'For Christ's sake, let me *in!* Joe's out here and he's crazy!'

Larry's fists pulsed with muscle as if they had a life of their own. 'I told you to get out of my way.'

'Don't you understand?' cried Will. 'She's killed him. If she hadn't she wouldn't be here—she'd be at the bottom of the lift shaft. She's safe out there. But in here she's lethal.'

The scant light was enough to show contempt in the athlete's face. With no light at all it would have been plain in his voice. 'Will, if she scares you that much, go and sit behind the couch and we won't tell her you're there. But I'm not leaving a woman to the mercy of a maniac because of some crackpot theory.'

'Oh God,' moaned Will, 'listen to me, please. She's lying. Joe isn't out there. He's dead. She killed him. She's the one we have to worry about. Wait and you'll see I'm right.'

'*Wait?*' bellowed Larry. 'While he rips her head off? Cower behind the furniture while he finishes the job? Jesus, boy, I never took you for anything much but I didn't realize how deep the yellow went.' Still talking he reached out, fisted one hand in Will's clothes and spun him across the room, attacking the barricade with the other.

Will fetched up in a heap against the wall. He didn't bother to rise. There was no point: even on peak form he was no match for Larry. 'Richard,' he begged, 'Tariq, stop him. People are going to *die* here!'

Richard had been prepared to explore the possibilities

when what they were discussing was hypothetical, a sort of grim game with no immediate practical consequences. On that basis he was prepared to accept that Will could be right. But asked to translate that into action, to deny sanctuary to a woman who could be in imminent danger from a madman purely because, debating in safety, they'd decided she probably wasn't, his voice rose incredulously. 'Will, you don't *know* that. What if you're wrong? You can't gamble her life on it!'

'I'm not wrong. And he's going to gamble all our lives.'

About then, though, the argument became academic because Larry threw the door open and Tessa fell inside.

'The torch!' Richard tossed it. Larry snatched it out of the air and stepped into the corridor in one fast, fluid movement.

He saw nothing. But the range of his vision was only a few yards in any direction. He could see that the lift doors were closed, couldn't make out the door of the nearest bedroom. Joe could have ducked in there, or he could have faded back into the dark. Just because Larry couldn't see him didn't mean he couldn't see Larry. Standing in the corridor, holding a pathetic little torch that did little more than mark his own position, Larry suddenly felt exposed. He retreated into the room and slammed the door, shoving the sofa into place behind it.

Finally he turned the torch on Tessa. Sheelagh caught her breath. The woman's face was deeply scored down one side. They weren't just scratches: the flesh gaped and blood had run down to her jaw. Her eye was puffy and her lip split. She was shaking.

Larry steered her towards the mattresses. 'Come and sit down. You're freezing. Mrs Venables, can we do anything about—?' He indicated Tessa's savaged cheek.

Before surrendering herself to their care Tessa took the torch in a shaky hand, scanning the troubled faces. Richard wondered uneasily if she'd been able to make sense of the argument she must have heard through the shut door, but the beam passed over Will with only a fractional dismissive pause. It settled on Tariq.

The big man bore its scrutiny for some seconds before he opened his mouth to speak. But with the words still in his throat Tessa slapped his face, hard. 'You bastard!' she spat. 'You useless frigging bastard.'

Tariq reeled but he kept his feet. 'Tessa—'

She hit him again. 'I trusted you! You said you'd protect me. You said I shouldn't be alone with him so you'd stay and protect me. And you went to sleep!'

'What happened?' Larry took the torch, sat her on the mattress and tucked a quilt round her trembling body while Mrs Venables began to work on her face. 'Will found Tariq out cold and you and Joe gone.'

She breathed a racked sigh. 'And Miriam?'

'She's all right. She started to come round, then she went back to sleep. She isn't making much sense yet but I think she's all right. Tessa, what happened?'

'I'm not altogether sure—I was half-asleep myself.' Her tone hardened. 'But I was there for my medical skill, not because I was big enough to control the patient if he went ape.'

'I'm sorry,' murmured Tariq. 'I didn't—mean—'

Her swollen lip curled but she said nothing more to him. 'The first thing I knew he was out of bed, swinging at me with a lemonade bottle.' She touched beside her eye. 'I didn't go out exactly but I lost touch for a minute. By the time I recovered it was too late. He'd stuffed something in my mouth and had my arms halfway up my back. He dragged me to the lift shaft, but as the doors opened we heard movement in here and the handle turning. He hauled me up the corridor out of sight.'

'That was Will,' said Richard. 'He had something to ask

Tariq. God knows what—it seemed important at the time. But he was out cold and you were gone. When we found some of your hair in the lift doors we assumed the worst.'

She eyed Will icily—so she had heard the argument—before continuing. 'The locked door round the corner—Joe has a key. He must have had it all along. He pulled me through the rubble by my hair. Then he pushed me down and told me to keep still. I didn't dare do anything else. He kept saying, "Don't think it's over, don't think I'm finished." He's crazy. I mean, really—I think he's insane.'

'How did you get away?'

'When everything was quiet he unlocked the door again. I knew we were heading for the lift—I'd nothing to lose. I hit him as hard as I could with fifteen inches of piping I'd found in the rubble and spent half an hour sitting on. He went down. I didn't wait to see if he went out. I came up that corridor as fast as I could, and when I got his goddamned hanky out of my mouth I yelled to let you know I was coming.

'Only when I got here the door was shut fast.' Her voice cracked with fury and remembered terror. 'What he took you so *long?* I could hear him behind me, I only had a few seconds' lead—and I was hammering at this door and yelling my head off, and *still* no one opened it. What were you waiting for—a password?'

There was an awkward pause. Then Larry said negligently, 'There was a lot of stuff behind it.'

'I'd have moved it fast enough if it had been on my side!'

Will spoke so softly as to be barely audible. 'It was my fault. I was afraid of letting a killer in here.'

'So you left me outside with him?' she cried bitterly. 'You abject bloody coward! Richard risked his life in a six-hundred-foot drop for you. And you wouldn't risk opening the door for me?'

Will said nothing more. Larry had the grace to keep the light off him, but it took no imagination to see him flinch under the lash of her tongue.

Tariq said slowly, 'Maybe this changes things. If there's a way through the rubble, all we have to do is break that door open and we can get out of here.'

They stared at where they thought he was. 'How?'

'There has to be a stairway,' he said. 'We know that. For emergencies. We thought we couldn't reach it for the rubble behind the door, but Tessa got through. To the far side?'

'What?' She wasn't sure what he was asking.

'Where Joe took you—was it an open corridor? Or just a space in the rubble? What could you see?'

'A corridor. Like the one outside.'

'Not blocked.'

'No.'

'All right,' said Tariq, his tone quickening. 'We know the stairs are on that side—the other way there's a brick wall. If we force the door and crawl through the rubble we'll find them. We can walk out of here. It's six hundred feet but it's downhill all the way.' They could hear him grin.

'What about Joe?' Sheelagh didn't share his confidence. 'You think he's going to let us go?'

'I don't know what he'll do. We'll have to watch our backs, be ready to defend ourselves. We'd better wait for daylight.'

'We'll need something to force the door,' said Larry. 'Anybody got a crowbar?'

'How about a battering-ram?' Richard nodded at the table. 'That's pretty solid.'

'Good,' nodded Tariq. 'Then as soon as it's light Richard, Larry and me'll go beat the door down. The rest of you stay here. When there's a way through we'll come back.'

There was a general chorus of assent. But Richard, listening for it, missed a voice. 'Will?'

Will was torn. He knew none of them was anxious to hear his opinion right now. But he was sure they were about to make another bad mistake. He said quietly, 'I don't think we should split up. Every time we do that someone gets hurt.'

Exasperated, Larry said, 'It's because people are hurt that we have to split up. You're not going to be much use breaking down a door, are you? And Tessa's had enough for one day. You'd be vulnerable hanging round in the corridor, and in the way if we have to fight him off.'

'And if we can't break through we'll have to come back here,' added Tariq. 'I don't like the idea of leaving the room empty.'

Tessa had neither forgiven nor forgotten. Her voice was a sneer. 'Don't worry, Will. We won't let you come to any harm. I'll take care of you.'

'I know you'll try,' he murmured bleakly.

'Oh dear God,' Sheelagh exclaimed, 'you're not back to that again? What does it take to convince you—a maniac sticking *your* head down a lift shaft? I know: go sit in the corridor. If you're right it's the safest place in the building.'

'What does she mean?' asked Tessa sharply. 'What did *you* mean?'

Sheelagh eyed him askance. 'Will thinks—'

He interrupted. 'Will thinks it's time we heard the truth from you, Tessa. Because he thinks you've been rather economical with it so far, and he wonders why.'

The sharp susurrus of breath all round was more eloquent than words. They were amazed that he'd say that to the woman's savaged face when events of the last few minutes had so plainly proved him wrong.

'Jesus, Will,' groaned Tariq. 'Can't you just—?'

Tessa cut him off unceremoniously. 'I know what this is about. It's between me and Will, and it goes back way beyond this weekend.' Her tawny head lifted, lion-like, her flecked eyes proud. She gave Will a little scornful smile that broadened as it took in the others, inviting complicity. Such was the power of her personality, so much stronger than his, that they found themselves smiling back before they'd heard what she had to say.

'He's right. I haven't been entirely frank. I did know Cathy—as well as he did and better than the rest of you. We were lovers, for a year. She left him for me. I don't know how he found out—discretion was important to us both—but he has and he can't forgive me. If I was a man he'd punch my lights out.' She gave a humorous little snort. 'If he was.'

The darkness all around crawled with tension. Larry didn't know where to point the torch. He ended up playing it between them so it captured both the rake of flesh down Tessa's cheek and Will's clenched jaw.

Some men might have sworn or struck her, or answered with insults designed to return hurt for hurt. Will responded, characteristically, with a scrupulous attention to the issue that cut through any amount of personal abuse and other distractions. He shook his head. His voice was oddly calm. 'This isn't about who Cathy preferred in her bed. It's about the fact that Joe is missing and other people are lucky to be alive. You're saying Joe's responsible—that he tried to kill you too—but that makes no sense. I think you killed him, and tried to kill Miriam, to keep a secret so damning it could blow your world apart.

'That you were in love with a girl? No. I may be the last person in the civilized world to be shocked by that. That you supplied her with drugs? Maybe—that could come back to haunt you, even this long after, if there was any proof. But why risk everything to hide something that can't be proved?' His voice was puzzled; he was thinking aloud, exercising the intellect that was his only impressive feature.

It was a rhetorical question but Tessa chose to answer. She said ironically, 'Hard to credit, isn't it?' She seemed more exasperated than alarmed.

Richard was growing more and more uneasy about the hypothesis they'd constructed in her absence. She wasn't behaving like someone with a terrible secret. She was behaving like someone who'd been cornered by a crackpot but trusted her companions would rescue her before things got nasty. 'Go easy, Will,' he muttered. 'You're not in court now. Anyway, I thought you didn't do prosecutions.'

Will's gaze was level. 'I don't. What I'm doing here is defending.'

'What you're doing,' said Tessa, almost tolerantly, 'is making an idiot of yourself. Everyone knows why. They may even sympathize. But they're not going along with your make-believe any more. Why don't you let it drop now?'

He sighed. 'Because it matters too much. Because if I'm right you want to kill me, and if I'm wrong Joe wants to kill us all. It's important to know which.'

She shook her head wearily but said nothing more.

'All right,' he conceded. 'I agree, for the moment, I don't know why you did it. But I'm pretty sure I know what you did.

'When you realized what was going on you assumed Miriam knew everything and tried to silence her. When it turned out Joe was behind it you created a diversion, got him away on some pretext and stuck a hypodermic into him. That's what he was trying to say when we found him—not that he needed an injection, that he'd had one. And we watched while you gave him another. God help us, we even held him for you. Was it insulin?'

'I told you it was,' Tessa said irritably.

'Because it shouldn't have been. Those weren't the symptoms of a diabetic collapse. They were the symptoms of hypoglycaemia. Dry skin, diabetic coma—yes?'

'No,' she said, meeting his gaze. '*Damp* skin, diabetic coma.'

Taken aback, Will looked at Mrs Venables but the housekeeper couldn't help. 'Not as I remember it.'

'Oh, I see,' Tessa said caustically. 'You're getting your medical input from the lady who makes the tea!'

'She made it for a diabetic. She had to know what to watch for.'

'Well, I hope he never went off in front of her because she got it wrong.'

It wasn't something they could clear up right now. When Miriam was awake she could give a casting vote. 'Was the first shot insulin too? Wouldn't an injection of insulin make a healthy person ill? And a second shot endanger his life?'

'He was ill when I found him,' Tessa said in her teeth. 'I treated him and he recovered enough to pick up where he left off.' She indicated her face. 'Do you think I did this myself, for God's sake?'

Will regarded the damage speculatively. 'Perhaps. I don't think Joe did it. He certainly didn't hit you with the lemonade bottle. If he hit you first he'd have woken Tariq, and if he hit Tariq first the bottle would have been shattered. Then there's the lift. Did it really just break up—generously waiting until no one was standing on it? Or did something hit it bloody hard?'

As with all trials, the room full of people distilled in essence to just these two: the defendant and the prosecuting counsel. The others were observers, witnesses, judges, but these two were the principals. Anyone else could have walked away and the thing gone on; but a backward step by either of these would signal victory for the other. Tessa knew it instinctively, Will because it was how he made his living. Accuser and defendant, mongoose and snake—there was no room for compromise. The only success for either lay in destroying the other.

'Why are you lying, Tessa?' Will's voice was soft, persuasive. 'All this must matter enormously to you—enough to kill for, more than enough to cut your face for. After all, you had your medical kit. With local anaesthetic and a scalpel you could have done it in a few moments. A scar isn't too big a price for your safety.' The glimmer of the torch showed his lips pursed, head tilted like a curious bird's. 'What is it, Tessa, that you can't let anyone know? That's worth committing fresh crimes, with all the risks of discovery, to conceal?' The silence was profound: a dropped pin would have battered like gunfire.

It seemed then that on the very brink of success the mongoose stepped back, lost conviction, went off the whole idea. Will shrugged and his tone was almost apologetic. 'Perhaps I was wrong about this. You're right, it suited me to think the worst of you—to blame you for what happened to Cathy. You took her away from people who cared about her, gave her stuff that made a monster of her and then walked away. She probably wasn't much fun by then, but I wouldn't have left her like that. None of us would. I blamed you for her suicide.

'And that was wrong, wasn't it? Cathy didn't commit suicide. You murdered her.'

TWENTY-EIGHT

THEY MAY HAVE believed it, they may not; they may have been waiting for proof. They may just have been too stunned to react. But no one spoke. No one objected, and to Tessa it seemed as if Will spoke for them all. As if she were surrounded by enemies.

She had never shrunk from her enemies. She met his gaze without flinching and her voice was diamond-edged with anger. 'You're a sick man, Will Furney, so maybe I should make allowances. But you're not getting away with that! I know you hate me. I understand why. But nothing justifies what you're doing to me. You're piling lie on lie in the hope that, without any kind of evidence, the sheer weight of them will bring me down. Well, I have news for you. I don't topple that easily.'

The tone of her voice changed as she appealed to the others. 'You're thinking I lied too and you're right—I said I didn't know Cathy when of course I did. I didn't consider our relationship anyone else's business. Maybe I was wrong. I wish I'd told you everything from the start—we wouldn't be in this mess if I had. But you must see what Will's trying to do. He's gambling that I can't prove my innocence. He's out to crucify me, because Cathy loved me more than she loved him.'

Will felt a ripple of empathy like a tide changing in her direction. It prompted a smile that barely made it to his lips. They were like a naive jury being swayed first one way, then the other by the heartstring arpeggios of opposing counsel. Disappointed in them he said tiredly, 'When we leave here we'll have all the proof you want. Either Joe will be alive and in a strait-jacket, or he'll be a corpse full of insulin on the atrium floor. You and I will never have to battle for belief, Tessa, except here and now.'

'But here and now is what matters,' she retorted, circling the group with fierce eyes, 'more than it ever will again. This fantasy of Will's is dangerous—not just to me, to all of us. If you start listening to him, to even half-believe, you'll start wondering if Joe's still out there. You'll get careless. A moment's carelessness is all it takes. Miriam turned her back on him and he almost killed her. I nodded off by his bed and he almost killed me. He may not be responsible for his actions, but that'll be no comfort if he gets his foot in that door. And if you stop thinking of him as a real and present danger, he will.'

Tariq found a voice that wasn't much more than a croak. 'Is she right, Will? You've no evidence for this? You're *guessing?*'

'She's right I have no evidence,' Will conceded shortly. 'But I'm not guessing. It's the only thing that makes any sense. Cathy wasn't the suicide type—we all felt that. It's why Joe never accepted her death, why it preyed on him. Maybe he didn't know it himself, but what he was seeking from us was an answer to a question no one had thought to ask—not why did Cathy take her own life but did she?'

'The inquest said she did. The post-mortem showed she died of drowning. The police found nothing to suggest that anyone else was involved.'

It wasn't Tessa speaking; for a moment they couldn't think who it was. Then Larry flicked the torch along the wall and Miriam was sitting on her mattress, her duvet tucked around her like an old Indian in his blanket, Mrs Venables fussing over her like a Buff Orpington. She sounded frail, but she was fully conscious and her mind seemed clear.

'Welcome back,' smiled Sheelagh. 'We were worried about you.'

'I seem to have missed rather a lot,' complained Miriam weakly. 'Do I gather somebody hit me?'

Larry gave a sour chuckle. 'We were hoping you'd tell us.'

Tessa said, 'Will thinks it was me. It wasn't, it was Joe—he had a go at me too. I think the guy's as near unhinged as makes any difference.'

'Joe?'

They were wandering in circles when it was vitally important to stick to the point. Richard tried to bring the discussion into focus. 'Miriam, what can you remember?'

She considered. 'Best friends. We were playing the best friends game. That's when you worked out why you were here.'

'That's right,' he said encouragingly. 'And you told us you were acting for Cathy's father. Joe. You didn't tell us that, he did, after you were attacked. Do you remember talking to him that night?'

'Yes.'

The mood quickened. 'In your room?'

'No, his. I told him I'd gone just about as far with this as I was prepared to.'

'Was he angry?'

'A little. But I think he was expecting it.'

'Do you remember going back to your room?'

'Oh yes.'

'And did you see anyone after that?'

Again a pause while she thought. 'Tessa.'

So many people caught their breath it sounded like a breeze. Richard kept his voice even. 'In your room?'

'Yes.'

'What did she want?'

For the first time Miriam's voice stumbled. 'I'm—not

sure. Something to do with papers. She wanted to read the paper? I can't remember.'

'Try to remember this,' he said. 'This is important. Do you remember her leaving?'

She didn't even have to think about that. 'Yes. We talked a little and then she went. I'm sure she did.'

Another corporate sigh as the pent breaths were let go. They'd thought the answer within reach but it was only a will-o'-the-wisp after all: they looked on it and it was gone. Miriam had nothing useful to report. Joe could have come to her room later and carried out the attack; so could Tessa; so for that matter could Midge or any of them. She genuinely didn't know. Perhaps she never saw her assailant.

Will said, 'What papers, Tessa? Miriam may not remember but you must.'

He had her against the ropes of her own credibility: if she refused to answer, certain conclusions were inevitable. She sniffed. 'The autopsy. Miriam said she had a copy of the post-mortem. I wanted to see it.'

'Why?'

'I wasn't at the inquest. No one approached me and in all the circumstances I saw no reason to volunteer. But we were lovers once. I wanted to know how she died.'

'It was in the newspapers. Admittedly I didn't see it. I was—' Will stopped abruptly, as if he'd blundered into a trap he'd dug and forgotten to mark.

Richard's scalp crawled. 'Abroad? That's what you said.' He hadn't believed it then, wouldn't believe it if Will repeated it now.

Will took a deep breath and slowly nodded. 'I did, didn't I? It wasn't true. I spent four months in a psychiatric unit in Norfolk. A combination of depression and exhaustion, they said. I was off on the Planet Zog when Cathy died. The only papers I saw in that time had ink-blot butterflies on them. But my secretary read about it. Cathy was famous once, there was a certain amount of interest in how she died. Linda—my secretary—broke the news once I got home.'

'But not in much detail?'

His narrow shoulders etched an embarrassed shrug. 'I didn't want to talk about it. I couldn't deal with it. It was too late to do anything—I tried to put it out of my mind. Not altogether successfully. I don't know how many times I picked up the phone and dialled Norfolk, and put it down again before they could answer. It's funny. I bet *you* think I couldn't wait to leave that place. But if it's what you need, you stop thinking of it as an institution and start seeing it as a sanctuary. Literally, an asylum. The difficult part is breaking away when they tell you you're fit to go. I think that's why I came here—for another taste of sanctuary.'

Richard stared at him, appalled. They'd listened to him. They'd gone along with much of what he'd proposed. They'd seriously considered the possibility that Tessa had killed two people and tried to kill others, on the unsupported suspicions of a man who'd spent four months in a psychiatric institution. They might have left her with Joe in the corridor because of what Will said.

Tariq too was thinking. But he was considering not Will's actions but Tessa's. 'What could you learn from the post-mortem report that you didn't already know?'

She resented being quizzed but had better reasons for answering than staying silent. She didn't want to leave any suspicion in their minds that she had something to hide. 'In the event, nothing. Cathy drove into the river and drowned—it was that simple. Suicide.' Her voice hardened. 'So can we *please* see these wild allegations for what they are? Will's a sad man with a history of mental illness set on punishing someone for his misery. Maybe he has cause to hate me, but he's wrong about me harming Cathy. The only thing I did wrong was fall for someone with no sense of proportion. Cathy spent ten years trying to be the best. When she realized she wasn't going to make it she preferred to crash in flames rather than make a new life for herself out of the spotlight. None of us is responsible for that.'

Trying to decide where the truth lay, Tariq was defeated by the dearth of facts. Neither version of events could be proved or disproved on what they knew for sure. But time alone would deliver a judgement and he saw no alternative to waiting. He didn't even know who he wanted to believe. If Tessa was telling the truth it only meant that Will was mistaken; but if he was right then Tessa had killed two people. He said tiredly, 'This is getting us nowhere. Can we leave it for now and concentrate on getting out of here?'

There was a general murmur of consent. No one wanted to judge, on ambiguous evidence, whether one of their number was paranoid or the other a murderer. With no facts they weren't prepared, weren't able, to make a choice.

Larry gave a rather phoney laugh. 'After all, nobody's going anywhere.'

Will shook his head obstinately. Like many small men he had a way, when he reached a line he wasn't prepared to cross, of digging in and looking as immovable as a rock. 'But that's not true, is it? We're hoping to leave here. Tessa'll be with us. If we're watching her we're vulnerable to an attack by Joe if I'm wrong. If we're watching for Joe, we're at risk from a killer in our midst if I'm right. We have to resolve this before anyone leaves this room.'

'I agree,' Tessa said, surprising him. 'Look, this is my neck too. When we go out there I want everyone concentrating on the real issue, not something dreamt up by a bitter, frustrated and unstable young man. Plus, I don't want to have to worry who's behind me on the stairs.'

Tariq stood up. His head ached, but if he added himself to the growing list of the unfit there wouldn't be enough strong hands left to do what needed doing. 'It makes no difference what either of you want,' he said flatly. 'We can't settle it here. But we have a chance to leave before anyone else gets hurt. If that means an armed truce until we can sort out who did what to who, so be it. But it's coming light and I'm going to have a crack at that door.'

He got the support he needed because he wasn't asking anyone to take sides. 'Good. Then I'll take Larry and Richard, and the table, and the rest of you stay here. Keep the door shut but stay alert. We really can't be sure if we're going to meet any trouble. If you hear us coming back in a hurry it won't mean we're missing you.'

The door was more massive than they remembered, solid as a house. They eyed it uneasily. 'Remember, we don't know what to expect,' said Tariq. 'Joe may be behind there, or he may be behind us.'

'Or he may be forty storeys below,' murmured Richard.

'Mm. And the door may go down as soon as we hit it or it may kick back. Can we try not to break any bones?'

They backed as far as the corner, lined up on the lock. 'Geronimo?' suggested Richard.

'Geronimo,' agreed Tariq.

'Oh, get on with it,' growled Larry.

They thundered down the short corridor and the table struck the door like cannon-fire. But it didn't spring open: the recoil caught Tariq, who was behind, in the midriff and he sat down with a surprised grunt, exactly as if he'd been kicked by a mule. The door suffered no obvious injury.

'We're doing this wrong,' opined Richard. 'If we break one of the panels we can climb through.'

The rubble would be densest at ground level. They chose the upper panel, on the basis that helping the less agile members of the party through would be easier than clearing a ton of bricks.

The edge of the table sliced into the door with a splintering sound. When they yanked it back it pulled half the panel away. They tugged the fragments out with their hands.

But as the hole grew only more rubble came into view. Bricks, blocks, leaning timbers, even a small cement-mixer, but no way through.

Finally Larry put their burgeoning misgivings into words. He stood back and said with certainty, 'They never got through here. She lied.'

TWENTY-NINE

WILL WAS LIKE A MAN with a chipped tooth: he couldn't leave it alone. The lack of proof only goaded him on. He knew he could have imagined a lot of this. He'd been hit so hard in the emotional solar plexus that all the old certainties had shaken. Had he been reduced to victimizing a woman whose only crime was to love the same girl he had?

He genuinely didn't think so. He believed Tessa had done most or all of what he'd accused her of because if she hadn't the outcome would have been different. Proof lay six hundred feet and perhaps only half an hour away, but he couldn't leave it alone for even so short a time. He was as obsessed as her father with the fate of Cathy Beacham.

Tessa was sitting on her mattress, knees held in the compass of her arms, only her tawny head above the folds of the quilt, the slashes down her face tacked with sticking plaster. She watched him speculatively in the strengthening light and Will, standing at the end of the mattress with his arms crossed over his ribs, watched her.

At length he said, 'I don't understand why she had to die. You were finished with her. There was nothing left worth having. All that promise, that vitality, wrecked by the garbage you fed her. She was desperate enough to risk her reputation on a last chance at success, and you helped her, but when it came to nothing you left her to deal with the consequences alone. That was cruel but there was nothing to stop you. Why did you need her dead?'

Tessa regarded him with dislike. For several seconds she said nothing; then she seemed to reach a decision. 'It's true that Cathy took steroids. I didn't start her on them—I advised against, but winning was all that mattered to her. Later I got them for her because it was safer than trusting a locker-room pusher. If she'd been caught, and if it had come out that she and I had a relationship, I'd have been in trouble anyway. A doctor can't afford to associate with people who abuse drugs.

'But she never got her form back, and over the next few months the situation deteriorated further. She was mean, unpleasant and manipulative. She started using our friendship against me, saying that if she went down she couldn't guarantee to keep me out of it. Finally I couldn't justify the risk—I had to get out before she ruined my life. We never intended to live together, you know. It may not sound like it but my marriage is important to me. The thing with Cathy was a frivolity, a bit of fun. I never meant to leave my husband. At first that suited her fine. But as her other friends drifted away she became more dependent, more demanding. I was sorry for her but her problems weren't my fault and I wasn't going to sacrifice everything to pay for them. I said goodbye.

'She wasn't murdered, Will: not by me, not by anyone. But that gives you a problem, doesn't it? She could have had you back any time but chose to die instead.' She chuckled unkindly. 'That wouldn't do anybody's self-esteem much good. No wonder you ended up milking moo-moos on the funny farm.'

Outraged, Sheelagh was about to intervene, the armoury of invective springing to her tongue with the oiled ease of regular use. Then she saw Will didn't need it.

'We used to call it Being Tired and Emotional,' he said, grinning faintly. 'As in, As tired and emotional as a fruit cake. As tired and emotional as a brush. A sense of the absurd is valuable in even a minimum security madhouse.'

Miriam said softly, 'You ought to go back sometime. They'd be proud of you.'

Will grimaced. 'That depends on whether I'm right about all this. If I'm wrong they might want to keep me.'

She shook her head, cautiously in case it came off. 'You're sane enough. Being wrong, even ridiculously wrong, is no measure of lost marbles.'

'What about believing you're right when everyone else thinks you're ridiculously wrong?'

'That could be a bit suspect,' she allowed. 'Unless you turn out to have been right all along.'

Tessa rolled her eyes theatrically. 'Don't encourage him! For a moment there a bit of common sense nearly reared its head.'

Sheelagh was watching her critically. 'Have you *no* sense of culpability? Of having contributed to Cathy's death? I have, and I'd hardly seen her for years. You were lovers. Even if that's the extent of it, don't you feel any guilt, any regret, about what happened to her?'

'Regret, yes,' nodded Tessa, 'but not guilt. I'm not responsible for the mess she made of her life or the way it ended—not how Will thinks and not the way you mean. Cathy died because she never grew up, never learned to take responsibility for her own actions. Maybe she drove into the river expecting someone to haul her out, dry her off and sort her out the way they always had. Maybe it really wasn't suicide so much as a cry for help—well, in Cathy's case a demand. But she misjudged that as, in the end, she misjudged everything. She thought she could get away with anything on the strength of what she once was.'

Will seemed hardly to be listening. His gaze turned inward somehow, as if what was in his head was more real, more reliable, than anything Tessa could say. A glint of understanding flickered in the grey irises and his voice was a hiss. 'She was *blackmailing* you?'

The absence of a reply was no more obstacle to his vault-
ing intuition than the lack of sure facts. His conviction was
absolute. It was the missing link, the piece that connected
everything else. Cathy a blackmailer? Everyone said she
changed. The drugs that made her strong also made her
aggressive; but what do you do with aggression when there
are no matches left to win? 'She was, wasn't she? She was
all washed up, she was never going to play tennis again.
She couldn't even get a job from a schoolfriend, and her
family had enough problems of their own. She'd cut herself
off from everyone she might have turned to. But there was
still you. And she had a power over you that she didn't
have over anyone else.'

He thought for a moment then went on, slotting the
pieces together. 'While she thought she could still win
she'd have died rather than talk about the drugs and where
she got them. But by now even she knew it wasn't going
to happen. She was going downhill fast. Sick, broke and
alone, she needed help and turned to the one person whose
strings she could still pull. You'd risked your career for
her, she'd always have that lever against you. The tabloids
would love it: Tennis Star in Gay Drugs Shocker with GP.
By now she had nothing left to lose. Except her life.

'She was killing herself anyway—all you had to do was
hurry her along. It wasn't difficult. She never guessed how
far you'd go to protect yourself. She expected you'd be
angry but she thought finally you'd pay. You couldn't afford not to. It didn't occur to her that you'd fight back.'

Again he paused, long enough for the women listening
to think he'd finished and remember to breathe. But Will
was just ordering his thoughts.

'You met to discuss it. You said where and when, so
you'd already considered Plan B. She wasn't worried—she
thought she'd won. She thought you'd pay her off and say
that was all she was getting; and she'd say it was all she

wanted; and you'd both know that she'd be in touch again whenever she needed some more. That's what blackmailers do. If you don't want to be in their hands for ever, sooner or later you have to deal with them.'

He waited for Tessa to deny it. But she didn't. He held his breath waiting for her to admit it but she didn't do that either. After what seemed a long time she said, carefully, 'Blackmail is a crime.'

'Yes, it is,' he agreed. 'A vicious one. It succeeds because victims don't know where to turn for help. If they could talk to the police, probably they wouldn't be worth blackmailing in the first place.'

There was another gravid pause. Will did nothing to end it, prayed no one else would. At last Tessa said pensively, 'That much is true. She was trying to blackmail me.'

Success was so close Will was afraid of frightening it away. He inched up on it. 'You met by the river?'

Under the quilt one shoulder lifted. 'I wasn't afraid to talk to her. We were good friends once.'

'You parked your car nearby and got in beside her?' Tessa nodded. 'She asked for money, you refused, she threatened to ruin you. Then—?'

'Nothing. I left.'

'No.' Will shook his head. 'Cathy ended up dead, and it wasn't suicide. What happened?'

Stubbornly she repeated it. 'I left.'

For a moment he seemed to change the subject. 'She was a strong girl. She was tall, powerful. You'd never have got the better of her physically. You needed an edge. What did you do—hit her over the head? That would have left a bruise, but the pathologist would expect as much—crash your car into a river and you're going to bounce your head off the windscreen or the side pillars.'

The peridot eyes were calm. 'You talk as if you were there—as if you saw all this. But it never happened. I met her by the river, heard her out, told her to get lost and left. When she realized I wasn't going to play ball, in despair— or more likely a fit of pique—she drove into the river. Maybe she thought I'd dash back and pull her out. But her timing was shot to hell. I didn't know what she'd done until I heard it on the news. And I'm not sure I'd have saved her if I could have. You're right, I was relieved she was dead. But I didn't kill her.'

Will had constructed a model in his head of events as he believed they'd transpired. He'd equipped it with every detail he knew or could extrapolate, and by now it had achieved a virtual reality. He talked as if he'd seen what happened because, in the theatre of his mind, he had.

But there was a price to pay. What he was describing was the murder of someone he'd cared for, and now the emotional burden of that broke over him, threatening to swamp him. He went to respond but the words caught in his throat.

Sheelagh laid a hand on his arm. Right or wrong, he was hurting and in need of comfort. The trials of this weekend had disclosed unexpected strengths in all of them, but none more surprising than the tenderness that bloomed when Sheelagh learned to step out from behind the anger that had shielded her so long from the risks of getting close to people.

It was the same with the others, she thought. Tariq, labelled as mercenary and unfeeling, had emerged as a sensitive and ethical man. Larry the alleged slave-driver had shown a tenacious loyalty that made nonsense of the accusation. Richard, whose courage one night fell short of the inhuman demands on it, had risked his life for a companion. And Will, condemned by himself as well as her father for letting Cathy go without a fight, had fought himself to a standstill on her behalf.

Sheelagh's cobalt eyes flew wide. Will was so exhausted

that he'd missed something. He'd asked the question when there was no means of verifying the answer; now there was. 'Miriam, you're a doctor. What are the symptoms of diabetic coma?'

The psychologist stared at her. *'Diabetes?'* Her voice cracked with incredulity.

'I know, it sounds crazy, but bear with me. I'll explain in a moment. How do you distinguish between the two sorts of coma that affect diabetics?'

Miriam must have decided to answer the question and find out why later. 'The symptoms are distinctive if you know what to look for. I suppose the easiest guide for the layman is whether or not the patient's sweating.'

'And if he is?' Sheelagh's voice was soft.

'If he is it's hypoglycaemia and you need to get some sugar into him.'

'You wouldn't inject insulin.'

It must have been obvious to her that none of this was academic. The waiting stillness in the big room confirmed it. She may not have known the precise significance of her answer but she knew it was important. Even so she spent no time thinking about it. 'Christ, no!'

Sheelagh nodded slowly. 'We found Joe in a state of collapse. He was barely conscious and sweating. Tessa diagnosed diabetic coma and injected insulin.'

Her lips parted but for a moment Miriam said nothing. When the words came they were flat, colourless and hard. 'Is he dead?'

'We don't know for sure. Tessa says Joe attacked her and is still outside waiting for us.'

Miriam didn't believe it. 'No.'

'Yes!' Tessa leaned forward over her bent knees, her face flushed with anger. 'It's true, I clipped his wings because he was dangerous, and lied in case some bleeding heart stopped me and someone died. When he came round he tried to kill Tariq and me both, and if he hadn't been disturbed he'd have killed you too. The man was insanely obsessed, and nobody's more to blame for that than you are, Miriam. You're a psychologist!—couldn't you see what he was doing, what was happening to him? Couldn't you see it was going to end in tragedy?'

Miriam's gaze was unyielding. 'I knew Joe well for a period of months. He was depressed and troubled, but I don't believe he was capable of violence. And if he wasn't violent you had some other reason for what you did.'

Tessa tossed the fox-red hair, impatience merging with despair. 'I can't talk to any of you, can I? You're not interested in anything I say. You've decided who's to blame—you don't want to hear the facts in case they get in the way. You tell me what happened, then, because I'm sure I don't know why I'd do the things you say I've done!'

The few moments' respite, the support of allies, gave Will new heart. 'All right, I'll tell you what I think happened next. To Cathy, beside the river. You had her helpless in the car beside you, and you weren't going to let her threaten you again. You started the car and as it headed for the river you jumped clear.'

He gave a little snort of laughter that had nothing to do with mirth. 'It must have scared the wits out of you when Richard hurtled past. He didn't see any of this, of course, never guessed there was someone else there. You kept out of sight and let him get on with it. You didn't think he could save her and you didn't care if he died trying. While he was fighting for his life you went home.'

His forehead creased. 'What *is* it you're so afraid could still come out? Joe didn't suspect Cathy had been murdered. Even if he had, even if he'd suspected you, what could he possibly have proved?'

Tessa offered no explanation. But understanding came from somewhere because Will's brow cleared and he exhaled a soft little sigh. 'The *seat?* The driver's seat was in the wrong place. In order to start the car you had to squeeze between Cathy and the wheel, so you pushed the seat back. The car would have been photographed when it was recovered. If the police reopened the file they'd spot what should have struck them at the time—that the driver's seat was too far back for Cathy to have reached the pedals.

'That should have rung alarm bells right away. It didn't because they thought they knew what had happened. But they only had to compare measurements to realize Cathy couldn't have been driving. And if she wasn't driving it wasn't suicide.'

THIRTY

HE BELIEVED IT UTTERLY, conviction growing with every chip he added to the mosaic. He couldn't be sure if the three-woman jury was equally convinced. Throughout the telling their eyes had turned like flowers following the sun, from his face to Tessa's and back; but though she had plainly lied it was a far cry from there to murder. He needed her to admit it.

She shrugged the quilt closer under her chin. In the ashy light of dawn her face was grey, bright hair and bright eyes leached of colour. Will waited for her response but the seconds passed and his hopes with them. He was going to have to finish it alone, trudge every last step with her silence dragging at him like lead. He drew a disappointed breath to do it; but she spoke first.

Her voice was colourless too, denatured, stripped of the vigour that had braced it through so many crises. But if Will was right they were crises of her own making: it was easy to be brave and witty and strong in adversity, thought Sheelagh, when you knew the only danger in the whole bloody building came from you!

Tessa's eyes rested half-focused on the quilt peaked over her knees. Softly, wearily, she said, 'I never wanted any of this. I never wanted to hurt Cathy—I was fond of her once. But she'd have bled me dry and then sold the husk. She had no sense of honour left. All that mattered was getting what she wanted. She'd have ruined my life. I had to stop her.'

In the soul-deep silence that followed they could clearly hear the thunder of feet, the crash of wood on wood down the corridor where the wrecking crew had yet to realize they were engaged on a fool's errand.

Finally Miriam said gently, 'Is Will right? Did you drive Cathy's car into the river?'

After another long pause Tessa looked up, her gaze defeated. She nodded. 'Yes.'

'Was he right about the rest?'

'Most of it.'

Will had seen people in this situation before. They lied and lied, staked their reputation and their liberty on a fiction that grew thinner and less plausible the more it was explored, and when it finally tore and flew apart they reacted with horror, anger and even grief, as if the invention was something tangible which had been stolen from them, like a purse.

But their second reaction was relief, as if the invention had been crushing them. As if they'd saddled themselves with a burden they couldn't hope to carry but didn't know how to lay down. They were grateful to be rid of it. When there was no more need for caution they wanted to talk about what they'd done.

Now she'd started talking Tessa wanted to tell it all. To explain things which showed her in a bad light, to have a little sympathy for the trials she'd endured. 'It happened faster than I expected. I barely got out before the car left the dock. Then there was that great splash, and a moment after that Richard—well, someone, I only found out who in the next day's papers—came sprinting past. If he hadn't been fully occupied he'd have seen me.'

She looked at Will then and her jaw lifted with a trace of the old arrogance. 'You were wrong about that. I didn't think he'd die. I thought he'd save her. I thought I'd have the police round as soon as she woke up. Oh, you were wrong about that too. I didn't hit her—it was ether.

'I went home. There didn't seem much point running so

I waited. John, my husband, was at work so I passed the time writing to him—an explanation, an apology. When the police still hadn't come I put the radio on.

'The first report gave no names, just said a woman was believed drowned and a man trying to save her was rescued after a car went into the Thames, and the police didn't suspect a crime. That was the first intimation I had that I might get away with it. I waited another hour, listened to all the bulletins, and the story didn't change and the police didn't come. So I burnt my letter and went to bed.'

'What happened next?'

'*Nothing* happened next,' she said, still possessed by the wonder of it. 'No one came anywhere near me. Cathy must have been as secretive about me as I'd been about her. When the inquest recorded it as suicide I thought it was over and tried to put it out of my mind. Cathy was the author of her own downfall. I genuinely didn't *feel* like a murderer. After fifteen months it no longer seemed real. I saw no reason not to come here when I was asked. I wouldn't have joined in a group confessional, of course, but nobody asked me to. I was here to research an article. The thing with Cathy wasn't—relevant.' Her gaze switched to Miriam. 'How did you *know?*'

'*What* I knew came from Joe,' said the psychologist. Her voice was quiet and controlled. Perhaps it wasn't the first time she'd heard a killer's confession; or perhaps the whole thrust of her training was to ready her for anything she heard, however terrible. 'He talked to Cathy not long before her death. She told him almost everything—all the disappointment, all the slights. But not that she was planning to blackmail you, so he'd no reason to think she was murdered. He wanted you here because you gave her drugs that ruined her life and then left her in the wreckage alone.'

'The mesambuterol wasn't my idea!' Tessa said indignantly. 'Really. She picked some up on the circuit, liked the results and asked me to get her a supply. I suppose that was her first shot at blackmail. She said if I wouldn't help she'd have to ask around, but if she was caught it could come out about her and me.' She sniffed sourly. 'She must have put it more subtly than that because I didn't get the subtext, and in the event she didn't have to spell it out. I thought it was the safest way if she was determined to have it. She promised I'd never be compromised, but it was the steroids talking. From then on she made a lot of promises she'd no intention of keeping.'

Will had kept quiet while she got used to talking. But it was too late for her to clam up now so he risked prompting her. 'You must have been as puzzled as anyone when this weekend took the turn it did. But you were the last to spend much time with Cathy. You knew about the rest of us. When you realized who we were you knew her ghost was up and walking. That's why you had to talk to Miriam.'

Tessa made an ambivalent gesture of acceptance—with her head: her arms were under the duvet. 'I needed to know how much damage had to be contained. I could cope with people knowing about Cathy and me—John would have been hurt but he wouldn't have left me, and my partners wouldn't have cared. I could field the drugs issue because this long after, nothing could be proved. But if someone was aware it might not have been suicide, then I was in trouble.'

'Did you try to kill me, Tessa?' asked Miriam. Her tone was still calm, non-accusatory, but the psychologist knew now exactly who she was talking to: a woman who, to protect herself, had killed two people and tried to kill more. Miriam had known Joe Lockhead for a few months; they had been friends; with all his faults the world was a poorer place without him. When there was nothing more pressing she would grieve. But for the moment it was imperative that she stay on top of what was still, in the absence of anyone equally qualified and without a sore head, her job.

'No,' Tessa said immediately—too quickly for it to be true. 'I tried to buy a little time. To think, to work it out. I thought you knew!'

Miriam shook her head sadly. 'Never suspected. Even when Will guessed I thought he'd got it wrong.'

'I wish I *had* got it wrong,' Will said grimly. 'But Joe's dead and his murderer tried to kill you too, to buy her safety with your silence. By the time she'd talked to you she knew nothing less would do. What you didn't know you could get at, and you weren't prepared to cover up for her. So she collected a blunt instrument from the kitchen, came back—your door wasn't locked, she'd taken all the keys earlier—and when your back was turned she hit you as hard as she knew how.'

His gaze came back to Tessa. Even now she had too much pride to avoid it. 'You thought you'd done enough, but she was still alive when Joe found her. His confession must have knocked you sideways. Whatever Miriam knew about you, he did too. Now you needed them both dead.

'Miriam shouldn't have been a problem. But Mrs Venables knew better than to leave her alone with any one of us. She only left the room when we were all in here.

'The neatest solution was to blame everything on Joe. You fused the lights, steered him away on some pretext and shot insulin into him. When he was found you diagnosed diabetic coma and gave him some more. None of us knew enough to stop you.'

In the shadows Mrs Venables bowed her head. She'd known, but not in time.

The end was in prospect. Will laboured on. 'That delivered him into your hands, but to make him a credible scapegoat you needed him physically out of the way. Sick in bed he couldn't be blamed for any more attacks, and by now you were aware that mass murder might be your only option. You no longer knew who knew what. We were putting together facts and deductions and intuitions so quickly you'd be in danger if any of us left here alive.

'You took whatever chances presented themselves. With better luck that smear of butter would have disposed of two of us and always looked like an accident. If we hadn't worked it out, by Monday you'd have been the terrified sole survivor of a massacre by a madman. The police would have accepted your account for lack of any other.'

He was done at last. He thought he'd covered everything, but it wasn't an achievement to take much pleasure in. He looked drained. 'Have I left anything out?'

Tessa regarded him almost without blinking. At length she said with quiet venom, 'I wish that stupid bloody boy had left you where he found you.'

Will gave a grim chuckle. 'I'll take that as a compliment, shall I?'

Her eyes narrowed at him. 'Don't you dare judge me! I didn't start any of this. I was defending myself—from a blackmailer, from her crazy father, from a nosy sod who couldn't leave well enough alone. Everything that's happened was Cathy's doing, even the things that happened after she was dead.'

'She was sick!' cried Will. 'Partly from the stress of her career, but mostly because what should have been her salvation—getting friendly with a doctor—turned out to be anything but. If she'd fallen for a steel-rigger, or a road-sweeper, or God help her if she'd stayed with a solicitor, she'd be alive now. This harpy you talk about—she wasn't like that until she knew you.'

'No? Or was it just that she never found anything you were useful for? What *are* you useful for, apart from digging up things that should have been left buried? I wouldn't mind so much,' Tessa added, her voice rising querulously, 'if I thought you did it for Cathy, because you loved her. That I could understand. But you set out to destroy me for no better reason than to see if you could. Mere cleverness. Never mind that lives were in danger, you had to show what you could do. You want to know why Joe's dead? Because of you. If you'd been just a shade less clever, maybe we could have got through this without anyone getting hurt.'

He recoiled as if she'd spat in his face. It wasn't true; but it was what he was afraid of and so he believed her. His lips parted on a little pant of grief. 'No.'

'Yes,' said Tessa savagely. 'You hadn't the guts to keep Cathy when you had her, or the sense to let go when she was gone, or the decency to put the needs of others ahead of your pride. People have paid for your arrogance in pain and in death, and my one consolation is that you're going to feel that, in here'—under the quilt she thumped her heart—'to the day you die.

'So maybe there's one last thing you should understand.' She produced it from under the quilt, held it up between the thumb and forefinger of her left hand.

He couldn't make it out. It looked like a cork. Stung by the contempt in her voice he leaned closer. It was a cork, the stopper from the neck of a small bottle. One end was darkly stained and there was a deep cut incised into it. 'What—?'

Perhaps if he hadn't been so tired, if he hadn't thought it was over, he wouldn't have made the mistake of leaning still closer in the effort to identify it. The stain on the cork was of no consequence. The incision *was* significant, and in another moment he'd have realized why. He'd have remembered what a cork was good for when you had something sharp in your pocket.

But the main function of the cork in Tessa's left hand

was as a decoy, to draw him in closer—and stop him wondering what she had in her right hand.

As he leaned over her the tawny woman rose from the
folds of the quilt like a snake uncoiling from a basket. In
weary bewilderment Will had put himself within striking
range, and as she surged to her feet Tessa stabbed fiercely
upward, driving her scalpel into his throat.

Blood fountained. Sheelagh gasped. Locked together, the
strong woman and the small man pitched over and rolled
across the carpet. Will's eyes flared whitely and a sound of
some kind, unrecognizable but for the note of horror, bubbled from his throat.

It was too late for Tessa to buy her freedom with his
death as she had once hoped to. If she could have continued
undetected perhaps she would have killed them all and
passed it off as the work of a madman, but she couldn't do
that now. So her only motive was personal satisfaction. Not
getting away with it. Just doing it.

There was no reason to suppose that when she'd finished
with Will she would turn her attention to someone else. So
when Sheelagh leapt on the back of a woman bigger than
herself, a woman armed with a lethal weapon, a woman
who had already killed twice, it was because of what she
was doing to Will not what she might do next.

But Tessa had nothing left to lose. As soon as she felt
the younger woman's arms she twisted snake-like inside
them, rolling her own body on top and freeing her right
hand. Sheelagh saw her face from a range of inches and
was appalled by the hatred there. Tessa had convinced herself that others were to blame for her situation, that she was
their victim, that all her actions were justifiable. She
stabbed the blade at Sheelagh's eye.

On a good day Sheelagh looked and even behaved like
a respectable woman, the proprietor of a thriving business,
a woman with a stake in society. But it was only skin-deep:

underneath she was an alley cat. She wasn't afraid of being hurt, only of being beaten. She couldn't get away from the blade so she did the next best thing: combined a last-ditch defence with a dirty counter-attack.

She thrust her left hand in front of her eye. The blade punched deep into her palm and Sheelagh yelled, as much in rage as pain, and struck out with her own weaponry—a right hand armed with talons filed to a point under a scuffed coat of blood-red lacquer. It was no time for scruples: she too went for the eyes.

She had the satisfaction of feeling her nails rake the torn skin of Tessa's cheek and hearing her screech. Then Tessa snatched back the scalpel—blood leaping from the younger woman's palm—and scythed at the exposed artery inside Sheelagh's right wrist.

THIRTY-ONE

ABANDONING their battering-ram the men headed back to the conference room. They peered cautiously round the corner, still wary of the madman who had tried to push Tessa down the lift shaft. When they realized how silly this was they looked away in embarrassment and moved up a gear.

Before they reached the door they heard screaming: a prolonged, high-pitched, soul-piercing scream that momentarily froze the marrow in their bones.

Larry recovered first. He hissed, 'Jesus Christ'—it may have been a prayer rather than a curse—and hurled himself at the door. It barely shifted, baulked by the sofa wedged behind it.

Richard hammered. 'Let us in! What's happening?' His voice cracked and soared but no one answered. Even after the scream grew thin and died no one came.

'We have to move it,' Tariq said tersely. He wasn't underestimating the task, only knew it must be done. They set their shoulders to it and pushed with every ounce of their strength; with their feet sliding from under them, the veins standing out on their temples, their jaws clenched and their eyes staring; with the bunched muscles trembling in their shoulders and braced thighs. And it wasn't enough. So they delved beyond strength into the very substance of their bodies and used that, knowing that if the door didn't give soon somebody's heart would.

The door eased. Just a fraction; then a little more. Encouraged to a final bruising effort they attacked it like draught-horses with a mired wagon to move, and as the aperture inched wider Larry snaked through and tugged at the sofa from the inside.

They came in on carnage. Will was on the floor, blood pouring from a wound in his throat. Sheelagh was in a chair, blood pooling in her upturned palm. Mrs Venables was on her knees, both hands clasped to her face, blood oozing between the fingers. Miriam, staring, mouth agape, had half-risen from her mattress before shock froze her there.

Tessa stood silhouetted by the window, her hands behind her, one over her shoulder and one up her back as if trying to scratch an unreachable itch. Larry stared round him wildly, dumbstruck. Richard said again, still in the same odd, high voice, 'What *happened?*'

Tessa made no answer. She seemed to bow to him; but instead of straightening she continued to lean forward until it turned into a slow-motion fall and she pitched to the floor at his feet. A single tremor shook her body, then she lay still. The back of her jacket was soaked with blood and the handles of the long-bladed kitchen scissors protruded from it.

Mrs Venables lowered her hands. The blood on her face was in the shape of her fingers: it was not her blood. She said, almost calmly, 'I had to do it. She was killing them.' Then she began to weep.

Sheelagh's injury was bloody but not dangerous: the blade never reached her wrist. She wrapped her hand in a towel and nursed it in her lap like an ailing child.

Tessa needed no help either. Her life shuddered out while Richard stared down at her.

But Will was an emergency. His windpipe intact, he was breathing and still conscious; but eyes great with shock and the bright blood pumping foreshadowed imminent collapse. He was bleeding a river: too much and far too fast. No one could bleed like that for long. He was trying to lever himself up on his arms as if sitting up would make a difference.

Larry knelt over him and clapped both hands to the incision. 'Get something to bandage it with. Lots of something! Even if we can't stop it we can slow it down.'

'Esme, help me up.' Short of top form both mentally and physically, Miriam was still a doctor and the wounded man's best chance. She forced the weakness from her limbs by sheer will-power, made herself turn from the tragedy which had happened to one which might still be averted. 'Good, Larry, hold it tight. The less blood gets between your fingers, the more there is keeping him alive. Esme, the First Aid box. I'll suture it though God knows if it'll hold. Esme! And then bandages—all you can find.'

Urgent demands on her were what Mrs Venables needed most. There would be time later to reflect on what she'd done, to weep and fall apart if she had to. But the present crisis made self-immolation an unaffordable luxury and she responded like a trouper, striding off to the kitchen and returning with a red box with a white cross on it. While Miriam quickly located the items she'd included in case somebody needed a stitch or two, Mrs Venables—using another pair of scissors—started cutting a sheet into strips.

Miriam turned to the strongest man present to hold the patient still. But Tariq had held Joe Lockhead while Tessa pumped death into his veins, and he backed away, holloweyed, shaking his head. Larry understood if Miriam didn't. 'I'll hold him.'

In the event Will took very little holding. His senses were fading fast, dulling even the awareness of someone sewing his throat back together. Larry steadied his head; that was all that was necessary.

'I don't know how well this is going to work,' Miriam said tersely. Her broad fingers were inserting the stitches deftly enough but there was a lot of damage and not much time: if she was meticulous with every single one he was going to be the neatest corpse in the morgue. 'I thought I'd left all this behind when I got out of medicine.' She finished suturing and started clapping dressings over the wound. Blood quickly stained the first; without disturbing it Miriam bandaged firmly over the top. A little blood seeped through. Again she bandaged over it, as firmly as she could without closing Will's airway. Then she sat back on her heels, eyes glued to his throat, and waited.

For five minutes no one spoke. Still the bandage held the blood in check. Will's eyelids flickered, a white line showing under each.

'It's going to hold,' whispered Miriam. 'Dear God, I think it's going to hold.'

They covered Tessa's body with a quilt, meaning to leave it where it had fallen. But it was still only Sunday morning, they could be here another twenty-four hours, and no one wanted to share their living-space with the woman who'd tried to kill them. Nor did they wish now to separate and return to their own rooms. Whatever comfort there was lay in one another's company. So after a while they moved the body into the end bedroom, Tariq taking one end and Richard the other. Neither felt the need to eulogize over her, but it was harder to hate a dead woman than a live one.

By now the people who had missed the final act of the tragedy had heard all the details. Tariq knew as much about what Tessa had done and why as anyone there. But he didn't understand, and he needed to. 'How did it happen?' he asked, bewildered. 'How did a woman like that—an intelligent woman, a woman in her profession—come to kill two people and try to kill more?'

Richard had spent much of his career trying to make sense of atrocities. And there was an answer, of a kind. 'It's like boiling a frog.'

Tariq's eyes swivelled and lit on him cautiously, as if he might be dangerous. 'Pardon?'

Richard grinned. It wasn't that funny; he was fighting a lunatic sense of relief that started welling up with the realization that it was over and everything was going to be all right. Even the presence of the dead woman under the quilt couldn't mar that.

'If you drop a live frog into a pan of hot water it'll jump out demanding to see its lawyer. But if you put it in a pan of cold water and light the gas it'll sit there looking deeply suspicious until it dies. It seems there's no precise moment, as the water heats up, when it's appreciably hotter than it was the moment before, and without that trigger the frog can't make up its mind to jump.'

Tariq was struggling to relate a scientific curiosity to events in the penthouse. 'So?'

'Tessa didn't set out to kill anybody. Cathy was blackmailing her: when she couldn't shake her off, to protect herself Tessa killed her. She tried to silence Miriam because she thought she'd found out, and Joe because she thought *he* knew. In fact neither of them knew Cathy was murdered. But Will would have worked it out, so Tessa tried to kill him, with the butter. In the end she had to kill everyone who knew anything. Nobody'd have been left by Monday if she hadn't met her match in a sixty-year-old housekeeper armed with a pair of scissors.'

Tariq still didn't understand about the frog. Richard made it simple. 'If we'd stood in a line eighteen months ago, Cathy and her dad and all of us, and someone had given Tessa a Kalashnikov, she wouldn't have used it. She'd have said nothing could make her murder nine people. But one at a time the murders were easier to commit than to avoid. There was never enough difference between what went before and what came next—between confronting a blackmailer and killing her, between killing a blackmailer and killing people who could expose her, between that and killing anyone who might know anything. There was never a clear enough signal for the frog to jump.'

'She must have been mad. Don't you think?'

'I doubt it. Not in any clinical sense. She could have stopped any time she was prepared to pay for what she'd done. That was the problem—she thought she could get away with it. That may be immoral but it's not irrational.' Richard shrugged. 'But then, you're talking sanity to a guy who falls apart if a car backfires. Who am I to judge?'

Slowly Tariq smiled. 'I could be wrong, but I wouldn't put money on that happening again.'

As they left the room, closing the door quietly behind them, someone was waiting for them in the corridor: Midge, shuffling from foot to foot like a dancing bear in his ragged clothes.

In the space of about forty-eight hours that boy had filled the roles of both demon and angel. The people stranded in his topless tower had been deeply afraid of him, of an unfathomable mind and unpredictable malice. With Will's rescue all that turned around: then he seemed a God-sent guide in a hostile wilderness.

Now the drama was over and a return to normality in prospect, Midge appeared before the two men decked in neither horns nor halo, as just himself: a youth on the brink of manhood, a transient, a squatter, a gleaner and scavenger on the periphery of human society. Something more than an idiot, less than a citizen.

He said, 'Someone fell.' He gestured jerkily at the lift.

Tariq nodded sombrely. 'Joe. The old man. Tessa killed him—the woman with red hair? She's dead too. It's over now.' He wondered how much explanation was called for, waited for an indication that the bare facts in a few words were insufficient. But Midge nodded, as if knowing who obviated the need to know why. Tessa had lied about almost everything but she'd been right about Midge. A boy of very little brain. Will owed his life to the fact.

Tariq indicated the conference-room door, closed to conserve the heat. 'We're all in there. Are you coming in? We'll be having breakfast soon.'

Midge shook his head quickly. 'No.' It wasn't fear; it might have been discomfort. After so long alone he really didn't enjoy company.

Tariq took a deep breath. He knew if he didn't try he'd regret it. 'Midge, you don't have to live like this. We can find you something better. Maybe a hostel—a nice room, and friends, and people whose job it is to make sure you're OK.'

The forget-me-not eyes widened. ''M OK now!'

'Midge, you're not! You're getting by, just. You're not eating properly, you've nowhere warm to sleep, and once this place is in use you'll have to leave anyway. Won't you let us help? We owe you that much.'

Midge blinked with surprise and a scorn he tried, politely but too late, to disguise. 'Help Midge? You?'

Tariq chuckled. 'You're right. What do I know? Except I know you deserve better than this. You can't want to spend your whole life this way?'

'Why not?'

'Because—because—' It was like trying to explain why rain's wet. Some things are so self-evident that the arguments for them don't exist. 'Rats live like this. People shouldn't have to.'

'Rats do OK!' Midge retorted hotly. 'Go where they want, do what they want. Don't starve, don't need social workers. Last thing rats need is a chance in life!'

Richard laughed out loud. 'Tariq, you're going to lose this one. Walk away while your dignity's intact.'

But Tariq genuinely felt the need to do something. His

eyes were unhappy. 'We can't just leave him here. God knows what'll become of him.'

'We can't kidnap him, either. Look, as near as damn it he's a grown man. He has the right to live like this if it's what he wants. Now, you may argue that he's not competent to make that decision. But then, by the same criteria, neither are half the people living rough in London today. You've got two choices: leave him to it, or send in the welfare hit squad. But they'll have to bring him down with tranquillizer darts, like a monkey.'

Tariq couldn't believe he was getting an argument on this. 'They could find him somewhere to live. They could train him to do a job.'

'Hey, terrif,' said Richard drily. 'They can teach him to push a broom, and wash his hands before meals, and get used to being the dimmest member of any gathering. That's an improvement? Maybe it is, for some people. But whatever you think of it, Midge's life satisfies him. You could break it up, but you couldn't guarantee to improve it. My guess is, five years down the road he'll be where he is now, doing what he's doing now, only maybe a bit less satisfied because he's had his expectations raised.'

With both of them looking at him, Midge approvingly, Tariq in dismay, he sighed. 'How about this? My station's got a pretty big building—nothing like this but there's a lot of corridors and basements and things. If I could fix up some kind of a caretaker's job, with room and board on the premises, would that suit you both?'

'I suppose it might be a viable compromise,' Tariq allowed reluctantly. 'If he's determined not to have a chance in life.'

'Midge?'

Midge thought about it. Gradually the suspicion in his eyes abated. 'Could work nights,' he shrugged. 'Wouldn't have to see people.'

'Can you fix it, do you think?'

Richard shrugged. 'Oh, I think so. After this fiasco they owe me. One condition, though.' He fixed Midge with a steely eye. 'You want to move around the building, you use the goddamned stairs!'

They were resigned to another twenty-four hours' incarceration. In the event rescue came mid-afternoon when one of the builders came back to borrow—that was the word he used—some equipment to do up his kitchen and found a man's body in the bottom of the clear shaft in the atrium.

Apart from Will, who was taken to hospital though by then he was already mending, the survivors spent the rest of the day talking to policemen. There was at first an understandable reluctance to believe them, but six people talking to six different officers in six different rooms and all coming up with the same answers eventually proved persuasive. By late evening they were allowed to leave their phone numbers and go home.

So Richard was home for Sunday supper not much later than originally expected. It didn't occur to Fran to ask what had kept him. She sat him at the table while she brewed some tea. 'Tell me all about it.'

He ruminated. 'It didn't go exactly to plan.'

'Of course not,' she said calmly. 'What ever does when you're involved?'

He debated briefly whether to begin the story and have his tea spoil or wait till he'd eaten. Duty prevailed. 'One of the other crazies murdered the organizer.'

The look on her face was all the reward he could have wanted; but his egg when he got it tasted like a fellwalker's inner sole.

DEATH

OF A DUSTBUNNY

CHRISTINE T. JORGENSEN

When Elena Ruiz disappears, five-year-old Steven Holman is convinced that a vampire has taken his nanny. Stella the Stargazer, astrological adviser to the lovelorn, is certain there are no vampires, and she also knows that Elena wouldn't walk away from her charge. Only Steven has the clues to her disappearance. So Stella has taken over Elena's job temporarily to find her friend.

Between comforting the boy and trying to put her own haphazard life in order, Stella discovers a trail that leads to monsters of a very human sort....

Available May 1999 at your favorite retail outlet.

Look us up on-line at: http://www.worldwidemystery.com

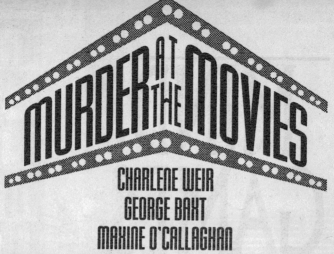

MURDER AT THE MOVIES

CHARLENE WEIR
GEORGE BAXT
MAXINE O'CALLAGHAN

MURDER TAKE TWO
by Charlene Weir

Hollywood comes to Hampstead, Kansas, with the filming of a new picture starring sexy actress Laura Edwards. But murder steals the scene when a stunt double is impaled on a pitchfork.

THE HUMPHREY BOGART MURDER CASE
by George Baxt

Hollywood in its heyday is brought to life in this witty caper featuring a surprise sleuth—Humphrey Bogart. While filming *The Maltese Falcon*, he searches for a real-life treasure, dodging a killer on a murder trail through Hollywood.

SOMEWHERE SOUTH OF MELROSE
by Maxine O'Callaghan

P.I. Delilah West is hired to search for an old high school classmate. The path takes her through the underbelly of broken dreams and into the caprices of fate, where secrets are born and sometimes kept....

Available March 1999 at your favorite retail outlet.

Look us up on-line at: http://www.worldwidemystery.com   WMOM305